The Quiet Earth

George looked at his mother in admiration. He didn't think he'd ever seen her stand up to his father before. Her colour was heightened and her chest heaved, until she raised one workworn hand to the base of her throat and pressed it there, to recover her composure. Taking a deep breath to steady herself, she moved swiftly back to her chair.

George met his sister Beth's eyes, and raised his brows in silent enquiry. She gave a slight shake of her head and raised her shoulders in the suggestion of a shrug. She didn't know what was up, either. George looked at Joseph, but his brother kept his eyes obstinately fixed on his breakfast. His colour was high and his arms lay at either side of his untouched plate, fists clenched...

THE QUIET EARTH

EARTH

Margaret Sunley

ROWAN

A ROWAN BOOK

Published by Arrow Books Limited
20 Vauxhall Bridge Road, London SW1V 2SA

An imprint of the Random Century Group

London Melbourne Sydney Auckland Johannesburg
and agencies throughout the world

First published in Great Britain by Century 1989
Rowan edition 1991

© Margaret Sunley 1989

The right of Margaret Sunley to be identified as the
author of this work has been asserted by her in
accordance with the Copyright, Designs and Patents Act,
1988

This book is sold subject to the condition that it shall not,
by way of trade or otherwise, be lent, resold, hired out,
or otherwise circulated without the publisher's prior
consent in any form of binding or cover other than that in
which it is published and without a similar condition
including this condition being imposed on the
subsequent purchaser

Printed and bound in Great Britain by
Courier International Ltd, Tiptree, Essex

ISBN 0 09 972120 1

Dedicated to my late father-in-law, Eddie Sunley, on whose stories of his forbears and their farming methods this fictionalised book is based

Acknowledgements

My grateful thanks go to

Mrs Gladys Jenson – George's granddaughter

Mr and Mrs Wildsmith of Aumery Park Farm,
Sleightholmedale

Mrs Holmes of Cherry Tree Farm,
Sleightholmedale

CHAPTER ONE

George Oaks sleepily opened his eyes, and nestled down further into the snug valley his body had made in the featherbed. Although he was engulfed in the warmth, his nose-end sensed the bitter cold of the February morning. He stretched out an exploratory hand to the other side of the bed, to find it deserted. Good! His younger brother Jonadab was up, taking his turn at tending the stock with the hired men.

Their father, Jonadab the elder, was a bit of a martinet. In fact, his reputation in the nearby villages of Fadmoor and Gillamoor was that of a harsh man – harsh, but *just*. This was why, on Sunday mornings in winter, two of his three sons were allowed an extra hour in bed. They took this strictly in turns, week by week; one rising at six as usual, and the other two luxuriating in a further hour's rest.

Today, it was the turn of Jonadab, the twelve year old, to get up at the normal hour and go into the buildings to help the men with the milking, foddering up and cleaning out of the animals. It was a great responsibility for a boy of twelve for, as his father saw it, the sons were not there just to help the men but to keep an eye on them. Childhood was a luxury which could not be afforded on the Oaks' farm in Sleightholmedale. Every member of the family worked as soon as they were able to walk; egg-collecting being the first childhood task.

George poked his nose over the eiderdown. Like everything else on the bed, this was homemade, being just a patchwork bag, the inside of which had been liberally coated with candlegrease to make it impervious to the goose-feathers with which it was filled.

Jonna had left the candle alight – a waste which would have enraged his father. In the flickering glow, George contemplated the frost patterns on the little window. They never ceased to fascinate him. The ferns, flowers and swirls which coated the insides of the windows on winter mornings seemed almost magical.

His glance then moved to the single bed in the opposite corner of the room. There was no hump there to denote that his other brother, Joseph, was still sleeping. Instead, the covers were thrown back, and Joseph was gone.

'By 'eck! Oor Joe's nivver wekkened mi!' George groaned, as he leapt from the bed. So great was his alarm at the thought of facing his father even a few minutes late for Sunday breakfast, that he didn't even notice the icy coldness of the bedroom. Forgetting, in his haste, to put on his Sunday shirt, he pulled on his best blue serge trousers and tucked in his workday shirt before tightening his belt.

His mam always made their clothes on the big side, allowing room to grow. In the case of the two eldest sons this was false economy, as Joseph at twenty and George at seventeen were stocky, well-built lads, who surely couldn't fill out much more. Nevertheless, there were always two or three inches of spare round the tops of their trousers so that, in addition to their braces, the sons always wore a belt.

George gave his face a perfunctory splash with the water from the basin on the wash-stand, thanking his lucky stars that his brothers had broken the film of ice on it. As he rubbed his face and hands on the rough towel, thriftily made from a flour sack, he reflected uneasily on the lack of sound from the kitchen below.

The three boys slept in a room which was separate from the rest of the house, being reached by a ladder from the kitchen. Normally, all the sounds from below floated up, accompanying the smell of breakfast but, on this day, nobody spoke. Still wondering why Joseph hadn't given him a shake, George gingerly descended the ladder, waiting for his father's wrath to burst upon him. Despite his uneasiness, he relished the kitchen's warmth which rose to meet him as he went down.

The long deal table, scrubbed white after each meal, was surrounded by its full complement of family, apart from his grandparents, Joseph and Jane. They, being in their seventies and retired after toiling all their adult lives on this self-same farm, were treated more or less as honoured guests, rather than family.

George glanced round the table, but no eye met his. All were busily engaged with their food, eyes down, knives and forks working. Was summat up, he wondered.

At last, George brought himself to look at his father, who sat at the head of the table, dominating it by his size and the strength of his character. He was a tall man, lean but sinewy, strong as whipcord. His almost-black hair was flecked here and there with grey and, from under his heavy brows, icy blue eyes glared out like shafts of steel. Now they focused on George, piercing him until he felt the blood rising in his cheeks. Try as he would to please his father, he knew that he and Joseph, looking as they did like his mother, Annie's, side of the family, always took second place to young Jonadab, who not only bore their father's name but was, even now, a miniature edition of him.

George's tongue nervously wetted his lips. 'Good morning, Mother, good morning, Faither,' he croaked. He felt foolish that his father could reduce him to such a state. After all, he was almost grown up.

'Thoo's late.' The accusing blue eyes never wavered.

'Aye, Faither. Aah'm sorry. Oor Joe nivver wekkened me.' George added the latter, feeling that Joe did deserve some of the blame.

'Give him some breakfast, Ann.' Jonadab nodded to his eldest daughter, who lived on the farm with her husband, John Waind.

Ann rose silently from the table and crossed to the large fire-oven, where George's breakfast of several rashers of fat bacon, two eggs and a slice of fried bread had been keeping warm. Placing it before him, she returned to her place on her mother's right, with eyes downcast and not a word.

George realised with a growing feeling of dread at the pit of his stomach, that no one but his father had spoken yet.

Today should have been a happy day. Yesterday, after almost a month of being cut off by snow in the little dale, they had managed to get out, up the steep hill almost a mile in length, which separated Sleightholmedale from the outside world. Under the care of his married sister and her husband, he, Joseph and Beth had gone to a concert in Farmer Butler's barn.

In these entertainments, arranged to help the severe winters to pass, everyone who could sing, play an instrument or recite a poem was called upon to entertain the neighbours. Joseph had sung in his rich baritone and with great feeling, *Drink To Me Only With Thine Eyes*.

George had noticed that the impassioned words

10

were being directed at the Butlers' second daughter, Mary, and wondered if his brother was a bit keen on her. He knew that at the Christmas barn dance, they'd danced together more than was really seemly.

However, the few farming families in the district rarely had a chance to meet outsiders, so husbands and wives were usually chosen from their own community. Perhaps Joseph would start courting Mary Butler when he was twenty-one . . . George dragged his thoughts back to the table, as his father's eyes swung from him to Joe.

'*Joseph*,' he stressed the full name, 'had more on his mind than waking thee!' As though to emphasise his words, he leapt to his feet, knocking over his Windsor chair. 'Goo on!' he bellowed, thumping with his clenched fist on the table. 'Tell thi brothers and sisters what's up!'

'Nay, Jonadab! Not in front of the childer!' exclaimed his wife.

Martha and Maria, the little ones, strained forward excitedly, knowing that their father's wrath was not directed at them.

'Off wi' thee! Into t'parlour, girls,' said Annie, rising to usher them away.

'Nay! Nay!' thundered her husband. 'Let 'em stop and hear what a brother they've got!'

Annie hesitated. She rarely went against her husband's wishes but this time she braved his anger. 'Nay, they're only bairns. I won't have 'em hear such goings on,' she protested, and hurried them from the table and into the next room.

Closing the door behind them, she stood leaning with her back to it, her hands rolling and unrolling her white Sunday apron in her agitation.

George looked at his mother in admiration. He didn't think he'd ever seen her stand up to his father before. Her colour was heightened and her chest heaved, until she raised one workworn hand to the base of her throat and pressed it there, to recover her composure. Taking a deep breath to steady herself, she moved swiftly back to her chair.

George met his sister Beth's eyes, and raised his brows in silent enquiry. She gave a slight shake of her head and raised her shoulders in the suggestion of a shrug. She didn't know what was up, either. George looked at Joseph, but his brother kept his eyes obstinately fixed on his breakfast. His colour was high and his arms lay at either side of his untouched plate, fists clenched.

'Well?' hurled his father at his lowered head. 'Thoo's such a man! Say what tha's got to say. Come on! Out with it, then!'

Joseph slowly raised his flushed face and looked defiantly round the table. 'Aah'm off ti marry Mary Butler,' he stated.

'Go on! Tell 'em t'rest!' came back his father's voice like the crack of a whip. Joseph flinched under the attack. 'Thoo means thoo's *got* ti marry Butler's lass. She's in't family way, carrying thi bairn. That's right, isn't it?'

George could not believe his ears! Their Joseph and Mary Butler . . . doing that! When – where? His thoughts were in a turmoil. He and Joe had been so close, and yet his brother hadn't confided in him. Of course, at seventeen, George knew that in the nearby villages there was many a hasty marriage and many a bairn born early.

The Oaks, however, were strictly brought up and so indeed were the Butlers. The Bible was read by Jonadab to his brood every evening after supper, and all had to learn the Ten Commandments and the Lord's Prayer at their mother's knee, as soon as they could talk.

'How dare thoo bring shame on our name?'

12

demanded his father. 'Not only are thoo an Oaks, but thoo bears thi grandfather's name and his faither's afore him. A Joseph Oaks has farmed this land as long as folk can remember. It's a name well-respected hereabouts and now thoo's brought shame on it!'

Joseph could bear it no longer. He rose slowly to his feet and looked miserably round the table. 'I love Mary and Mary loves me,' he said, staring defiantly at his father.

'Love?' scorned Jonadab. 'Thoo's loved not wisely, but too well, young man.' His eyes fastened on George, who was sitting with knife and fork poised, mouth open. 'Stop thi gawping and let thi meat fill thi mouth!' he barked.

George, for the first time ever, felt a twinge of pity for his father. The Oaks had farmed Aumery Park Farm for at least three generations and he knew his father was proud of the family name. Now his eldest son, the bearer of the name passed down from eldest son to eldest son, had brought disgrace to the family. Jonadab had always regarded himself as lucky to get the tenancy of this land which meant so much to him. His own elder brother, Joseph, had died soon after birth and he himself had treasured his inheritance, farming it wisely and bringing up his children strictly. He found it hard to believe that one of his own blood could be a sinner.

Glancing at those still at the table, Jonadab spoke again, dispiritedly, even sadly. 'Let thi brother's conduct be a lesson,' he instructed. Drawing himself up to his full height, he reached for the family Bible, which lay on the dresser behind him. As he slowly turned the pages, his listeners glanced uneasily at each other. Joseph sank again to his chair.

'Psalm fifteen – the gentleman's psalm,' his father began. ' "*Lord, who shall abide in Thy tabernacle?*

13

Who shall dwell in Thy holy hill? He that walketh uprightly, and worketh righteousness in his heart . . ." '

Before he could continue, Joseph sprang to his feet. 'I don't need a Bible, Faither, ti speak my psalm!' he interjected. ' *"O Lord, rebuke me not in Thine anger, neither chasten me in Thy hot displeasure. Have mercy upon me, for I am weak."* ' With that, he pushed his chair away and ran out of the kitchen, banging the door behind him.

All eyes turned to Jonadab, who looked most discomfited at being bettered in his own house, where he was the expert in the Lord's word. He looked down the table at his wife, but she threw her apron over her head and began to sob.

Their father stared piercingly at each of his children. 'That's the last sinner this family will produce,' he said heavily. 'Thoo'll apply thissens to thi work and thi Bible and when thoo goes out o' this valley, thoo all sticks together.'

Turning to the parlour door, which had opened a crack during the latter part of the proceedings, he said to Martha and Maria: 'I heard thi at t'door. I reckons thoo couldn't mek much on it, but thi brother's done wrong and I hope as how God can find it in His heart to forgive him. Aah doon't know as how I can.'

At this stricture, Ann, Beth and Tamar joined in their mother's quiet sobbing while, not to be outdone, Maria and Martha began to wail.

'Shut thi row!' Jonadab ordered, with impatience. 'Trust womenfolk ti mak a meal on it, when owt goes wrong.'

George hastily bolted the rest of his breakfast, now congealed and unappetising. The only other people at the table who were not sobbing and puffy-eyed were his brother-in-law John Waind, and his younger brother Jonna, who now caught his eye and smirked slightly.

George felt his anger rise. The family would never be the same again and yet that silly gawk could do nowt but grin. John Waind's face was set and George thought he knew the reason why. His sister Ann had been married to John for over a year now, and there was no sign of a bairn. Yet here was Joseph, begetting one without a marriage-band.

His father looked round the table. 'Come on, Mother. Get thissen ready. We'd best be off up ti Butlers', an' see what's ti be done.' Turning to his eldest daughter, he instructed: 'Now, get on. Aah'm trusting thoo and John to keep them at it. There'll be no service up at Fadmoor for you lot. Carry on wi' t'Bible as we've done this last month.' Turning to Maria and Martha he went on, 'Have you lasses fed t'hens yet?'

'No, Faither,' they chorussed.

'Well, off thoo goes then, and wrap up warm. Aah knows they're not laying, but they've got to be fed.' He then addressed George. 'Goo find thi brother,' he commanded. 'Tell him to look sharp. Butlers has ti be seen and t'hoss won't mek it up yon hill. It'll have ti be shanks' pony.'

Not even waiting to put on his coat, George ran out into the bitter cold with just a washed sack over his shoulders. There were always plenty of these hanging behind the kitchen door, to be used as aprons for dirty jobs or hoods, capes and covers for the men in foul weather.

He avoided the stable, knowing that the two farm lads would be in there, the warmest place on the farm, playing Merrills on the lid of a cornbin with some pegs or polishing brasses; passing the time until the hind's wife eventually called them in for dinner.

George flushed when he realised that this crisis not only affected them and the Butlers, but would be the talk of the neighbourhood. Some of their neighbours would be secretly gratified, he was sure, that this could happen to two families who considered themselves so virtuous.

Rapidly running from building to building, and peering into the gloom of each, he skidded round, finding it difficult to keep his balance on the icy paving stones. When he came at last to the cowhouse, there he found Joseph leaning against Blossom, his favourite cow. His arms were wrapped round the gentle beast's neck and his face was buried in her warm side.

Seeing that his brother's shoulders were heaving in silent sobs, George put an arm round him. 'Come on, Joe, Faither's waiting. Thoo's got ti face t'Butlers.'

Joseph straightened up and smiled ruefully through his tears. 'Aah've mucked things up good an' proper, haven't I?' he murmured self-consciously.

George had to acknowledge that this was true. He couldn't imagine what the outcome would be. 'Where'll you live, when you're wed?' he asked.

'Aah don't know,' groaned Joseph. 'Aah just don't know what's tiv 'appen.'

'Doesn't thoo love 'er, then?' queried George.

Joseph looked at him in amazement. 'Love 'er?' he repeated. '*Love 'er*? I worships 'er – she's all t'world ti me!'

'Oh, well.' George was rather embarrassed at his brother's intensity. 'Aah reckons it'll all turn oot all right, if thoo loves each other.'

With that, they turned and went back to the house, Joseph's arm resting across George's shoulder.

CHAPTER TWO

When the two boys went back into the kitchen, all was bustle. Ann had set the two elder sisters on to do the vegetables while little Martha had been despatched to her grandparents' bedroom with two mugs of tea.

'Now don't you say owt to 'em,' she had been admonished by her eldest sister. 'Just ask if they're coming down yet. Faither doesn't want 'em upset, at their age,' she explained, as Joseph came in. He flushed, but didn't answer as he mounted to the lads' bedroom.

As his feet disappeared overhead, George looked at his sisters. 'This is a pretty kettle of fish,' he said. 'What's goin' to happen?'

'Ssssh!' murmured Tamar. 'Our Mam and Dad's coming.'

Jonadab and Annie entered from the parlour, arrayed in their Sunday best. His black Sunday suit had been brushed until not a speck remained thereon; his best boots were so highly polished as to mirror the glow of the fire. In his hand he carried a stovepipe hat while, above all his finery, his face was set in stern lines. Annie was also in black, from bonnet to her gleaming boots – shoes were not worn by the Oaks. Jonadab considered them to be 'fancy fol-de-rols' – of no use to hardworking folk. Annie's funereal garb was relieved only by a white lace collar, and even this was fastened by a brooch of jet, purchased in a weak moment by her husband on a rare visit to Whitby. She treasured this as a visible sign of his affection, which he otherwise rarely displayed, mistaking gentleness for weakness.

'Come on, young man!' he bellowed up the ladder. 'T'walk'll tek us long enough, and we don't want to be all day.' As Joseph scrambled down in his blue serge suit with a white silk scarf knotted round his neck with deceiving casualness, his brothers and sisters looked on him in a fresh light. The girls could understand Mary Butler being swept away by him. Though stocky of build, he was not short, being just over medium height. His fresh, open face still bore traces of last summer's tan, never lost through time spent indoors. He had tried to sleek down his unruly chestnut hair with water, but it sprang back in places in wayward cowlicks, as they were called in those parts. He stood looking at his parents, nervously twisting his cap in his hands.

'By gum!' thought George. 'He's not a bad-looking lad – in fact, he's a man!' This came as a revelation to him: although Joseph was twenty, his brother had never noticed the maturity which had lately come upon him. To George, he was just 'oor lad'. Their father also, although he expected a man's work from them, had kept them young through his domination and expectation of implicit obedience.

His mother looked tenderly at her eldest son. She knew he had done wrong, but she also recalled her husband's passion, held in check before their marriage only by his iron will and her fears. 'Is thoo ready, lad?' she enquired, softly.

'Aye, Mam,' he muttered.

'Get thissen a stick, then,' instructed Jonadab. 'Yon hill'll tek some mounting wi' all t'ice on it.'

With that, he led the way, wielding his crook like some patriarch of old, his wife and son following silently behind.

Leaving the comfort of the warm kitchen, they

passed the duck pond, still beneath a sheet of unbroken ice, and made their way without speaking to the bottom of the steep hill which led out of the dale.

'Keep an eye on thi mother,' said Jonadab. 'It's nobbut slippy up t'hill.'

The silence having been broken, Annie and her husband carried on a desultory conversation, mainly discussing the work on the farm, and wondering if this was the end of the heavy snowfalls which had isolated them from the outside world for the last few weeks.

Joseph could not bring himself to join in the talk, partly because he did not wish to draw his father's attention to himself and also because his mind was teeming with thoughts and conjectures. He was over-joyed to be marrying Mary, but bitterly sorry about the circumstances. Though he remembered with delight their passion in the stolen moments in the hayloft at Christmas, he knew he had brought dis-grace to both his family and hers. He realised that they must marry as soon as possible in the hope that people's memories were short, but knew also that there would be plenty of old biddies and young ones, too, for that matter who'd be counting on their fin-gers when the bairn arrived.

Where would they live? There was no room at Aumery Park Farm, he knew that full well. All five bedrooms were occupied so that even Uncle George, his father's brother, was forced to sleep at the hind's house where Dorcas, the wife of Bert Weald, the farm foreman or hind, provided lodgings for some of the farmworkers. Perhaps the Butlers would give them a home. Poor Joseph's thoughts whirled round in his head, as they trudged up the steep road, slith-ering and sliding on the icy patches.

The way to Fadmoor had never seemed so long

and yet, on the other hand, it seemed no time at all before his father was knocking on the solid oak door of the Butlers' farmhouse.

Constructed of local stone, the house was large and far more prosperous-looking than their own long, low, thatched home. John Butler, he knew, was in a secure financial position, being a yeoman farmer with a vote. As they waited, they heard footsteps echoing down the stone-flagged passage. Then the bolts were drawn back. That they had come to the front door was an indication of the importance and solemnity which Jonadab attached to their visit.

The heavy door swung open, and John Butler stood before them, a stout man in his mid-fifties with a heavily-bearded, ruddy face. His usual jovial expression was now replaced by a grave look and his normally twinkling eyes were clouded. There were a few seconds of silence while he regarded them.

'Now, John,' said Jonadab, in embarrassment at their errand.

'Now, Jonna,' he answered, stepping aside. 'Come thissen in Mrs Oaks, out o' t' cold.' Without a word to the scarlet-faced Joseph, he ushered them into the front parlour and to seats by the fire. Annie glanced round surreptitiously as she settled herself, never before having been in the Butler's best room. She was rather mortified to see that it was better furnished than her own parlour, having some bought rugs on top of the linoleum, not the traditional clip rugs which she and her daughters made during the winter evenings.

As John Butler took her heavy cloak, his wife bustled in. 'Good morning Mrs Oaks, Mr Oaks,' she greeted them. 'Now then, Joseph,' she added, and Joseph was relieved to see the trace of a smile on her face. 'I'll bring us some tea, and then we'll all sit down and have a talk. Meanwhile, get yourselves warm,' and she went out of the room.

Joseph sat away from the fire, feeling in no need of warmth, bathed as he was in perspiration. He saw his father's eyes fix him sardonically, as he passed the back of his hand over his brow.

Jonadab sat back in his chair, one hand on each knee, talking in a low voice to John Butler. As they discussed the hard winter and the merits of their own particular animals, Joseph found himself longing for a glimpse of Mary. He ran a finger round the inside of his neckerchief, grown unaccountably tight, and glanced across at his mother for a look or smile of comfort.

Annie, however, was still covertly eyeing the room, trying to remember the details to pass on to her daughters. Not all the chairs were wooden-seated. Some were upholstered in a rich, plum-coloured velvet, which matched exactly the tasselled drapes festooning the mantlepiece. In one corner of the room was a whatnot, its shelves crowded with dainty dishes, ewers and pottery; far finer than anything in her house. To her right was a pedestal table of rich, dark wood, polished to a high lustre. Though her own daughters spent hours polishing the oak furniture in the parlour with the best beeswax, they never achieved a sheen like that. Could it be that mahogany wood, she wondered.

She only had time to take in the black marble clock on the mantlepiece when Ann Butler returned, carrying a teapot and water jug. Close behind her followed Mary with a tray containing teacups and saucers. She kept her eyes down as she crossed the room, placing the tray on one of the tables.

Joseph's heart leapt at the sight of his love. Her soft fair hair swung in ringlets, hiding her face as she bent over the tray, arranging the teacups. Stare

21

as he might, Joseph could not draw her eyes to his but, as she busied herself with the cups he noticed that her hands were trembling.

'Come back, Mary!' her father instructed as she made for the door. 'This concerns thee and t'lad more than anyone else.' He turned to the Oaks. 'We know why thoo's come. She told her mam this morning.' Mary reluctantly turned back into the room, her eyes brimming over and her cheeks rosy as she took her seat next to Joseph, whose hand found hers and squeezed it reassuringly.

He cleared his throat. 'Mr and Mrs Butler, Mother, Faither,' he began. 'Me and Mary's sorry to bring this upon you, but we do love each other and I would have asked for her hand even if this hadn't've happened.'

Turning to John Butler he added, 'I'm strong and hardworking Mr Butler, sir, and I'll tek good care o' Mary and t'bairn, nivver fear.'

'Aye, lad,' John Butler replied, 'I knows as thoo's a powerful lad and can work wi' the best of 'em. Mary couldn't have done better, but I wish it could have happened different.'

'Well,' said Mrs Butler in a businesslike voice, 'what's done cannot be undone and the best thing now is to get them wed as soon as we can. Don't you agree?' she added, turning to Annie Oaks.

As Annie later confided to her eldest daughter, she was 'fair flummoxed'. Obviously the young couple would have to marry and, just as obviously, the happy event must take place without delay. However, she knew her husband and realised that the Butlers were not reacting as he had expected.

Jonadab placed both hands on the chair arms and strained forward, his blue eyes blazing in disbelief. 'Nay, John! We're here on the Lord's day, faced wi' a pair o' sinners and is that all thoo's got ti say?' he spluttered. 'Wrong's wrong, and we cannot condone it.'

Ann Butler leaned towards him, her hand placed placatingly on his arm. 'Now, Mr Oaks,' she interrupted, as he half-rose to begin his thundering condemnation of the young couple. 'To forgive is not to condone. We can forgive our children, even when they've sinned, without condoning their actions.'

As Jonadab sank back into his seat with a look of bewilderment on his face, he turned to his wife for support but she, not to be outdone, opposed him for the second time that day. 'Come, Jonadab,' she murmured soothingly, 'to err is human, to forgive is divine.' She looked round, rather proud of this statement. She wasn't sure where she had heard it, but it certainly sounded good.

For their part, Joseph and Mary sat side by side on the sofa, content to be together and only too happy that the arguments were not, as yet, aimed at them. Seeing that all attention was diverted from them, and seated as they were at the back of the room, they gave each other a shy smile that said more than a whole bookful of words. Mary blushed and gave Joseph's hand a squeeze. Their eyes were then drawn back to the group by the fire, where the atmosphere was tense.

John Butler had risen to his feet. 'Do Aah take it, Jonadab, that thoo isn't for t'marriage?' he asked incredulously. 'Surely thoo won't see our Mary disgraced?'

'Nay, nay, John. Aah just don't think they should get off that easy,' muttered Jonadab.

'*Easy*?' gasped Mrs Butler. 'Our Mary hasn't had it easy. Your lad only found out last night, but our Mary's known this past month, while you were snowed up down in t'dale!'

'Oh, poor lass,' whispered Annie.

All Jonadab Oaks' dominance had deserted him. He had been prepared to see John Butler take a whip to Joseph and thrash him but now it seemed that events were being taken out of his hands. 'Where'll they live?' he queried. 'We've no room down in t'dale.'

'We've a room empty. It's only a little one next to the apple room, but it's cosy,' countered Mrs Butler.

'Thoo means thoo'll find him work?' demanded Jonadab.

'Of course.'

'But what am Aah to do without him? Aah can't get a man in his place till t'Martinmas hirings.' Jonadab was losing ground and he knew it. Since hearing Joseph's news that morning, he had been bent on revenge and punishment for the slur on his family's good name. And the Butlers', of course, he hastened to add to himself. Now it appeared the Butlers were not out for vengeance on Joseph. As long as the wedding could take place quickly, to protect their lass, they were content to let things go. Not only that! He realised that he was about to lose his eldest son, one of the strongest lads and best workers in the district. Joseph suddenly grew in stature in his father's eyes, and became a most desirable and dependable worker.

There was yet another shock in store for the Oaks, however. John Butler stood with his back to the fire, thumbs tucked into his braces.

'Aah sent me lad early on to Gillamoor with a note to t'parson. Aah've got an interview this morning. If we go over now and sign t'papers, t'first banns might be read tonight, at Evensong. That way, the young folk can be wed within the month.'

Annie gasped and raised her hand to her throat, in an involuntary movement. 'So soon?' she whispered, looking across at her firstborn son. Was she to lose him so quickly?

'Aye, Mrs Oaks. It's a ball that unwinds itself. There'll be no hiding our Mary's condition if we hang about, so we must be quick.' He looked at Jonadab. 'Thy lad's under twenty-one, so thoo'll have to sign and give permission,' he added.

As if in a dream, Jonadab rose to his full height. 'Thoo's got it all arranged, then?' he challenged.

'It's for the best, Mr Oaks,' said Mrs Butler. 'What has to be, will be – and we don't want to stand in their way, do we?'

'No . . .' Jonadab answered. Of course he wanted the wedding, but he was master in his own house and was not used to being gainsaid. He liked to hold the reins with a firm hand and drive his family along his chosen track. Now the initiative had been taken from him and he found it hard.

'I told my lad to get the pony and trap ready when you arrived. If we tek the young couple now, we can leave the womenfolk to make the rest of the arrangements.' John Butler strode to the door and held it open. 'Come along then,' he said, gathering them in with his glance. He swept them out into the passage, when they barely had time to put on their outdoor clothes before he whisked them into the pony trap and away towards Gillamoor.

Time passed quickly for the two mothers left behind. Annie Oaks was shown the room where Mary and her son would sleep, and she was surprised to see that, though none of the Butlers used it, it already held a bed and some furniture.

'Funnily enough, we've been making a clip rug for t'bedside and it's nearly done,' observed Ann Butler. 'They'll be cosy here, and there's room for a crib when t'time comes.'

Annie Oaks felt rather strained and embarrassed.

Although outgoing and friendly, the other woman used little of the dialect common in the dales. Annie wasn't sure whether she was putting it on, or was really what she herself labelled 'a bit uppity-like'. When they returned to the parlour, she noted once again the differences between this room and her own. She knew that the land down in Sleightholmedale was fertile and highly-productive and that Jonadab was a good farmer, and yet their house had changed little since his father had inherited it from old Grandad Oaks. The furniture was good, solid, English oak. She and the girls kept it spotlessly clean and highly polished but, though they tried to soften the chairs with patchwork cushions, and the room was brightened by windowsills crowded with geraniums, she had to admit that her home fell far short of Ann Butler's in elegance.

She wished that Jonadab thought a bit more about the house, but realised that as long as he was comfortable and well-fed, any more was dismissed by him as fancy and beneath contempt. Nevertheless, she determined that on her next visit to Kirkbymoorside market, she'd buy one of those japanned trays with flowers on, to prop up on the dresser.

It seemed no time at all before the rest of the group were back, both husbands with set faces and the newly-betrothed pair looking downcast.

'Is all fixed then?' asked Annie Oaks, looking from one face to another, in perplexity. 'Mrs Butler's just been saying t'wedding'll be a bit early in the year for some nice sprigged muslin she's seen – '

'It's not too early for owt, woman! Not too early at all,' Jonadab broke in, his face set in a frown and his eyes flashing.

The two women looked at each other. Surely nowt could have gone wrong? John Butler's face was ruddier than ever; in fact, it was beginning to mottle with purple. 'We forgot Lent!' he explained.

'What about Lent?' Annie Oaks knew it would soon be Pancake Day, but couldn't see why it should affect Joseph's marriage.

John looked uncomfortable. 'T'vicar won't marry 'em in Lent. Certain things,' he reddened even more at having to explain in mixed company, 'certain things has to be done wi'out in Lent. Thoo knows,' he finished lamely.

All now looked uncomfortable and embarrassed, avoiding each other's eyes. They all made personal sacrifices for Lent, but had forgotten in their stress of the day that no marriages took place in that period.

'It's because we're Dissenters,' burst out Jonadab. 'Aah even offered ti tek Joseph home wi' us, straight after t'wedding breakfast, till Easter, but he'd have none of it.'

'That's nonsense, Jonna, and tha knows it.' John Butler interrupted his neighbour's outburst. 'Easter it's to be an' we must mek t'best on it.' He was lapsing into the vernacular, in his annoyance.

'There's one thing,' Ann Butler said. 'It gives us longer to get Mary's things ready. All my girls have been working on their bottom drawers since their twelfth birthdays, so it's only clothes she'll need.'

'Same with mine,' Annie Oaks said with satisfaction.

Every bride's bottom drawer was a matter of pride. From an early age girls sewed, crocheted and embroidered until they had a sufficiently large collection of household linen to last them many years of marriage. As they grew older and were allowed a portion of the egg-money by their mothers, they bought jugs, plates and other crockery from the stalls on market days.

Although the country markets were mainly for the

sale of farm produce – eggs, honey and the like – there were always a few stalls selling pots, tinware, besoms and other items.

'Come on, Missus. We've done all that can be done this mornin'.' Jonadab was grim-faced and rather resentful at the way things had gone. He felt that John Butler had been a bit high-handed in the way he'd handled the whole affair. He still felt that the couple, whose actions he could only think of as wanton, were escaping too easily considering the way they'd misbehaved.

His attitude to Joseph was, however, tempered when he realised he was soon to lose him, and he appreciated for the first time the lad's efforts on the farm. Up to now, he'd tended to take them for granted. Anyway, Mary Butler was older than Joseph, and should have known better. It was a maid's duty to resist a man's advances, he considered.

As Mary brought Annie's cloak in from the passage, he regarded his future daughter-in-law for the first time, with interest. She was a bonny enough lass, he grudgingly admitted. Her complexion was fair and her eyes an unusual shade of hazel, flecked almost with green. These were enhanced by the green plaid dress she wore – a bit fancy for his liking, nipped in well at the waist, showing off her trim figure. A bit on the slight side for childbearing, he considered. However, she'd soon be Joseph's wife and a handsome pair they'd certainly make.

'I'll see that the word's spread round the villages that they've been betrothed since Christmas,' said Ann Butler. 'With the weather as it's been and you fastened in down there, they'll not think it odd that there's been no announcement made.'

Mary spoke for the first time. 'How many brides-maids can I have, Mam?' she asked nervously.

28

'Just our Elizabeth, I think,' Ann answered consideringly. 'We don't want a big splash, under the circumstances.'

As the Butlers ushered them to the door, Joseph looked back at Mary. Eeh, but she was lovely. He could hardly believe that in seven weeks they'd be wed. He wondered what it would be like living here. He knew that John Butler, albeit a strict employer, lacked his father's harshness, and his dedication to the land. Maybe he'd have it a bit easier, but he thought guiltily of his two brothers. 'It'll be hard on oor George and Jonna,' he pondered.

It was now past noon, and a pale sun had struggled through, melting the ice which had coated the road but not making the hill any easier to negotiate. They made their way down in silence, each deep in thought as they struggled through the cart tracks, the mud clinging to their boots with tenacity, as though to hold them back. It was with relief that they reached the valley floor and knew that the last couple of hundred yards were on level ground.

Each reflected on the morning's events. Each saw them from a different viewpoint, but each came to the same conclusion: 'It's been a rum morning.'

CHAPTER THREE

As they entered the porch, Jonadab motioned to Joseph and Annie to pull off their sodden boots and leave them there until after dinner. When his father pushed open the door into the kitchen, Joseph sniffed in appreciation of the warmth and appetising smell which greeted them. The table was set and the elder sisters began to bustle about with steaming hot pans.

'We s'll gan an' change oor stockings and expect t'dinner ti be on t'table when we comes down,' Jonadab instructed his daughters as he strode across the room. He was back in his own domain, where his word was law. 'Maister in mi own house', as he would have put it. He paused by the far door, his gaze directed towards the two little girls playing on the rug beside the fire.

'Now, oor Martha and thoo Maria! Thoo knows better than ti have thi dolls out on t'Sabbath. We'll have no wayward maids in *this* house!' He glared round at his family before following his wife and banging the door behind him.

Meanwhile, Joseph had scuttled up the ladder to change his own long woollen stockings. He felt he could be in for a rough time, and wanted to avoid his father for as long as possible. George shot after him. 'What's gone on, Joe? What's happened?' he asked anxiously. 'We expected thoo'd come back black and blue from old Butler.'

'Nay,' answered Joseph, rubbing some warmth into his feet with the coarse towel, before pulling on a pair of clean, dry socks. 'They were all right, really. Not mad or owt. In fact, when Faither lost his temper, they cooled him down.'

'When's thoo gettin' wed, then?' asked George. He had never known such a day in his life. Here was their Joe, only three years his senior and yet already looking a man. He was off to be wed and had fathered a bairn, and all. It defied George's imagination. He couldn't believe all that had happened since he first woke up. No wonder Joe had forgotten to wake him!

'Easter,' hissed Joseph. 'Come on, or Faither'll be back.'

Down in the kitchen, Jonadab and Annie had not yet made a reappearance, but Ann Waind was carrying a huge platter, bearing a joint of salted beef and a prodigious amount of suet pudding. This she placed before her father's seat, while her sisters, Beth and Tamar, set out the vegetables. Ann felt a sense of, not exactly resentment, more of disappointment. She was a quiet, home-loving young woman, who was longing for a baby.

'If only it could have been me,' she thought sadly.

George and young Jonna helped their grandparents, Joseph and Jane, to the table and all stood, waiting behind their chairs, for Jonadab's entrance. When he strode in, he stood at the head of the table and glared sternly round. Little Martha, the seven year old, scraped her foot on the floor in her anxiety to stand up straight. As her father's disapproving gaze moved to her, she blushed and hung her head.

'Well?' he demanded.

'Sorry, Faither,' she whispered.

Once silence had fallen and all eyes had closed before his, he surveyed his flock. Seemingly satisfied, he closed his own eyes and raised his head slightly. There was no bowing of his head before the Lord for Jonadab Oaks. He respected his God, but more as an equal.

'Oh Lord, bless this food tiv oor use, and us ti Thy service,' he intoned.

'Ame. . .' began voices from various places round the table. They were cut short, however, when, with a raising of his voice, he continued: '. . . and forgive them among us who has sinned.' He then whipped open his eyes, to catch with satisfaction the flush which darkened young Joseph's neck. The family all drew back their chairs and stools and took their places, ready to enjoy the belated meal. As was the custom, they ate in comparative silence, the only voice to break it being, predictably, that of Jonadab senior.

'Noo then, them as eats maist puddin' gets maist meat.' It was one of his few witticisms. The older boys and girls were now wise to his words, but Martha and Maria still believed their father, outdoing each other in their efforts to eat great portions of the suet pudding.

The older children had learnt that those who ate most pudding had no room for much meat, and so there would be plenty left to be eaten cold. Maria and Martha, however, still tried to consume as much suet duff, or Yorkshire pudding, as possible, being then unable to tackle much of anything else.

As on every Sunday, a fire had been lit in the parlour and here, after finishing off their dinner with a pint pot of tea, the parents and grandparents betook themselves. While they sat around the peat fire, banked up with logs to give a cosy flame, Jonadab intended to break the news to his parents of the catastrophe which had struck the family.

The rest of them cleared the kitchen table, where they would all gather when the girls had washed up the pots. This was not a straightforward task, especially as no less than twelve people had sat round the table for the midday meal. After the plates had been washed with water heated over the fire, the knives and two-pronged forks were rubbed bright with sand from the sand-jar. It was one of young Jonna's jobs to see that there was always a good supply in the jar. This he provided by scraping a piece of sandstone with a flat knife. The iron cooking pots and pans were also scrupulously cleaned with sand, before being rinsed and then dried with yet another recycled flour bag. Once they had passed Ann Waind's inspection, they were hung from the rafters of the kitchen ceiling; the plates were arranged on the dresser and the cutlery placed in a wooden box on a shelf above the stone sink.

Taking off her apron and placing it in the top drawer of the dresser, Ann motioned her sisters to do the same. She realised that, like herself, the others were dying to hear Joseph's tale. There was, however, one more task before they could settle down.

'Goo across ti t'spring, lads, and fetch t'water in,' she instructed. The three brothers seized the two great water barrels which stood on the floor near to the sink, and rolled them through the door. Once outside, they were loaded on to a sled for the short trip across the road. Taking them across was an easy job, but bringing them back, full, was a different matter.

The spring which gurgled down the hillside was caught when it reached the road, in a long stone trough. The Oaks were fortunate in that the spring never dried up, no matter how hot the summer, and the water was always sweet, cool and sparkling. 'T'best water in all t'county,' was Jonadab's boast, though how he could substantiate the claim without tasting all the rest was debatable.

The three boys had what were called 'lading cans',

like spoutless metal jugs. These they used to scoop up the water from the trough and empty it into the barrels. Both George and Jonna were dying with curiosity as to what had happened at the Butlers' that morning, but Jonna daren't voice the question which swirled round in his mind and, as for George, he'd already gleaned one bit of information which he felt would satisfy him until Joseph unburdened himself to them all.

As they worked, they heard the sound of a horse's hooves coming towards them from further down the valley. As the rider drew near, he reined in his horse and halted. Looking up, the brothers saw that he was obviously one of the aristocracy. His horse was a fine specimen and the cut of his immaculate fawn coat and the sheen on his highly-polished riding boots proclaimed that money was no object.

'Is the water fit to drink?' he drawled.

'Why, yes, sir!' young Jonna was eager to answer. 'We drinks nowt else!'

'Get me a drink of it, then,' he commanded. Joseph felt resentful at his attitude but passed up a lading can full of the clear, ice-cold liquid. To his anger, it was dashed from his hand by the stranger.

'Good God, man! Surely you don't expect me to drink from that?' he sneered. 'Is it too much to expect you to get a tumbler from the house?'

Joseph flushed but did not reply. He crossed the road and opened the kitchen door. 'Will you bring a cup?' he called, and returned to filling the water-barrels, studiously avoiding looking at the stranger.

Tamar came over and held the cup beneath the spring to catch the water. The stranger eyed her appreciatively as she approached him with the drink. She had a neat, trim figure and her merry, elfin face was framed by curling tendrils of dark hair. Her eyes were of an unusual amber shade, fringed by black lashes.

As she held the cup up to him, the rider clasped her hands for longer than was necessary, and smiled deep into her eyes.

'Thank you. That was truly refreshing.' He raked her figure boldly with his eyes as he handed the cup back to her. Tamar lowered her lashes over the fascinating tawny eyes and gave him a coquettish glance as she returned reluctantly to the house. As she entered, she looked back over her shoulder to find that, as he moved slowly off, he was still watching her. As his eyes met hers once again, he raised his riding crop and spurred his horse to a canter.

Tamar re-entered the kitchen with a secret smile. It was the first taste of the power over men which was developing in her, and she relished the feeling.

Once the two barrels were full, the wooden lids were pushed firmly on and then the two elder brothers seized the leather strap attached to the front of the sled and pulled it across to the house, while Jonna followed behind, steadying the barrels. With the skill born of long practice, Joseph and George rolled each barrel on its rim, keeping it as upright as possible, into the kitchen. By the time the barrels were standing in their place, Jonna had propped up the sled by the house wall and, as he entered, the three turned to see the rest of the family sitting round the table, waiting expectantly.

'Come on, Joe! We're all dying to know what's gone on!' exclaimed Tamar.

George looked across at her. 'It's not seemly to be making sheep's eyes at any man, especially one of t'gentry,' he chided. Although Tamar was only his junior by a year, he felt that somebody should check her behaviour.

Her eyes narrowed and she glared across the table

at him, before bursting out: 'Aah did no such thing!'
George did not bother to reply. There were far more
important matters to be discussed.

Joe looked round. 'Well,' he began, 'it were odd,
really. I expected Mr Butler ti take a stick ti me.
Aah knows our Dad would a' done if it had been
t'other way round.'

There was a murmur of agreement round the
table. 'Any'ow, t'Butlers were all right. You could
see they weren't suited, but bent on makin' t'best
on it.'

'Did they shout at thi, or owt?' interposed Jonna,
seemingly disappointed that there'd been no high
drama.

'No. Mistress Butler seemed nice as pie.' Here,
he came to a stop. It was awkward with the three
younger ones there, all ears. John Waind, too, had
been a bit funny, not saying much. Joseph was well
aware that his conduct had been inexcusable but, by
'eck, he thought, it hadn't seemed like sin.

'Aah'm sorry. I know what Aa've done will reflect
on all t'family,' he said earnestly. 'Aah disn't want
folk sayin' as 'ow t'Oaks is a flighty lot, or owt.' He
was a sensitive lad and knew well enough that his
own actions might well affect Beth and Tamar's marriage chances. Many families in the district were,
like themselves, Methodists, rather narrower and
stricter in outlook than 'Church folk'.

They met, more or less regularly, in a little room
in Fadmoor, where local preachers came round,
shouting of Hell and Damnation with much table-
thumping and finger-pointing. Joseph was uneasy
about what would happen to him in Hell, but consoled himself that he was young and strong. It would
be a long time before he had to face the Afterlife, so
he determined to make the best of this one.

'When's t'wedding, then?' asked the ever-practical Ann.

'Easter. It can't be afore. T'parson won't wed us i' Lent.'

Ann did a quick calculation in her head. She knew that Joe was a good-living lad and that his lapse from virtue would have been a single occasion, most probably at the Christmas dance. Easter was at the end of March, so Mary Butler wouldn't be showing. That was a blessing, at any rate, though folks would be doing their sums when the bairn put in its appearance. Poor Joe, she thought, caught the first time, yet she and John had no children on the way after more than a year of marriage.

All the girls had helped in the Butlers' kitchen whenever there'd been a concert or dance in their barn, but though the families were fairly friendly, none had ever seen the rest of the house.

'Did thoo go in t'parlour?' asked Beth.

'Aye.'

'What's it like?'

Joseph was stumped. He'd had too much on his mind to take much notice of his surroundings.

'Well,' he gazed round for inspiration. 'It's fancier than oors. All ornaments and bits and pieces – pots an' things,' he finished lamely, realising that he'd let his avid listeners down. 'Oor Mam'll know. By 'eck, she were takin' it all in. Er eyes were all ower.' He chuckled at the thought.

That chuckle left his audience speechless. That Joe, whose day had started so devastatingly, who'd been denounced by their father as a sinner and whose soul must surely be heading for Hell-fire, could laugh, was utterly beyond their understanding.

Joseph, however, was under no illusions. He knew that the next few weeks at home would be made intolerable by his father. Not only would Jonadab

37

make his displeasure felt in various ways, perhaps not even addressing him personally, but he would be determined to get as much work as possible out of his son before he left the family farm.

Ann Waind now came to what had been bothering her all day. 'Where are you and Mary going to live?'

'Up at Butlers'.'

This was like a bombshell to his brothers and sisters. George felt stunned.

'Thoo means thoo's leaving t'farm?' he asked incredulously.

'What else is there ti do? It's full 'ere.' Joseph bit his lip, realising what effect his words would have on Ann and John Waind. As the eldest son, Joseph's place was on the family farm. Upon her marriage, Ann should really have moved to the Wainds' farm in Bransdale, but they had the same problem – a house bursting at the seams. John was not the eldest son, and so Jonadab had taken them in, finding work for John, as John Butler was to do for Joseph. When they became too old to work, the dale and moorland farmers remained on the farms, handing over the reins to the eldest son, but giving him the benefit of their vast experience of the land which had been their lives. So, houses were packed, with three and often four, generations living together under the same roof.

John Waind spoke for the first time. 'Mebbe Ann an' me could get summat on our own,' he ventured.

'Nay, John. On what our Dad pays thee, thoo'll be a long time saving up for owt,' replied Joseph heavily. John did receive a wage, which was more than Jonadab's own sons could expect. This was why their Uncle George still worked on the farm where he'd been born. Never having received a wage from old Joseph, his father, and never having married, he had remained there as a farmworker when Jonadab took over the farm.

Joseph looked round at his brothers and sisters. He would miss them all, he knew, and yet he was relieved in a way to be leaving. His father had made it clear that he could never forgive his conduct and he felt that the less they saw of each other, the better it would be.

'George,' he ventured shyly. 'Aah'd like thee ti stand for me at t'wedding. Be a witness, thoo knows.'

George was flattered. 'Thanks, Joe,' he said, flushing with pleasure. 'By, Aah s'll be honoured.' He considered a moment. 'What about Faither? Won't he expect ti be a witness?'

'Aah dissent care what 'e expects.' Joe was in a defiant mood now, having safely got through the ordeal of facing the Butlers. 'It's my wedding and Aah s'll have who Aah wants.'

The more they heard, the more his audience marvelled at the change in their brother. Only that morning he'd run from the house, discomfited and embarrassed by his father's taunts, but now he was staunchly talking of disobeying Jonadab. Whatever had been said up in Fadmoor that morning had certainly put some mettle into the normally placid and obedient young man.

At that moment, there came a knock on the kitchen door. 'Jonna!' called Will Ransome, one of the two lads who worked on the farm. 'Mr Weald says to tell thi it's time for milkin' and fotherin'-up.'

'Aye, Aah's coming,' answered Joseph, pushing young Jonadab down by placing a hand on his shoulder. 'Aah'll do it. Thoo might as well mek use of me while Aah'm still 'ere.' With which sentiment, he went out of the kitchen. Joseph wasn't taking on Jonna's turn only to do him a favour, but to take the opportunity of telling the men what had happened. He realised that they'd find out soon enough and he wanted to tell them himself.

When they were all in the meal-house measuring out the portions for the horses, cattle and pigs, Joseph cleared his throat.

'Aah've summat ti say,' he announced uncomfortably.

The two men and two lads turned to regard him with interest. The normal conversation on the farm was to do with the weather or stock, with very occasional references to news of the outside world, brought into the dale by someone who'd been to market. Seeing four pairs of eyes fixed upon him, Joseph's newfound courage deserted him for a moment. He swallowed audibly and then began.

'Uncle George, Mr Weald, Will and Rob, Aah've summat to tell thi.' He paused once more.

'Aye?' enquired his Uncle George kindly.

'Aah'm ti be wed at Easter,' Joe blurted out.

The look of disbelief and amazement on each face would have seemed comical in any other circumstances.

'Wed?' echoed Uncle George. 'Aah didn't know thoo was walkin' out.'

'Well,' explained Joseph, rather shamefaced. 'It's Mary Butler up at Fadmoor, an' it's a bit of a rush job, like.'

Uncle George looked at the youth with sympathy. He knew his brother and could guess Jonadab's reaction to the news. The two farm lads were silent, not knowing how to react. They'd only worked at the farm since November, having been chosen by Jonadab at the Martinmas hirings in Kirkbymoorside, but they considered t'Maister a hard man and had made a secret pact not to work for him a further

40

year. Their hearts went out to Joseph, who couldn't escape his wrath.

Bert Weald, the foreman, looked at the lad with a kind of admiration. 'By gum, thoo's a dark 'oss,' he commented. He couldn't believe that one of Jonadab Oaks' flock had strayed. He'd worked for him now for over seven years and stayed because, although a demanding master, Jonadab was scrupulously fair. The tied cottage occupied by the Wealds was pleasant, and not too near the farmhouse. His wife provided bed and board for any hired workers, and they'd a good-sized garden for vegetables. However, being able to escape to his own house when his day's work was over was a far cry from being under the master's watchful eye all day and every day as Jonadab's own family were.

'There's one thing, lad. Thoo's showed guts in facing us and telling us thissen,' he complimented Joseph, guessing what courage it must have taken to do so. 'Come on, now, let's be on,' he continued, bustling them about their allotted tasks.

When Joseph returned to the house for tea, his presence was completely ignored by his father. Sunday tea was always the same – boiled ham and pickled onions, huge plates of bread and butter, with jam to use up the bread and, finally, a fruit or seed cake. All this fare was, of course, home-produced. One thing Jonadab prided himself upon, among the many, was that his wife kept a good table.

After tea, the whole family repaired to the parlour for prayers and a Bible reading. Jonadab had insisted that his children learned to read and write at Sunday school, while their parents were at chapel. Both he and Annie had mastered their letters and Jonadab had painstakingly practised every evening in his youth, until he reached a high enough standard to read aloud from the Bible.

A lot of farmers known to him could only just write their names, or even put their mark, but Jonadab had always been ambitious and, after an early grounding, had determined to better himself through self-education. By his continual insistence, all his children could, at least, write their names, and the three boys could pen a letter if need be. It was his custom to call upon even Martha, the youngest child, to read a verse or part of a psalm, aloud, at the evening service. While considering too much education of little use to females, he was determined that his daughters should learn the basics of reading, writing and numbers, if only to pass them on to their sons.

His own parents, old Joseph and Jane, were unable to read, but Jonadab had taught both to write their own names when they were younger. They always listened in admiration to their grandchildren reading and often discussed with each other how well their son had raised his family. After the nightly prayers, the old couple would go off to their bed, where one of the granddaughters brought them a cup of hot milk.

On weekday evenings, the three boys usually went for an hour to the stable, to play Merrills or brush the horses and polish the brasses. This was warm, cosy and a man's world. While they were occupied there, the girls would sit round the fire knitting, sewing, or just gossiping, though this latter pastime did not find favour in their father's eyes.

On Sundays, however, only essential work was permitted and, after prayers, while they sat round the kitchen table drinking a cup of milk in the candlelight, Jonadab would question them on what he had read to them. His favourite passages were from the Old Testament but tonight, he had read the parable of the Good Samaritan. He felt that the girls, the two young ones in particular, had had enough to put up with for one day, so he had chosen little Maria's favourite story as a special treat. She and Martha were excited at being able to answer all his questions, making the atmosphere at the supper table lighthearted and in direct contrast to the gloom of breakfast. The older ones, however, noticed that no smile lightened Jonadab's features, but the younger children were happy, as their father had intended.

Young Jonna tried to capitalise on the softening of the family's mood, and sidled up to his mother.

'Mam,' he cajoled, 'can I have t'big bed all to myself when Joe goes, an' let oor George move into t'little 'un?'

Annie was annoyed at being reminded of Joe's eventual departure. 'No!' she snapped, taking him aback by her tone. She sought for inspiration. 'You'll both stay where you are, and Uncle George'll move into t'little bed. Aah've nivver liked it – him having to lodge in t'hind's house.'

Jonadab's attention was captured by the sound of his brother's name. He turned from Martha and Maria. 'What was that, Mother?' he queried.

'Aah'm just saying as 'ow Uncle George can come back after Easter.'

'Aye. Aye, that 'e can,' said Jonadab with satisfaction. It would be good to have his brother to talk to in the evenings. 'Off ti bed with thoo all,' he ordered now, looking at the grandfather clock in the corner. 'It's half-past eight and time all honest folks was in their beds.'

The eldest in each room took a candle and candlestick from the dresser, lighting it with a spill of wood from the fire.

'Goodnight Faither, Mother,' all said as they went from the room.

Jonadab banked up the fire with peat to keep it until morning. As his wife picked up their candle, he made the statement which had been repeated every night for the last fifteen years of their marriage. 'Aah'm just off ti look at t'stock. Aah s'll be up in a minute.'

Having visited every barn, stable and byre assuring himself that all was well, he followed his wife upstairs. His feet were heavy and his brow was lowered as he entered the bedroom.

'Eeh, Mother,' he said, sinking down on the bed. 'Aah nivver thought ti see a day such as this in all mi life.'

'Husband,' ventured Annie, 'aah knows thoo's a few golden sovereigns in t'tin box in t'thatch. T'lad'll have ti have a new suit and things. If you could let me have five guineas, or even five pounds, I'll tak him into Kirkby next market day ti be measured for a suit and some boots.'

Jonadab shot up as though he'd sunk on to a bed of nails.

'Five guineas?' He was incredulous. 'Does ta think Aah'm made o' money, woman? What's in t'thatch is for a rainy day – not ti be frolicked away on wantonness.'

Drawing a deep breath, Annie stuck to her guns. This was the third time today that she'd defied her husband and each time she was finding it easier. 'This day's bin a stormy one, not just rainy,' she rejoined with grim humour, 'and 'e's not going ti t'Butlers without being proper fitted out. Aah s'll get some stuff and each girl can mek a shirt – Aah'll mek him a best one for t'wedding missen. Martha and Maria can knit some socks.'

Reluctant as he was to part with his money, Jonadab's pride was at stake and he realised that Annie must have her way. He knew she wouldn't waste his hard-earned brass and no lad of his was going out from the farm threadbare.

As they got into bed and blew out the candle he kissed her cheek.

'Aye, all right. As long as five guineas covers it,' he capitulated.

At the far end of the house, Joseph's voice came across the lads' room: 'George?'

'Aye?'

'If it's a lad, Aah shall call it after thee!'

George settled down with a sigh of satisfaction. 'By gum, Joe, it's been a day and a half,' he said.

'A day and a half? More like a week!' Joe replied.

CHAPTER FOUR

The bitter winter gave way early to a fine, warm spring. Within a week or two of the fateful journey to Fadmoor, Annie Oaks decided that it was time to stand the market at Kirkbymoorside once more. During the hard winter months, she had been confined to the dale, unable to earn the money which was her sole income. The egg-money had got rather low, much of it having been spent on Christmas gifts. Her hens had come into lay with the warmer weather, so she could make up a few baskets of goods to sell.

Calling to Joseph to bring the pony and trap to the front, she gathered four large, flat-bottomed baskets from the pantry.

'How many pounds of butter has thoo got, our Beth?' she called.

'Just coming, Mam,' said Beth, entering from the dairy and carrying a tray on which were arranged several pounds of butter, each expertly patted into shape with a pair of Scotch hands and then embellished with a milkmaid wearing a poke bonnet and carrying a pail.

This wooden mould had been bought for Annie by Jonadab early in their married life, and on market days it identified her particular butter for potential customers. Though Beth was now in charge of the butter-making, it was made strictly to her mother's instructions with not a grain more or less of salt than Annie laid down. Beth was nineteen now, and would make a good farmer's wife, Annie thought with pride.

She loaded up one basket with the butter, several jars of curd and some homemade jam. Into a second basket she tucked half a dozen dressed chickens, and then, the two last baskets were lined with hay. Into one were carefully placed all the newlaid eggs she had. The family could finish off the ones she'd preserved at the end of last summer. The second of her hay-lined baskets held several sittings of goose eggs, in the hope that some of the cottagers at the market would buy them to pop under broody hens. When hatched and reared, the geese not only provided a substantial Christmas dinner, but the surplus would be sold to buy extra food. A broody hen would cover and hatch four goose eggs.

Annie surveyed them critically before covering each basket with a snowy white cloth. Later in the year there would be more eggs, cheeses, honey and nosegays of flowers to add to her stock. Her market-day earnings clothed her and the girls and bought in groceries which they could not provide for themselves, such as tea, soap, salt and baking powder. Every few weeks she would bring back a stone of dried fruit and a quarter of carroway seed, together with a pound of yeast for the breadmaking.

With the wedding coming on she felt, ruefully, that she could have done with twice as much to sell. However, she'd have to make the money stretch she told herself philosophically.

'Art ready, Joseph?' She went to the door, carefully carrying one of the egg baskets, while her three eldest daughters followed with the others. As Joseph held the horse's head, the girls stowed the baskets under the wooden seats at each side of the trap.

Tamar looked at her pleadingly. 'Will it run to new gowns, Mam?' she asked.

Annie hesitated. Better not let them become too optimistic. 'No, Aah don't think so, lass. We'll have a look tonight at what we've got. Some of you've grown since last year, but there'll be tucks to let out. Aah'll see what Aah can get in t'way of a bit of lace and some ribbons.' She smiled. 'Aah'll see thoo looks all right, nivver fear.'

The girls were satisfied. They knew their Mam would do her best. As they returned to the neverending tasks of the house, Tamar remarked, 'It disn't look as though Mary's wanting any of us for bridesmaids.'

Ann Waind gave her sister a little shake. 'Noo, oor Tamar! We'll have none o' that. She's only having their Elizabeth – even their Christie and Jane aren't being bridesmaids. It's for t'best that there's not a lot o' fuss made.'

'Aye, you're right,' conceded Tamar. 'Anyroad, she's a nice lass. In fact, all t'Butler lasses are.'

With a last look at the trap, turning the corner by the duck pond, they re-entered the house.

When Annie and Joseph arrived at Kirkby, the bustle of the market on such a bright, sunny day made a welcome change from the dark winter in the valley and the tension of the last week or two. Joseph helped his mother to unload her baskets and then went to stable the pony and put the trap in the big yard behind the Black Swan. Going through from the back, he had a word with the landlord, Joseph Jackson, and paid him for the stabling, plus a halfpenny for the hire of a chair. This he carried out through the back door – as a Methodist he couldn't be seen coming out of an alehouse.

When Annie was settled on her chair, her baskets spread about her and other farmers' wives around her to talk to, she looked at Joseph.

'Goo ti t'tailor's and get measured for a suit. It mustn't cost above a guinea and tell Thomas Dobson we wants it for next market day. Tell him it's cash on t'nail,' she added proudly. 'Same at t'shoe-maker's,' she called after him.

Joseph strode purposefully through the busy market place. It was the first time in his life that he'd ordered anything for himself and it made him feel more of a man than ever. On his way to the tailor's shop, he passed a stall full of pretty linens, where his eye was taken by a handkerchief embroidered with blue flowers. He paused. 'How much is that?' He indicated the handkerchief.

'Tuppence, and cheap at the price, sir.' The stall-holder knew that a 'sir' always flattered the young bloods, as he dubbed them. Made them more likely to buy, he told himself.

Joseph dodged back to where the farmers' wives sat.

'Mam! Can Aah beg tuppence?' he whispered. 'It's for summat for Mary.'

Annie had already done well, having sold two clutches of goose eggs and several scores of hens' eggs. She slipped her hand into the pocket of her voluminous white apron and passed the coppers to her son. She wished that Jonadab would give the lads a wage, no matter how small, but knew that all the farmers held the same view. The farms were the family's concern and the family should run them. Hired men were the ones who received the pay, while the children's loyalty and hard work was accepted as their parents' due.

When Joseph reappeared, the stallholder congratulated himself on being a good judge of character. The youth again picked up the handkerchief.

'It doesn't look very big for tuppence,' he observed, stroking the fine material.

'It's pure Irish linen, made in Ireland,' stressed the salesman. He added a final accolade. 'They're fancy-worked by t'nuns in a convent.'

Joseph dropped the scrap of linen as though it were red hot. 'Made by Papists?' He looked shocked to think that he'd almost bought it.

The pedlar could suddenly see the loss of his sale. 'Is it a favour for a maiden?' he queried.

'Aye. Leastways, it was,' Joseph answered sheepishly.

'Go on, then! For you, I'll knock an 'apenny off. Three halfpence to you.'

Joseph looked at the kerchief consideringly. He'd never seen linen so fine, nor needlework so beautifully done. As far as he could gather, his soul was already spoken for by old Nick, so what difference could another lapse make?

'Goo on, then, Aah'll have it,' he made up his mind. 'Leastways, if thoo'll wrap it up fancy-like.' Clutching his parcel, he pushed his way down the market to the tailor's shop.

He was always intrigued by the three apprentices, who sat cross-legged in a row on a bench, busily stitching and snipping. Looking round, he saw Thomas Dobson bending over a long table, cutting out cloth with a huge pair of shears. He straightened upon noticing Joseph.

'Now, Joseph, what can I do for you?' he enquired kindly. He liked the Oaks, considering them to be hardworking and thrifty. The farmers were among his best customers, even though they might not have as much money as many of the town's inhabitants. However, they always paid their bills on time, which was more than could be said even of some of the gentry.

'Aah've come ti be measured for a new suit, please, Maister Dobson,' Joseph answered.

Thomas Dobson raised a quizzical eyebrow. Joseph had had one suit bought last autumn. Was

50

Jonadab Oaks suddenly becoming generous, he wondered.

'Another suit, Joseph? Have you come into money, then?' he teased.

'Nay, Mr Dobson. Aah'm gettin' wed at Easter,' he announced, with a mixture of pride and shyness.

'Who's the lucky lady, then?' the tailor enquired, as he reached for his order book.

'Nay, Aah'm the lucky one,' Joseph protested. 'It's Mary Butler, from Fadmoor.'

'One of John Butler's daughters?' asked Thomas Dobson.

'Aye,' breathed Joseph, his thoughts dwelling fondly on Mary.

'Take off your jacket and I'll just check your measurements.' The tailor took his tape measure from round his neck. 'You've broadened out a bit, but otherwise there's not much difference,' he said, as he checked the measurements with those for Joseph's last suit.

As Joseph put on his coat again, he suddenly remembered his mother's instructions.

'Can it be ready by next Wednesday please, Mr Dobson?' he asked. 'Our Mam'll be in later for some shirting, and she says to tell you it'll be cash on t'nail,' he added.

'That it can, Joseph. I'll see that she gets a bit of extra material for patching, or longer laps.' The shirts were also used as nightshirts, and the men liked them nice and long.

Joseph blinked as he went out into the bright sunshine of the crisp, spring day. The shoemaker they always patronised was James Hill, whose shop was in West-end, so he hadn't too far to go. With this order placed, he wandered about the stalls, greeting people he knew and whom he hadn't seen for several weeks, while the snow had confined the family to the dale. He found that several of them had already heard of his forthcoming marriage and he accepted their congratulations with embarrassment. Would they be so eager to convey their good wishes if they knew all the circumstances, he wondered.

He made his way back to his mother to find her animated and satisfied, having sold everything but a couple of jars of curd. She slipped him another two pennies.

'Goo and get us a couple of penny mutton pies,' she instructed. 'By the time we've had a bite, Aah should be ready for off.'

True to her word, when Joseph came back with the pies, her baskets were empty and the cloths neatly folded in one of them. Mother and son ate their pies in companionable silence, each savouring the respite from the routine work of the farm.

As they finished eating and brushed the crumbs from round their mouths, and from their clothes, Annie suddenly remembered.

'What did you get Mary?' she enquired.

Joseph pulled his parcel from his pocket and carefully unfolded it. Annie examined the workmanship critically. It was beautifully done, she admitted, but tuppence was a lot to pay. As though reading her thoughts, Joseph held out the halfpenny.

'He knocked me an 'apenny off,' he said.

While Annie took her leave of the farmers' wives with whom she'd spent the morning, Joseph returned the chair to the inn and stowed three of the baskets away in the trap. Then they returned to the market-place to do the shopping. In addition to the shirtings and the thread with which to sew them, Annie bought a packet of needles. It was no use getting home and finding herself short, when they'd all be needing them at the same time. She then bought enough wool for a few pairs of socks and packed the lot into the fourth basket.

'Aah'm running a bit short of yeast,' she said. 'Aah'll just slip back to Hugill's and then we'll get on home.'

Now that the winter was over, she knew that she would be standing the market each Wednesday, so had no need to stock up with a large amount of groceries.

'What about t'ribbons and laces that you promised t'lasses?' Joseph suddenly remembered. 'Yon chap where Aah got t'kerchief had some right bonny things.'

They paused at the stall and Annie appraised the goods laid out. She'd made over a guinea through the sale of her produce and felt that she could afford a shilling, or even a bit more, on bits of finery. Once her purchases were made, they returned to the inn-yard.

There, Joseph removed the pony's nosebag, harnessed her up and yoked her to the trap. The journey home soon passed as they talked with animation about whom they'd seen, and discussed all the snippets of news they'd picked up.

As the trap began to descend the steep hill down into the dale, they looked round with pleasure at the impressive scenery, of which they never tired. On the left-hand side, the land fell away in a sheer drop, so that the road was level with the tops of some of the trees which covered the sides of the steep escarpment. To the right, the ridge continued upwards, so that the road seemed to wind down, clinging to the cliff side. Just before the road began its steepest drop was a small quarry, which had supplied the stone to build the three or four farms in the valley below.

'Stop by t'quarry a bit, Joe,' requested Annie.

Joseph, like his mother, was unwilling to draw this period of companionship to a close, so he pulled on the reins and stopped the pony, pulling off the precipitous road on to the quarry floor, which was level with it.

'We can't be long. Your faither'll be wondering what has happened to us,' Annie said. 'Aah just wants ti say, Joe, as Aah'm sure all will go well for thoo and Mary.'

'Thank thoo, Mam,' Joseph answered. 'And Aah'd like ti thank thee, an' all, for what thoo's done. Aah don't deserve it, but Aah wants thi ti know as Aah'm grateful. Thoo's stood up ti Faither for me, which can't have been easy. There's all this stuff an' all,' – he indicated the basket, laden to overflowing. 'Where's money come from, for it all?'

Annie smiled mischievously. 'Thi faither! Only nivver let on as thoo knows. He'd tek it amiss if thoo caught him out being soft.' So saying, she handed him the reins. 'Come on, we'd best be off. We've plenty to do afore Easter!'

The days that followed seemed filled with work from sun-up to sunset, and even into the night. The shirts which Annie had cut out were busily stitched by her daughters during every moment they could steal from the constant round of housework, dairy work, cooking and baking. The two younger girls applied themselves with diligence to knitting the socks, needing help with the turning of the heels, but otherwise managing to struggle on quite well.

To Joseph, it appeared that his father was determined to squeeze as much labour out of him as was humanly possible before he left the farm. Each night he fell into bed too exhausted even to hold a short conversation with George and Jonna.

The weeks tumbled past with an unbelievable rapidity. His mother had unearthed the deep woven

54

basket which had brought her belongings to the farm almost twenty-five years earlier. A larger basket fitted over the base, and the whole was secured with leather straps. Joe's new suit and boots were carefully packed at the bottom, and then as each shirt or pair of socks was finished, they were laid on top.

Joe was impressed. At least Mary wouldn't have any mending or darning to do for a bit, he thought. He'd never had so many shirts before and knew that they'd last him for several years. He realised that his mother was worried as to whether or not John Butler would pay him a wage, or treat him as one of the family, working for just his keep. She was trying to ensure that he wouldn't lack for clothing and, of course, wanted to impress the Butlers with the way her lad was turned out.

On the Wednesday after Palm Sunday, only a couple of days before the wedding, Jonadab went into Kirkbymoorside. This was the day of the biggest horse and cattle market of the year, when dealers came from all over Yorkshire.

Knowing that one pair of draught oxen were now into their third year, and would be killed for meat at the end of harvest, his family presumed that he'd gone to buy two more. Most of the heavy work on the farm was done by oxen, although Jonadab owned four horses in addition. In order to plough a straight rigg, Jonadab liked a horse harnessed with an ox. Oxen could work for longer hours but tended to wander if yoked together. The guidance of a horse kept them straight.

Just as they were going into the house for tea, the sons heard the sound of hooves on the road. Although oxen going on roads were shod, there was something about the rhythm of these hooves which made them stop and look expectantly towards the corner. As the pony and trap rounded the bend,

55

they were amazed to see, following behind with their halters attached to the back corners of the trap, a pair of magnificent, matched, grey shire-horses.

'By 'eck!' murmured young Jonna. 'They're beauties! They'll have cost a pretty penny.'

Not for the first time, George wondered what their Dad was worth. He knew that his father was a good farmer, husbanding his land well, and yet they all scrimped and scraped as though he only just managed to pay the rent. As Jonna had said, this pair of well-matched horses would have cost a fair amount. They hadn't sold off any foals either, this year, for they were being kept to build up the stock. Although Joseph preferred the traditional oxen, both George and young Jonna were drawn more to the horses. In fact, George had often thought that a day might well come when horses replaced oxen, rather than working alongside them. That wouldn't suit their Joe, he thought, glancing at his brother.

After tea, the main topic of conversation ousting even talk of the wedding, was the new arrivals.

'By, they're bonny, Faither,' said George as he settled down, feeling replete.

'They're an investment, lad,' answered his father. 'Aah'm intending to build up t'quality of t'stock. There's a demand for big draught-horses ti work for t'breweries and t'railways and they fetch a good price!'

'They'll not be in foal yet?' enquired Joseph.

'No. Aah've had a word with a chap who's got a good entire and he'll fit us in on his round in a week or two.'

This statement reduced his listeners to a respectful silence. A high-class stallion calling to serve their mares? It made them all look at their father in a fresh light. It would raise him above the neighbouring farmers with their sturdy little Galloways.

'Aah bet they cost thee a lot, Faither,' ventured young Martha.

'Pence ha'penny, mi lass, pence ha'penny,' her father smiled. This, they knew, closed the subject. Jonadab Oaks confided his financial affairs to no one – not even his wife, not even his father. He'd a lot more hidden in the thatch than they ever suspected and not even Annie knew that he had money deposited in the York Union bank in Kirkby.

That had been a wise move on his part, he congratulated himself. The money just sat there, earning more without him having to work for it – a fact that never ceased to amaze him.

There were a few driving about in fancy carriages who hadn't as much brass stored away as Jonadab Oaks, he thought with satisfaction.

CHAPTER FIVE

The wedding was fixed for noon on the Easter Saturday, but all the routine jobs had to be done before they could make a start. The menfolk were out by half-past five, hurrying to get the horses, cattle and pigs fed, while the girls did the milking.

After breakfast, while Martha and Maria fed the hens, collected and washed the eggs, their sisters washed up and put the milk into skimming pans in the dairy.

Then they were free at last to get into their finery! Though no new gowns had been made, they were all satisfied that they looked their best. With the help of new lace, ribbons and artificial flowers, they congratulated themselves that their old gowns and bonnets had taken on a new lease of life. Hair which had spent the night in curl rags now danced under their bonnets in unaccustomed ringlets and tendrils. As they chatted excitedly, Jonadab came downstairs, consulting his watch.

'Stop all the row! Thoo's like a gaggle of geese!' he admonished. Nevertheless, he surveyed them with satisfaction. Not many fathers had a better-looking family, he thought. But then, Annie was still a fine-looking woman. He glanced across at her and they smiled.

'Where's Joseph?' he suddenly demanded. Looking round and doing a hasty head-count, Annie realised that all were present and ready to set off, except the groom. He couldn't have got cold feet and run away, surely, she wondered. Then she chided herself for the unworthy thought. Her lads weren't cowards: they'd face up to owt that came, she told herself.

Just then, Joseph entered the kitchen. 'Aah've just been for a last look round,' he murmured self-consciously.

'Thoo's not going to t'other end o' t'world,' chided Annie briskly. 'It's only a couple of miles.'

'Are we all ready?' asked Jonadab. 'Best be off. It's a longish walk ti Gillamoor.'

As the family made for the door, he caught Joseph's eye and motioned with his head for his son to join him in the parlour. Joseph's heart sank. His father had treated him more normally of late. Was he going to spoil Joseph's happy day? Jonadab, however, fished in his waistcoat pocket and drew out five guineas. Holding them out to Joseph, he said gruffly: 'It's a wedding present.'

Joseph couldn't believe his father's generosity. 'By 'eck, Faither, Aah can't thank thee enough,' he said fervently. All this money and all his clothes paid for!

'Aye. Well see tha' disn't fritter it away,' came the answer. 'Look after thi brass, lad. Thoo'll find it's thi best friend.'

When they joined the others outside, they looked at the pony and trap in amazement. Unbeknown to anyone else, George and Jonna had spent every spare minute since their father had returned from market on the Wednesday afternoon, working in the waggon shed. The trap had been thoroughly cleaned and then newly varnished. Peggy, the pony, had been brushed until she gleamed and her mane and tail were plaited and interwoven with red, white and blue ribbons. All the leather was burnished and every piece of brass shone like gold.

'Thoo's done a good job there, lads.' Jonadab gave rare praise, making the two flush with pleasure.

With Grandma and Grandad leading the way in

the pony-trap and the two younger girls having a ride to the top of the hill, the procession wound its way up and out of the valley. All but Jonadab were full of chatter, and the girls laughed excitedly as they wondered what Mary would wear.

Jonadab was by nature a taciturn man, given to thinking much and talking little. Today, moreover, he had much to think about. Not only was he losing his eldest son and best worker with lambing, haytime and harvest still to come, but he didn't like leaving the farm for a whole day. True, Bert Weald was a good hind. He'd employed him for seven years and had left him with a list of instructions as long as his arm.

However, it wasn't like leaving your own kin in charge, he thought morosely. He'd had to give his brother George the chance to come to the wedding and of course, he'd grabbed at it. Jonadab did think he could have stayed to keep an eye on things. All in all, it was going to be a rum day, he considered. He was suddenly irritated by the chatter and laughter going on around him. 'Hold thi noise!' he bawled. 'Empty cans mek maist rattle.' So it was in comparative silence that they completed the three-mile walk to Gillamoor.

Entering the cool church, they found they were there before any of the Butlers, although there was a sprinkling of friends and neighbours at the back.

Joseph and George occupied the front pew, side by side, neither speaking. Joseph glanced down and saw that his brother's knees were shaking with nervousness. 'It's not thoo that should be nervous,' he whispered.

'Aah knows,' hissed back George. 'Anyroad, thoo's a bit red in t'face.'

Joseph knew that this was supposed to be the happiest day of his life, but all he could feel was utter fright at the thought of the changes which would begin this day – a new home, a new maister and a new wife . . .

Her deep involvement with the wedding arrangements during the last few weeks had filled Mary with pleasurable excitement. Joseph realised that her happiness at the prospect of marriage was unmarred by any doubts or fears. There would be no basic change in her life as there would be in Joseph's, and he knew that she was longing for him to become her husband and move into her home.

Suddenly, there was a rustle of excitement at the rear of the church. As the vicar motioned them to stand, Joseph craned his neck and peered round towards the door. His first feeling was one of shock. While he and George had been seated, dithering, in the front pew, the church had filled up. Joseph was astounded at the number of people who were crowded in.

He caught his breath when his gaze at last reached Mary. As she came down the aisle on her father's arm, she gave him a tremulous smile. Joseph couldn't have said what she was wearing. He only knew that she looked like a vision – the loveliest sight he had ever seen.

She was, in fact, wearing the sprigged muslin mentioned by her mother to Annie Oaks. It was of the palest lilac and sprinkled here and there with tiny bunches of violets. Her bonnet brim was underdrawn with lilac-coloured silk and was trimmed at one side with a bunch of violets. It was tied under her chin with deep purple ribbons. To finish off the picture, she carried a tiny posy of fresh violets, picked that morning, and surrounded by leaves. Joseph's thoughts were in a whirl. She looked so lovely and so delicate that he felt quite dizzy as he turned back towards the parson to wait for her arrival at his side.

George's gaze had passed over Mary to her sister, Elizabeth, who followed her up the aisle. 'By, she's a good looker an' all,' he thought.

Elizabeth's gown was similar to her sister's, but of a rich apricot, which set off her dark colouring. She carried no flowers but walked with her hands clasped in front of her. George knew that she was about four years older than Mary. 'Getting on a bit,' as he would have put it, but she was certainly exceedingly attractive. In George's eyes, indeed, she made Mary look a bit insipid, having black hair, tawny skin and dark, flashing eyes.

After the ceremony, and when they had signed the register, George was rather shy and confused when Elizabeth Butler took his arm and he found that he was to accompany her down the aisle. As he glanced at her, he saw the flash of white teeth and realised that she was amused by his embarrassment.

They came out of the church, blinking in the sunshine after the gloom to find that, true to custom, the village children had tied up the churchyard gate.

Joseph and George knew all about the custom, but pretended to be amazed to find the way blocked for the bride and groom. The village children made out that they could not open the gate. Then, as though suddenly struck by a thought, Joseph took a handful of sweets from his pocket.

'Will this pay the forfeit?' he called, as he flung them to the waiting children. George followed by tossing the contents of his pockets to them also, and while they scrambled on the grass for the goodies, the ropes were unfastened and the bridal party was free to leave.

George took Peggy's reins and led the way back to Fadmoor and the Butlers' farm, his passengers being Joseph, Mary and Elizabeth. They were a grand-looking quartet, and brought many a compliment as they passed through the villages. The four parents followed in the Butlers' trap which was also decorated and, after the pony-traps of the invited relatives, the younger boys and girls brought up the rear in one of Farmer Butler's ox-waggons.

It was a merry cavalcade: the adults were laughing and chattering and it wasn't long before the younger members began to sing. Only in the first carriage were the occupants quiet. All but Elizabeth seemed to be suddenly overcome by shyness and, for her part, she appeared to be quietly amused by the whole business. Joseph sat and gazed at Mary, overwhelmed by her beauty and, indeed, by the whole occasion. George, on the other hand, while pretending that the placid Peggy needed far more of his attention than was really true, kept stealing a glance at Elizabeth Butler out of his eye-corner. Her greater maturity had given her a self-confidence lacked by the others, bringing home to George his callowness and inexperience.

Being still unmarried at twenty-four, he supposed she was an old maid but, to his eyes, she looked no older than the bride and just as lovely; indeed, even lovelier. Poor George felt totally confused by the whole proceedings and especially by the close proximity of the two girls in all their wedding splendour.

In the eyes of the fashionable world, their outfits would have been regarded as pretty, but simple and countrified, but George and Joseph had been brought up to regard clothes as a necessity, for the sake of decency – to be made as plain, hardwearing and longlasting as possible. When outgrown, they should have still enough wear in them to be passed on to a younger brother or sister.

The village of Gillamoor was bathed in the pale

sunlight of early spring, which warmed the grey stone cottages lining the road. The one street of the village was unusually broad and straight, flanked on each side by a wide grass verge. Many of the cottagers owned a single milk cow and the summer months saw them tethered along the roadside grass. Now, however, the turf was starred with daisies and celandines while the tiny, neat gardens in front of the houses were bright with spring flowers. Many of the villagers who had not gone to the church came to their doors, to wave as they passed by.

As they left Gillamoor, George clicked his tongue and the pony picked up speed on the way to Butler's farm in Fadmoor. Two riders, coming in the opposite direction and realising that this was a wedding party, drew their mounts on to the roadside grass to watch the little procession pass.

'It's Sir Francis Sturdy's son,' commented Joseph.

'Aye, and yon chap with him is t'one who wanted a drink.'

Elizabeth and Mary looked across at the stranger with curiosity. His glance travelled over the bride and came to rest upon her sister. His superior expression gave way to one of appreciation as he eyed her boldly and he made a remark to James Sturdy, which drew a laugh.

Elizabeth bit her lip with vexation as she felt herself redden under his scrutiny. Why should this man make her feel embarrassed, she wondered. Over the years, she had encountered all types and ages of men and considered herself capable of coping with any of them. Now to her annoyance, she felt unsure, almost gauche, under his stare.

'Who is that most impossible young man?' she queried.

'We don't know,' ventured George. 'He came

64

down t'valley when we were filling t'water barrels and asked for a drink.'

Elizabeth felt uncomfortably naked under the rider's lecherous appraisal. Seeing her flush, he raised his hat to salute her mockingly, as he passed another murmured comment which caused James Sturdy to laugh out loud.

In the second vehicle, the two mothers were carrying on a spirited conversation, wallowing with relish in every detail and tuck of the gowns, every murmur and response of the service, and the hats, bonnets, trimmings and furbelows of the congregation.

John Butler, on the other hand, was finding his partner heavy going. To begin with, Jonadab was not in his own trap, in charge of his own pony. He disliked being a passenger: this mirrored his whole attitude to life. He liked to be in charge and able to control not only his own destiny, but that of his immediate family.

Now he sat, straight as a ramrod, one hand on each knee, and his stovepipe hat firmly on his head. His eyes were fixed straight ahead and he acknowledged not one of the villagers who came on to their doorsteps and waved to the bridal procession. Indeed, Jonadab never even noticed them. His brow was furrowed and his mind was engrossed with his own thoughts.

A right parade of it, John Butler was making, he opined. The whole deed would have been better done quietly, with just two witnesses. That way, folks wouldn't have been too sure as to when exactly, the wedding had taken place. As it was, with all this performance and at Easter too, the date would be firmly fixed in everyone's minds.

He suddenly felt a pressure on his knee and looked down to find Annie's hand there. She was leaning forward and looking at him solicitously.

'Are you all right, Jonadab?' she enquired anxiously.

'All right?' he repeated. 'Of course. Why shouldn't Aah be?'

'You're quiet. I thought you might have a headache.'

'A headache?' He was offended that she would venture such a thought. 'Me – have a headache? Don't be daft, woman!' With that, he retreated once more into his own thoughts.

Annie smiled apologetically at Ann Butler. She loved her husband dearly, but she did wish sometimes that he would relax and be a little less rigid in his attitudes. Whatever Jonadab's faults, though, she certainly would not wish to change him – especially not for John Butler she told herself, glancing at her host.

John Butler was too stout and florid for her taste. He was, of course, a good deal older than her own husband and must be well into his fifties. He was certainly enjoying himself, though, smiling, calling and waving to the bystanders. No one seeing him would ever have suspected the true circumstances of the wedding.

As they approached the farm, Ann Butler said, 'We are having the wedding breakfast in the barn. The numbers of invited guests crept up and up, until there was no room in the house.'

She had no need of apologies. The barn had been scrubbed until the floor was immaculate. The stone walls were newly limed to a sparkling whiteness, and decorated with swags of ivy and other greenery. Down the centre stood a series of trestle tables placed end to end, and draped with crisp, white tablecloths. To judge by the amount and variety of food, Ann Butler and her daughters must have worked nonstop all night, as well as for several days beforehand.

The farmers of the riggs and dales of North York-shire were proud of their ability both to produce and also consume food, and the table bore testimony to this. There was a whole ham, cooked to pink perfection; a large joint of salted beef beside it, ready for John Butler to carve. There were pork pies, game pies and chicken pies. When these savoury dishes were finished, the guests could move on to the sweeter things: cakes of every description, custards, curd tarts, junkets and syllabub and, the crowning glory of the feast – the bride-cake.

Although proudly made by Mrs Butler herself to her own family recipe, this had been taken down to Kirkby to be professionally iced. Its swirls and curls were topped with a tiny silver vase, filled with violets to reflect the theme of Mary's outfit.

'Come along, Mr and Mrs Oaks, take your places at the head of the table,' called John Butler. Joseph drew back to allow his parents to pass, and then realised that he and Mary were now Mr and Mrs Oaks. After a moment, he lost all his shyness in front of this roomful of guests.

'Come on, Mrs Oaks,' he teased Mary, as they went down the room to take their places at the end of the table, in front of the wedding cake.

Once the guests were seated, the food and drink began to disappear rapidly and the conversation grew gradually louder and livelier. When the young couple cut the wedding cake for Ann Butler and her daughters to carry to the guests, John Butler leaned towards Joseph. Raising his voice so that all could hear, he held out his hand to his new son-in-law. 'Here you are, Joe. There's two guineas, lad, to start you both off on the right foot. No lass of mine will enter marriage empty-handed.' With the boast ringing round the room he sat down again, casting a self-satisfied smile round the tables.

Joseph half-opened his mouth to tell of his own father's generosity but, as he caught Jonadab's eye, he received an almost imperceptible shake of the head.

'Thank you very much, Mr Butler,' he said clearly, instead. 'Me an' Mary's grateful, sir.' As he sat down, his eyes were caught by Jonadab's vivid blue ones, this time dancing with uncharacteristic but unmistakable humour. Joseph knew what pleasure his father would gain from outdoing John Butler, and especially when the other man's gift had been what the Oaks called 'loud-mouthed generosity'.

When the tables were cleared away, and the benches moved round the walls, the young people began to dance to the tunes of a fiddler brought over from Bilsdale. As they enjoyed the old country dances which were still popular in those parts – *Circassian Circle, Sir Roger de Coverley* and others, Joseph and Mary began to circle the room, having a word with each of the guests. More than one old man fished in his waistcoat pocket and gave Joseph a crown or even half a guinea. He began to feel that he was the luckiest and richest man in the whole world.

By the time he reached his own parents, he reckoned he must have about ten pounds, or even guineas in his pocket. While his mother kissed Mary and began to compliment her on her outfit, Jonadab drew him aside.

'Well, t'knot's been tied and thoo's made thi choice, lad. Or rather, it's been made for thi,' he added with a grim smile. 'What's started badly can often end well, if thoo buckles down ti work. Aah means both on thoo, an' all.'

'We shall, Faither, nivver fear,' Joseph assured him. 'Mary's a worker an' all.'

'Aye, well, Aah've a bit of advice for thi,' his

father continued. 'As soon as thoo can, get thissen into Kirkby and put yon money into t'bank.'

'Aah thought as how only rich folks went into them places,' protested Joe.

'Them as puts their brass i' banks, ends up rich,' his father asserted. 'If thoo keeps it under t'thatch or in a tin box, thoo'll dip into it. If thoo puts it in t'bank, they'll add some to it for thi!'

Joseph digested this piece of information with amazement. 'Thoo means they pays ti look after thi money, Faither?' He found this idea incredible.

'They pays ti use thi money, lad. Anyroad, this isn't the time nor place ti be talking money. Go see George Frank, t'agent for t'York Union Bank and tell 'im Aah've sent thi.'

Somewhat to Joe's chagrin, these revelations from his father were interrupted by Mary.

'We should have a word with everybody, Joe,' she said, laying her hand on his arm. 'Some will be leaving before long, to get home to see to their stock.'

As she led him away, his father's voice came, quietly. 'Noo don't forget what Aah've told thee. Thi best friend's thi pocket and make no mistake on that.'

As Joseph went through the motions of greeting the rest of the guests, his mind was in a whirl. Fancy his father knowing about banks and actually being acquainted with the agent. That meant he must have some money in one. All the family knew that Dad had a good few golden sovereigns and guineas in the tin cashbox hidden in the thatch of his bedroom, but the thought that he must have more – enough to put in a bank, in fact – was an idea which took a bit of swallowing.

'By, he's a close one,' thought Joseph admiringly.

'Eeh, oor Joe!' came George's voice. 'Disn't old married couples dance, then?'

'They do an' all!' he exclaimed, sweeping Mary into the circle of exuberant young people.

George, partnering Elizabeth Butler, was thoroughly enjoying himself. He was a good dancer, light on his feet despite his thickset build, and had lost his shyness of her. It was a pity she was so much older, he thought, eyeing her up and down. She was certainly good-looking.

Just then, she caught his eye and threw back her head, to laugh out loud. George blushed. Surely she couldn't read his thoughts? Not that he'd put anything past her. Her eyes were so dark and luminous that he felt she could see into his soul when they looked deep into his. She was all right, though. 'Don't be daft, man,' he thought to himself. 'She'd nivver look at a lad like thoo.' He knew that Elizabeth Butler had been fancied by many a man but, as far as anyone knew, had never considered marriage.

His own little sister, Martha, had had the temerity only that afternoon, to ask her if she was an old maid. His mother had tried to cover Martha's question with a bout of coughing, but Elizabeth had only smiled.

'No, Martha,' she'd answered, 'I'm not an old maid. I'm a maiden lady. An old maid has never had the chance to be married. A maiden lady has had the chance, but has had the good sense to refuse.'

With a laugh and a swish of her skirts, she'd seized George's hand and led him back into the swirling throng of dancers. George just didn't know what to make of her. He certainly had never met anyone like her before.

Joe's Mary was pretty and sweet, but similar to the other girls of his acquaintance – like his own sisters, really. Elizabeth, on the other hand, was outstanding among the girls as they danced. She seemed to carry herself straighter and hold her head higher, as though she acknowledged her own beauty

70

and revelled in it. 'She's like a queen should look,' thought George and gave himself up to the delight of partnering her in the dancing. He could not imagine why he'd never really taken any notice of her before. In his mind, he had classed her with the older women and never really looked at her. Now, dressed in her bridesmaid's finery and given the role of his partner for the afternoon, she was a revelation and George was flattered by her attention.

It seemed no time at all to both George and Joseph before Jonadab began to gather together his family.

'It's time we were off, John,' he apologised to his host. 'It's been a good do, Mrs Butler, but we've t'stock ti see to. Come on, Mother, round up t'youngsters while Aah help wi' Mother an' Faither.'

George was sorry that his day in the limelight and in Elizabeth Butler's company was drawing to a close. He would count it as one of the best days of his life up to now, he thought – except that their Joe wouldn't be going home with them.

When Joseph realised that they were leaving, he felt panic-stricken. He had always expected that, upon his marriage, his bride would return with him to the family farm. Now the family were getting ready to go home without him and he was cut off from the only life he had ever known. He thought with longing of the cosy farmhouse down in the dale, where he'd been cocooned from the world. He knew their dad was over-strict with them but, in the past weeks, Joseph had grown to realise that it was Jonadab's way of expressing his love for his family. Now they were going home and leaving him up here with the Butlers.

This was his home, now, he supposed, but it didn't feel like home. He'd never really courted Mary, so hadn't built up a knowledge of the Butlers over years or even months. 'I don't know how they

71

behave, what they do, or even what they eat,' he told himself. 'I don't know their land, their animals nor how they go about things.'

In his misery, he turned and looked at John Waind. This must have been how John had felt when he'd left his own family farm in Bransdale and come to them, he supposed. There was, however, one big difference. The faithful John had courted their Ann over a period of almost three years. He had come after chapel and had Sunday tea with them. He had helped around the farm and gradually slipped into their routine, before he'd married Ann and come to live with them. John caught his eye and saw the misery and apprehension mirrored in his brother-in-law's face.

'Thoo'll be all right, Joe,' he smiled, slapping him on the back.

'Aah hopes so,' thought Joseph, though he dare not utter the words aloud.

Mary realised a little of what he must be feeling though she could never have guessed the depths of his despair at that moment.

'Come along, Joe. Let's go and see them off,' she said, taking his arm and drawing him behind the family.

As they gathered at the rear of the pony-trap, which was to carry Grandma and Grandad and two very tired little girls, George suddenly felt a deep desolation at the loss of his brother. He daren't look at Joseph's face, feeling as he did the tears pricking behind his own eyes and not wanting to look unmanly in front of Elizabeth Butler.

'So long, Joe,' he said huskily. 'Aah expects we s'll see thee at chapel next week.'

There was the trace of a lightening of Joseph's gloom. As his mother had said, he wasn't going to the end of the world. His home was only a couple of miles away and he'd see them every week at chapel.

'Goodbye, all,' he murmured. 'Goodbye, Mam.'

His mother put out her arms as she had done in his childhood and Joseph pillowed his head in the comforting softness of her bosom.

As he straightened up, the little procession moved off and he and Mary turned away.

'Will your Dad expect me to start work today?' he wondered.

'Oh, no, of course not. Let's go for a walk, now most people have left,' answered Mary.

'Oh!' Joseph felt in his pocket and produced the parcel containing the kerchief. 'Aah'd forgotten Aah've summat for thee.'

Mary opened the parcel. 'It's lovely, Joe!' she cried with delight. 'Thank you!' Stretching up, she gave him a kiss.

Joseph realised that she was now his legal wife and that from now on, they would share the same bed and he could enjoy the delight of possessing her body as often as they wished, without any feelings of guilt.

'By 'eck! Aah'm going ti enjoy being wed, Mrs Oaks,' he murmured, putting an arm round her waist. 'Come on, let's go for yon walk – somewhere lonely,' he added.

He remembered the parson at chapel once, glaring round at the congregation and thundering at his cowering flock, 'The wages of sin is death!'

To Joseph, at this moment, the wages of sin seemed to be not only happiness but riches beyond his wildest expectations.

CHAPTER SIX

As the rest of the family made their way home in the gathering darkness, the younger ones were eagerly discussing all they had seen, the clothes and the details of the wedding feast. George walked a little apart, wrapped in thoughts of Elizabeth Butler. His parents, too, walked in silence. Annie's thoughts were with Joseph – the first of her children to leave home. Jonadab's thoughts were also on Joseph. That his son should now be living and working on John Butler's farm filled Jonadab with increasing resentment, the more he dwelt on the situation.

As they trudged towards home, Grandad Joseph suddenly called back, 'Look, Jonadab! Look! T'farm's afire!'

Startled, they all followed the line of his whip and saw, with horror, the glow of flames ahead.

'Oh, no!' Jonadab groaned aloud, as they began to run towards the farmstead. Upon drawing closer, they realised that the house itself was not alight. The fire, as yet, was confined to the cow-house, which stood apart from the rest of the buildings.

On entering the fold-yard, they were met with a scene of confusion. Although Bert Weald was shouting directions, the two farm lads were panic-stricken and refusing to enter the burning cow-house to try to rescue the animals.

Jonadab took in the situation at a glance. 'George! You and Jonna get t'cows out. Once they're out o' t'byre, let 'em run loose.'

Not sparing even his parents or the two youngest girls, he marshalled the family to pass buckets of water from both the spring and the duck pond. A blow from his open hand to their ears quelled the hysterics of the hired lads and they were pushed into the chain, to pass the water-buckets to the heart of the fire.

George grabbed Jonna by the arm. 'Come on, lad! We must save yon beasts,' he urged, as the bellowing of the cows came to them above the crackle of the flames.

Quickly tugging the kerchiefs from their necks, they dipped them in the horse-trough and swathed them across the lower half of their faces. George looked into his brother's eyes and saw the naked fear there, mirroring the flames.

'All right, oor kid?' He suddenly realised that young Jonna was no more than a child and that he was demanding of him a man's job and a man's courage.

'Aye, Aah'm all right, George.' Jonna was a younger edition of his father and would never be bested.

Clutching each other, the brothers hesitated when the heat from the cow-house met them, but then ran forward together into the burning building. The thatch was burning fiercely and sparks showered down upon them.

In their stalls, the frightened beasts thrashed about, eyes rolling wildly and necks straining at the chains which held them. It was as much as the brothers could do to avoid the tossing horns as they struggled to release the neck-chains which fastened the captive cows. George saw Jonna's two cows were loose and making for the doorway, before he had managed to free the other two. Jonna ran to help him. At last they were loose and turning, the two brothers made for the door, only to find that the wooden frame was, by now, alight. With bellows of terror, the cows attempted to draw back, but a blazing roof-beam crashed down behind them, sending a curtain of flame up at the rear. George gave a mighty thwack on each rump and, suddenly, he, Jonna and the two cows were through the inferno and into the fold-yard.

His father had given the cow-house up for lost and had concentrated upon damping the thatch of the house and then the other buildings, to stop the fire from spreading.

The stables were at the opposite side of the yard, so that Bert Weald and old Joseph Oaks had managed to lead the frightened horses to safety.

By the time George and Jonna had succeeded in saving the cows, Jonadab was satisfied that the fire would not spread to the thatched roofs of the house and the other buildings, so he redirected his fire-fighters' efforts to the burning cow-house once again.

The roof had been well alight before their return, ignited, they were later to learn, by the dry straw in which the cattle had been bedded down for the night. Young Will Ransome had filled an oil lamp in the cow-house and accidentally kicked it over. In his panic, as he tried to retrieve the lamp, he had knocked over the can of oil, which had spread amongst the straw.

It was one of Jonadab Oaks' rules that no uncovered lantern and no naked flames were allowed where there was either hay or straw. He insisted that lanterns were always filled in the meal-house.

'As soon as mi back's turned, they does as they likes!' He glared at his brother as he spoke. He could not but feel that if Uncle George had stayed back from the wedding and been down at the farm, the calamity would not have occurred.

After a few moments' respite, gulping in breaths

of the night air, George and Jonna joined the others in tackling the blazing byre.

'Thank the Lord it's a bit away from t'other buildings.' His father's exclamation was fervent.

'Aye! We could have lost the lot,' answered George, realising how close they had been to losing, not only the horses and draught oxen, but the stored hay and straw and even the house itself. Had the fire begun in any other spot but the cow-house, the outcome would have been disastrous.

As it was, although the roof and the woodwork had been destroyed, the thick stone walls, albeit blackened, had remained standing.

When Jonadab was satisfied that the fire was finally quenched, he led the way to the house. 'Thoo'd better come an' all, Bert,' he instructed Weald. 'Then thoo can tell me how it happened, over a mug of tea.'

As they trailed wearily into the house, George reflected on the difference between the start of the day and its end. While Weald explained the accident which had started the fire, he and Jonna washed their smoke-begrimed faces at the kitchen sink, before swallowing a mugful of tea.

'Come on, Jonna,' George murmured. 'Yon cows'll have ti be rounded up and put somewhere. It looks as though it's up to us ti do it.'

Looking round at the rest of the family slumped wearily over their steaming mugs of tea, Jonna followed him without argument. George knew that Jonna was flattered to be treated as an equal by his elder brother and would work for as long as was needed.

Luckily for them, after their first headlong flight from the fire, the cows had stopped in a huddle and were now making their way back along the road towards them.

'We'd best put 'em in wi' t'oxen. There's room in there now for us ti tie 'em up and then we'll get 'em milked,' said George. Jonna groaned. Milking was woman's work, but he was fully aware that his mother and sisters were utterly exhausted.

By the time they went back to the house, everyone was in bed except their father, who sat brooding by the fire.

'Get thissens ti bed, lads,' he said dispiritedly.

'Thoo'll have ti see Sir Francis Sturdy in t'morn, won't thoo, Faither?' asked George.

'Aye, lad. That Aah will. He'll want ti know t'thread through t'needle. Anyroad, there's nowt that t'estate joiners can't put right. It's a blessing we managed ti keep it contained.' He passed a hand wearily across his forehead as he spoke.

'Aah'll sit up, Faither, and keep going out and having a look round,' George offered. 'If thoo's ti go ti t'Towers tomorrow, thoo'll need some sleep.'

Jonadab looked up into the steady brown eyes. Reluctant though he was to leave his farm in anyone else's care, he realised that he could depend upon George. 'Aah thinks it'll be safe enough, but Aah'd appreciate an eye kept on it tonight.'

George was filled with pride that his father should even contemplate going to bed and leaving the farm in his charge.

'Aah'll keep awake, never fear, Faither,' he promised.

'Aah knows, lad! Aah knows.' His father patted his shoulder and went up to bed. George placed more peat on the fire and settled down in his father's Windsor chair, to keep his vigil.

Although he went out to inspect the dead ashes in the cow-house several times during the hours of darkness, it was not the fire which filled his thoughts, but Elizabeth Butler. George conjured up her face

78

in the firelight and dwelt on her vivacity and striking good looks. 'She'd never look twice at me,' he thought and yet, he continued to dream.

CHAPTER SEVEN

Joseph's presence lightened the workload of all the labourers on Butler's farm, but he was sorely missed down in Sleightholmedale. All the men, including Jonadab himself, worked from dawn to dusk, harrowing and tilling the land, ready for the sowing of the spring corn and the root crops.

Although both George and his father loved the valley that was their home, this spring they had no time to drink in the awakening beauty of the dale. The woods which massed along the hillside behind the farm burgeoned into tender leaf, unnoticed by the men who toiled on the valley floor. The birds which flitted among the branches, on their early business of nestbuilding, filled the air with trilling calls, unheeded by those who worked on the land.

Only Maria and Martha had time to enjoy the delights of the awakening season. Depending on where their father happened to be working, they chose their routes to avoid his notice. Sometimes they wandered along the beck to fill their arms with bright yellow Kingcups which grew in the water. These they would arrange in bunches, with twigs of pussy willow, to take home to their mother. At other times, they would run, doubled up and giggling, along the hedge which bordered the roadside. Finding a gap, they would squeeze through into the woods. Once in the sun-dappled shelter of the trees they played hide and seek, or tried to track down the woodpeckers which they heard but rarely saw, as they tapped out their signals on the bark. After a couple of carefree hours away from their father's stern gaze, they would trail home, bearing tangles of hazel catkins or little posies of sweet-smelling primroses. If they were unlucky, their progress would be halted by a shout from their father.

'Here, lasses! If thoo's nowt ti do, get a bucket and go picking up stones in yon field.' Then they would turn back, the delights of freedom forgotten as they bent their backs to work with the others.

When they were not being used by his father, George made a point of getting to know Violet and Rosie, the two new shire-horses. Whenever he could, he worked with them and, in the cosy stable, no longer joined in the games of Merrills or the singing to the accompaniment of Bert Weald's concertina. Instead, he preferred to spend his time grooming the two magnificent greys.

Though they towered above him as he rubbed and burnished their coats, they were far more docile and gentle than the fiery little Galloways. His father had, of course, other heavy horses but none to equal these two. To George, the newcomers were special.

'By,' he often told them, 'thoo's two beauties.' He was convinced that they were twins, though his father insisted that twins were rare in horses. In fact, he had never heard of twin foals. They were, however, so much alike as to be indistinguishable to the unpractised eye. 'As like as two peas in a pod,' he often murmured to them.

George, however, had no difficulty in knowing which was Rosie and which Violet. He spent so many hours grooming and polishing their coats, combing the tangles out of manes and tails and washing and fluffing the feathering which graced the huge feet, that he was sure he would know if one lost so much as a single hair.

In the weeks that followed the wedding, the pair proved to be a great comfort to George. They helped

81

to fill the gap which the loss of his brother's companionship had left in his life.

It was George who gave them their first feed of the day, at five-thirty. When they came in at noon, no matter whether he or his father had been working with them, George was the one who rubbed them down and gave them their hay. Gradually, he was building up a bond with the pair, and this pleased his father. Jonadab encouraged pride in the farm and stock and was content that George, whom he now regarded as his eldest son, should devote his spare time to the mares.

Until Joseph's departure, George had not realised how much his older brother had meant to him. At twelve, Jonadab was five years his junior and the two farm lads were also well below him in age. Since Joe's marriage, George was thrown more upon his own resources and found the running of the farm filling his thoughts more than he would ever have believed possible.

He no longer regarded himself merely as one of the work force, there just to do his father's bidding. He assessed the work and stock with a view to the future and prosperity of the farm. George had passed the subtle line between boyhood and manhood in a short space of time, so that he suddenly felt considerably older than his seventeen years, and had become more mature and serious in his outlook.

'Oor George's grown up fast,' Annie sighed to Jonadab.

'Not afore time, woman,' he was quick to respond. 'It'll do him no harm to know what life's about.'

One crisp, sunny morning when there was still a trace of late frost, George was looking forward with pleasure to a day's ploughing in the long field.

'Shall Aah tek Rosie and Violet, Faither, or will you be working 'em?' he enquired.

'Nay,' answered Jonadab. 'Leave 'em in t'stable. T'lad'll be bringing t'entire round this morning.'

The entire, or stallion, spent the spring travelling round the farms to serve the mares and get them in foal. George felt a surge of excitement at the thought of a visit from the pedigree stallion. With his proprietory interest in the two grey mares, he was eager to see their prospective mate.

As he walked up and down behind the plough, he relished the swish of the ploughshare as it cut into the crisp ground, turning it over in sharp, straight furrows. In the peace of the valley, broken only by the clink of the metal traces, the creak of leather on leather, as the harness rubbed against itself and the heavy breathing of his team, he could allow his thoughts to wander. The patient beasts had ploughed for almost as many years as he had himself, and needed the minimum of guidance.

He was, as so often lately, thinking of his brother Joseph. He and Mary usually walked down into the dale on Sunday evenings after chapel, and George was concerned to notice the change in Joe. He realised that marriage and the thought of the coming bairn placed a new responsibility on his brother, but sensed that something more than this had brought about an alteration in Joe's temperament.

It was plain that he was still head over heels in love with Mary, but something had quenched the spark which had been part of Joseph's nature.

When George tried to put this into words to his father, he merely received a grunt and the response, 'Joseph has had to grow up, George. A lad can't take on a wife, with a bairn on the way, and not become a man.'

George, however, felt that there was something more troubling Joe and saw, by his mother's face, that she shared his concern. 'Aah'll have a word with him next week, and see if Aah can get owt out of him,' he consoled himself, and having made this resolution, felt easier in his mind.

For a time, he tidied his thoughts away and concentrated on the ploughing, murmuring to the team, who flickered their eyes sideways and softly blew out their lips, as though in answer to him.

The day was still and calm, disturbed only by the plod of the horses and the sounds of the plough and harness. Suddenly, however, a flock of seagulls wheeled above them and the peace was broken by the birds' mewing cries, shrill and high-pitched as they tumbled and squabbled behind him.

George knew that many ploughmen found the following flocks of gulls irritating but, to him, their constant company was one of the facts of the ploughman's job and he was able to shut out their screeching and ignore them. So it was that he clearly heard the sound of a heavy horse coming down the hill. 'By 'eck!' he said aloud, so great was his excitement, 't'entire's here!' Although he was eager to see the stallion, he was conscious of the fact that there was still some time to go until he could break off for dinner.

Even this momentous occasion – the first visit of a pure-bred stallion – would not excuse him in his father's eyes if he so much as paused, much less go to the hedge to see the animal pass by on the road.

'Aah would be going t'wrong way,' he groaned, biting his lip in vexation as he headed towards the farm buildings. He could hear the sound of the hooves on the road, growing ever louder to the rear.

'Gee up! Gee up!' he cried, knowing full well that his team would not reach the end of the field any quicker, no matter how much he urged them.

What he didn't realise was that, upon seeing him in the field, the stallion and his lad had slowed to a saunter. As George swung the plough round on the headland, he caught sight of the noble head and arched neck of the stallion above the hedge. 'Oh, be blowed ti me faither!' he thought and shouted to his team, 'Whoa! Whoa!' Nevertheless, he gave a quick glance towards the farmhouse to be sure that he had not been observed.

Quickly looping the plough-strings round the plough handles, he then tied the halter shanks to the branch of a young sapling growing in the hedgerow. Hoping that his horses were fully secured, he leapt across the furrows towards the field gate.

At his cry, the stallion had also stopped. 'Hold on,' George called to the lad and leaned on the gate, gasping from the sudden exertion. 'By 'eck! 'E's grand!' he panted.

The boy gave the halter a quick twitch and the magnificent animal paraded majestically along the road. Muscles rippled beneath the sheen of his hide and though his head was carried proudly on his strong, arched neck, his eyes were sensitive and luminous.

His great size dwarfed the lad who walked beside him holding the halter, and yet he was easy to control, being willing and eager to please. George realised that his father had chosen the ideal mate for the two greys, even to matching their colour. He only had time, however, for a quick appraisal before he heard his team begin to whinny and snicker, scenting the stallion's presence.

'So long, mate,' he grinned to the lad as he shot back to the plough, thankful that his father had not seen his lapse.

His encounter with the stallion filled George's thoughts for the rest of the morning, pushing his worries about Joseph to the back of his mind. He hoped that when the lad walked his charge to the farm again on his next visit, he would be working on some job that would give him the time and opportunity to ask about the great horse's temperament and pedigree.

He allowed his imagination to dwell on the forthcoming foals, which Rosie and Violet would eventually produce. 'They should be good 'uns,' he gloated to himself, 'wi' them parents.'

He'd heard that in some parts of the country there were agricultural shows, where farmers could show off their stock and produce. If only there were one in the area! George visualised himself, proudly leading round the two greys and their progeny. 'I'd show 'em,' he thought, with no limits on his imaginary triumphs. He could see himself being awarded rosettes, medals, cups and even money prizes, going from show to show with his superb team, decorated and groomed to perfection. 'We'd be in t'paper,' he marvelled.

'George! George!' He came down to earth with a bump, to hear his sister Tamar's voice. 'Our Mam says don't you want any dinner?' she shouted, hanging over the field gate.

'Is it that time?' he called incredulously.

'It's ten past twelve and Faither's waiting,' she admonished as she jumped down and ran back to the house.

George groaned. Since Joe's departure, his father had tended to be less of a martinet towards him, at least, but he knew that Jonadab was a stickler for punctuality.

Upon reaching the headland, he unhitched the plough and led his team towards the gate. When they reached the road, he urged them into a trot, making for the stable. The air was suddenly split by a stentorian shout. 'Whoa!'

Both the horses and George immediately slowed

to a walk, and he looked towards the door of the farmhouse to meet his father's eyes, as steely as only they could be under lowered brows. 'Them 'osses has done a morning's work, young man. Don't you make 'em rush just because you're dilatory,' he growled. 'Rub 'em down and see to their feed an' all, before you come for yours,' he added, as he turned back indoors.

By the time the team had been put into their stalls, rubbed down, fed and watered, George was half an hour late. He took his place at the table as the rest of the family were finishing their pudding. His mother brought his loaded plate from the range, where it had been resting on a pan of boiling water, covered by a basin.

'Thank you, Mam,' he murmured, as he began his meal.

'Can we take it thoo was enjoying thi work?' came Jonadab's voice. Knowing better than to speak with his mouth full, George tried to swallow the lump of meat he was chewing, only to dissolve into a paroxysm of coughing as it became wedged in his throat.

His father waited with exaggerated patience, spoon poised, while George had a drink of water and recovered his breath.

'Yes, Faither. It was a pleasant morning and t'soil was turning over well,' he replied.

'So thoo lost track o' time,' persisted his father.

'Aye, Aah did an' all,' answered George.

'Or was thoo making up for t'time wasted, goggling at yon entire and gossiping wi' t'lad?' his father finished in quiet triumph.

Seeing the smile of satisfaction on their father's face, the others dared to smile at George's discomfiture.

'Aw, Faither,' he protested. 'Aah wasna' gossiping and it only took a minute to look over t'hedge.'

'Time's time, young man,' chided Jonadab. 'If all on this farm wasted a minute, that would be more than a quarter of an hour's work lost.'

George knew that to say any more would be a waste of time and probably only annoy his father, who was delivering his homily in reasonably good humour.

While he applied himself to his dinner, he listened to his father, John Waind and young Jonadab discussing the stallion and his merits. The girls, of course, were not allowed out during the stallion's visit. Indeed, his mother always locked the doors, on her husband's instructions, so that his daughters could not accidentally stray outside and witness 'something they shouldn't', as she referred to it.

George had been allowing the conversation to wash over him, paying little attention to what was being said, but suddenly heard his brother, pleading, 'When t'foals come, Faither, can I look after 'em, like oor George does Rosie and Violet?' he wheedled.

George felt a stab of dismay. Although, deep down, he knew it wasn't so, he'd always regarded the two grey mares as his, and had never envisaged anyone but him caring for their foals. He held his breath, waiting for his father's answer.

'We'll see, we'll see, Jonadab,' came the promise.

George felt his younger brother's eyes on him, to judge how well he would take this turn of events. He swallowed. 'Let's hope they're both fillies, and then we'll both be in charge of a matched pair. That'd be grand,' he smiled.

His father looked at him with approval, knowing what the gesture had cost him. George felt that in some way he had successfully passed a test and had risen in his father's estimation.

When Jonadab had said Grace at the end of the

meal, he addressed George. 'Can thoo get yon field finished this afternoon?' he enquired.

'Why yes, Faither, I should think so,' he answered.

'Good. I want rid of t'rest of them lambs afore t'ewes come into lamb again. When we get shut of them, it'll give us more room at lambing time. I've sold 'em to John Leeman from Wombleton. I want you to tek 'em into Kirkby in t'morn and he'll meet you at about eleven.'

George felt quite excited. Although life in the dale was fulfilling and he found the farm work satisfying, it suddenly occurred to him that he was now seventeen and this would be the first time he'd been away from the farm on his own.

As he collected his team from the stable and returned to his ploughing, he was whistling. Life suddenly seemed far rosier than it had done when the day had begun.

In his buoyant mood, the afternoon slipped away and it seemed no time at all before the field was finished and he was stabling his team. Even the fact that, during the evening, his mother was busy making a list of small purchases which could be brought back in his pockets, did nothing to lessen his enthusiasm for the following day's excursion.

'I only hope as it's fine,' was the last sleepy thought, as he snuggled between the sheets that night.

CHAPTER EIGHT

George's last drowsy wish was fulfilled and the next morning brought another clear, cloudless day. There was a nip in the air at first, but by the time he went down to the Black-gate field to round up the last remaining fifty or so of the previous year's lambs, the sun had quite a bit of power.

His mother had split an oven-bottom cake, as she called it. This was a flat breadcake, about the size of a tea-plate which, buttered, filled with boiled ham and wrapped in a clean white cloth, now reposed in one of his capacious pockets.

Accompanied by Jess, the experienced and dependable sheepdog and her son, Shep, George soon collected the sheep and set off up the hill leading out of the valley. Though Shep was younger and more excitable than his mother, he was 'coming along nicely', as Jonadab was wont to say and, on the whole, the two dogs worked well together.

At the top of the hill was an avenue, about half a mile long, at the end of which the main road passed, going left for Fadmoor and Gillamoor and right for Kirkbymoorside. This was the only difficulty until he actually reached the town, so George found that he needed all his concentration along this stretch. Keeping Shep with him, to round up any stragglers, he skilfully sent Jess ahead, by means of whistles and shouts, until she crouched in the centre of the main road, blocking the way to the left. As the flock poured out of the end of the avenue, chivvied along by Shep, it needed only the merest hint of hesitation on the part of a single sheep to cause Jess' lip to curl and, with a faint growl, she slunk low to the ground, moving from one side of the road to the other.

George breathed a sigh of relief as his charges turned as with a single mind, and headed for Kirkby-moorside. He knew that John Leeman would be waiting at the entrance to the town and the two of them, with two pairs of dogs, would manage the flock through, with little difficulty.

So thinking, he settled down to enjoy the walk. The lambs flowed before him like a river of wool, filling the width of the road. The stream of rippling backs widened and narrowed with the road, reaching from hedge to hedge. The silence was broken only by the semi-sound of the puttering of sheep-feet on the hardness of the road, and the occasional bleat as one called to another.

The attendant dogs silently ushered their charges along, appearing whenever needed like noiseless canine wraiths. Any laggard was spurred on by the threat of a quick nip at the heels. Any sheep which got a bit above itself and tried to lead the flock from the front would suddenly find that Jess had run ahead, at the other side of one of the hedges which bordered the road, and leapt out, facing him, to slow him down.

George was content to be walking behind with his crook, secure in the knowledge that Jess and Shep had the sheep under control. He felt a niggling sense of disloyalty to his family in that he was revelling in the unaccustomed feeling of freedom. Here he was, away from the farm on his own, and trusted by his father to carry out a responsible business transaction. 'Aye, that's what it is,' he reflected. 'A business transaction.'

Upon setting off that morning, he had been called aside by his father and learned, to his incredulity, that not only was he being entrusted with the deliv-

91

ery of the sheep, but that he was to collect the money for them and deposit it in the bank. Joseph had confided to George that, advised by their father, he had opened a bank account so it was no surprise to George that Jonadab had money in a bank. However, he had never envisaged that he himself would ever enter such a place. This was far more responsibility than had ever been placed upon Joseph, when he was living at home. George had almost stammered his thanks and assured Jonadab: 'Aah won't let thi down, Faither.'

'Aah knows thoo won't,' his father answered drily. 'T'first time'll be t'last, nivver fear.'

Reflecting on the morning's events and dreaming of the day when, all being well, he might be his own boss putting the proceeds of sales into his own bank account, George suddenly discovered that he'd dropped well behind the flock. Not only that, but as they surged round a bend in the road ahead, he realised that what had brought him to earth was the sound of horses' hooves. Breaking into a cold sweat, George began to run. 'Jess, Jess'' he called. 'Get away, by,' hoping that the dog could get in front of the lambs and turn them, before they met up with the pony and trap. It was a vain hope!

As George rounded the bend, he was filled with dismay. Jess had certainly turned the flock, but not before they had reached the horse. The sheep milled round and round in the narrow road, hemmed in by a hedge at each side and a dog crouched menacingly at the front and rear. The skittish pony was rearing on its hind legs, whinnying in terror at the sheer numbers of sheep surrounding it.

As George pushed through the thronging sheep to reach the threshing pony, the two-wheeled trap tipped backwards. The driver, who had risen to her feet in order to control the animal, was caught off-balance and toppled on to her back in the well of the trap.

Shouting instructions to his dogs to move the sheep further along the road, George caught hold of the pony to steady it. He then ran round to the back of the trap, calling, 'Can I be of assistance, ma'am?'

There, on the floor of the trap, was a sight which caused George to flush with embarrassment. The occupant lay flat on her back, her skirt up over her head, and a pair of pantalooned legs waving in the air. As he reached over to help her, she tugged her dress down to cover her drawers and he was confronted by the crimson face of Elizabeth Butler.

'Oh! 'eck!' he gulped. 'Aah'm sorry.'

Elizabeth knocked aside his helping hand, scrambled to her feet and took hold of the reins. 'You! You great lummox, George Oaks!' she flashed. 'If you can't control animals, you shouldn't be in charge of them!'

'Aah hadn't noticed how far in front they'd got,' he muttered in discomfiture.

'Noticed!' she answered scornfully. 'You wouldn't notice your head if it were loose.'

'Aah've said Aah'm sorry, Elizabeth,' he answered, but she would not be mollified.

'Get yourself off and control your sheep, and leave me to control my pony,' she retorted.

So saying, she straightened her bonnet and was just about to click her tongue to the pony, when a horseman rode round the corner towards them. Both Elizabeth and George recognised him as James Sturdy's companion on the day of the wedding. George also remembered the man's arrogance and bold looks at Tamar, when he had asked for a drink at the spring.

'Whatever is wrong? May I be of assistance?' asked the stranger, raising his crop to his hat and giving

Elizabeth a slight bow as he directed his horse through the press of the sheep.

Elizabeth glanced across at him coolly. 'I'm afraid that this young man lost control of his sheep. My pony was startled, but is settled now. Thank you for offering to help, but I can cope.'

George seethed at the way the stranger ignored him, having eyes only for Elizabeth. She was flushed with temper and her heightened colour and flashing eyes added to her attractiveness. Feeling awkward and inadequate, he turned to Elizabeth, beseechingly. She, however, busied herself with the reins and would not meet his eyes. He needed to be taught a lesson, she considered.

The rider addressed George for the first time. 'Come along, man! Get these animals rounded up and out of the young lady's way,' he ordered.

George felt his face redden under the rush of blood which accompanied his resentment. His brown eyes blazing with anger met the disdainful blue ones for a split second. He then lowered his lids and looked groundward, not daring to show his true feelings. James Sturdy's father was their landlord and George was unwilling to allow the accusation of insolence to be levelled at him.

'Elizabeth,' he began tentatively, but Elizabeth still considered him to have been inadequately punished for causing her undignified fall.

'Come along, please. Round up your sheep and move them on,' she demanded.

'On your way, man,' insisted young Sturdy's aristocratic friend. Turning to Elizabeth he added, 'With your permission, I will accompany you along the road until you and the pony are recovered.'

To George's chagrin, she gave the stranger a bright smile and answered, 'Why, thank you, sir. That would be so kind, as I am feeling rather shaken.'

George, normally so placid, was amazed at the feelings of rage and jealousy which swept through him as he turned away, sick at heart. Miserably, he checked the lambs to see that in the confusion none had leapt over into a field and become separated. All were there and he moved off once more, to continue the journey to Kirkby. That they were still together and more or less under control again, was only due to the dogs, he recognised.

'It would be her,' he sighed.

Since the wedding, he'd often allowed his thoughts to dwell upon Elizabeth, while telling himself that, being older and more sophisticated, she would never give him a second thought. 'Now I've blotted mi copy-book good an' proper,' he thought ruefully.

When George had gathered up the lambs and rounded the next bend, Elizabeth adjusted her bonnet and addressed the pony.

'Walk on,' she directed.

'I'm so sorry,' the stranger said, removing his hat for a moment. 'I should have introduced myself. Sir William Forster, at your service. I'm staying at the Towers, with my friend James Sturdy.'

Elizabeth's previous dislike of the man melted. He was undoubtedly attractive, being well above average height with fair, almost golden hair. His wide, light blue eyes were rounded and appeared guileless now as he regarded her. She was flattered by his open admiration and by the fact that he was titled.

'My name is Elizabeth Butler, sir, and my father farms at Fadmoor.' She smiled as she answered him and noticed his appreciation.

'Is he one of Sir Francis Sturdy's tenants?' he asked, as they began to move off.

'No. He owns our farm. He is not a tenant-farmer.'

What William omitted to say in his introduction, was that he had been spending some weeks at the Towers, hunting but chiefly paying court to Rowena, James Sturdy's young sister. She was a quiet, mouse-like little thing only recently out of the schoolroom, but upon her marriage at some suitable time in the future, would inherit a considerable fortune from her fond maternal grandmother. Realising that he must marry within the next few years to produce an heir for his own estate in Leicestershire, William had settled on his best friend's sister as the perfect solution. He had to admit to himself, however, that Rowena was rather childish yet, and boring – and he was enjoying the company of this attractive and sparkling woman.

Now, he glanced at her pony and drawing on his reins, he signalled Elizabeth to stop. 'Your pony's lame,' he said. 'I'll see if she has picked up a stone in her hoof.'

Elizabeth's annoyance with George rose once more to the surface. 'I do hope she hasn't strained a fet-lock. Heaven knows, she was thrashing about and rearing enough, when the sheep frightened her.'

The fall in the trap had shaken Elizabeth more than she had realised and not only was her back aching, but her head had developed a pulsating throb. Now she had the added worry of the pony's lameness. She stood, nibbling her lip and frowning in annoyance as she watched Sir William tie his bridle to a sapling in the hedge.

As he approached the rear of the trap to hand her down, Elizabeth turned towards him. Unfortunately, she failed to notice that the harness she had collected from the saddler's had slipped forward from beneath the seat and her foot caught in the tangle of straps. Stumbling forward, hands extended to save herself, she found herself caught in Sir William's arms. For a moment he held her, their faces level, and then, smiling, he swung her round and deposited her gently on the ground.

Elizabeth found herself smiling, too. 'Thank you. I'm afraid this isn't my lucky day,' she gasped, feeling rather breathless at his closeness.

'I'm sure it's mine,' he answered, looking into her eyes before going to examine the pony's feet. Was she deliberately egging him on, he wondered. She was certainly vibrantly attractive. 'Luckily it's only a stone.' He spoke over his shoulder as he bent to remove it. 'It's a blessing it's no worse and no thanks to that fool with the sheep.'

Elizabeth bridled. Although she had been rude to George, it was an entirely different thing for Sir William to disparage him. Nobody was going to slight him if she could help it.

'He's actually a very good stockman,' she said stiffly.

'He was giving a good impression of an idiot when I saw him,' came the reply.

Elizabeth's eyes flashed. 'You're speaking of a very good friend of mine,' she almost snapped.

William Forster looked curiously at her. He knew by her face that she was indeed angry. He could see the chance of a pleasant half hour in her company slipping away and felt annoyed.

'You set your cap at any man, do you?' He used his most supercilious voice for the insult.

Elizabeth stopped in the act of climbing back into her trap. 'Setting my cap? Whatever do you mean?'

'Oh come! Don't play the innocent with me. You can't deny that you threw yourself into my arms a moment or two ago,' he half-laughed.

She drew herself up before mounting the trap. 'I tripped, as well you know, sir.' She was as angry with herself, as with him, knowing that she had enjoyed the moment when his arms had held her. Seeing that he had really stung her, he followed up his advantage. She would not play fast and loose with him and get away with it.

'Nonsense! Have you forgotten the inviting look you gave me, when I saw you in that wedding procession at Easter?' he goaded.

Elizabeth was so furious that she could hardly speak at first. Her head was pounding as she glared at William Forster. She seized her long carriage whip and he thought, for a minute, that she would strike him.

'You – you insufferable popinjay!' she hurled at him and, giving the startled pony a flick across its haunches, she was off, leaving him standing in the road, staring after her.

It was fortunate that Bella the pony knew the way home. Elizabeth's eyes overflowed with tears of humiliation. How dare any man presume that she had thrown herself at him? By the time she reached home her head felt on the point of splitting and her face was pallid with a combination of temper and pain.

To her mother's consternation, her usually composed eldest daughter rushed through the kitchen and straight upstairs, announcing as she went, 'I'm going to lie down. I've got a bad head and don't want to be disturbed.'

Her mother and sisters looked at each other in disbelief. 'What on earth's up with her?' demanded Mrs Butler, but nobody could give an answer.

When George reached the outskirts of the town, he was relieved to see John Leeman waiting patiently. The older man was leaning on his crook, staring into space, his dogs at his feet. As the flock of lambs approached, he snapped his fingers whereupon his dogs leapt eagerly to their feet, ears pricked, awaiting their master's command. At his word, they separated, each positioning itself at a side road, to keep the flock in the main street.

John waited for George and the men ambled together down the street, each controlling his own pair of dogs to ensure that no headstrong lamb strayed.

'Noo then, George,' said John.

'Noo, John,' he answered.

'Is t'family all right?'

'Aye, they are that. Mind you, mi Gran and Grandad's getting on a bit.'

'Aye. They will be, an' all,' came the reply. This seemed to exhaust any conversational topic which they had in common, so they proceeded through the town in companionable silence.

When they reached the main Scarborough road, John paused only for a moment. Reaching into his pocket, he took out a small leather bag of coins. 'Thoo'll find that's right,' he said. 'So long, lad.' And, with a tip of his hat, he went on his way.

'So long, John,' called George and, whistling to his dogs, he retraced his own steps up through the market place.

As he went towards the York Union Bank, he kept one hand in his pocket, clutching the precious bag of sovereigns tightly. He could not imagine being robbed in the little town, especially when it wasn't market day, but he was not going to take any chances.

Once inside, he heaved a sigh of relief. He hardly knew George Frank, the agent, who looked up as he entered.

'Good morning, young man. What can I do for you?' enquired the clerk.

George was somewhat abashed at the sight of the high desk and piles of ledgers. He cleared his throat.

'Aah've come to make a deposit for mi faither, Mr Jonadab Oaks,' he announced, producing the bag of gold.

The bank agent shuffled through the ledgers and brought one out, which he opened on the desk. 'How much is there?' he asked.

George felt foolish. 'Aah didn't rightly know,' he confessed, 'but mi faither knows,' he added triumphantly. Nobody was going to diddle an Oaks, if he could help it.

The white fingers undid the strings of the money bag and tipped the gold coins on to the desktop. After quickly counting and putting them in neat piles, George Frank reached for one of several quills and dipped it into the inkwell, before entering a sum in the ledger. George had pushed his workworn hands deep into his pockets, ashamed of their roughness but, realising that the agent was trying to impress him, believing him to be illiterate, he leaned towards the desk, as though examining the entry.

The pen finished its scratching and the bank clerk passed over a receipt made out in his copperplate handwriting. George read it carefully before stowing it away in his pocket.

'Aye, that's right, Mr Frank,' he observed as he turned away. 'Good day t'you.'

'Good day, Master Oaks. Perhaps I shall have the pleasure of your account, some day,' said Frank.

'Aye. Thoo might, an' all.' George paused at the door. 'Mi faither banks 'ere and so does mi brother, so Aah can see no reason not to keep it in t'family.' Just before leaving the bank, he bobbed back and put his head cheekily round the door. 'Just as long as thoo disn't mix t'money up,' he grinned, as he went out into the street.

He walked up the market place, feeling rather pleased with his handling of the bank business. 'At least Aah showed yon chap that us Oaks isn't daft,' he thought.

His mother had asked him to buy yeast, sewing needles and linen thread. If he went to Hugill's in the market place, he decided, he could get everything in the same shop. This was contrary to his intention when he had first started out. He had meant to spend half an hour strolling round the little town, looking in shop windows and enjoying the unaccustomed freedom and leisure.

Since his encounter with Elizabeth Butler, however, another plan was circulating in his mind. If he set off for home straight away and went at a good pace, could he, he wondered, go to Fadmoor and see her? The fact that he could even contemplate such a step seemed not only daring, but foolhardy. What if his father found out? Worse still, what if Elizabeth would not forgive him for making a spectacle of her that morning. 'Oh well, nothing ventured, nothing gained,' he decided and, having completed his errand, set off at a good pace, eating his lunch on the way.

Upon reaching the turn-off to Sleightholmedale, he only hesitated for a moment before continuing on his way to Fadmoor. Knowing that he was unlikely to meet any of his family away from the farm, he had decided to chance a visit to the Butlers.

The dogs sat by the gateway at his command and George walked round to the back of the house. His knock was answered by the youngest daughter, Sarah, a pretty little thing of nine or ten.

'Mama, it's George Oaks,' she called.

'No! Er – it's your Elizabeth I want a word with.' George felt embarrassed when the child's eyes widened in surprise.

'He wants a word with our 'Lizabeth,' called Sarah, back into the kitchen. Then, looking at the

101

flush which crept over George's face, she began to giggle.

'Stop that silly noise this minute and get yourself inside,' said her mother sharply, appearing at the door. Sarah was obviously hurt by this reprimand in front of George and went back into the house with her lips quivering.

Mrs Butler pulled the door shut. 'Well?' she queried, arms folded and brows raised.

George felt awkward and wished with all his heart that he had not given into the temptation to come. 'It was your Elizabeth I wanted to see,' he muttered, feeling uncomfortable under her scrutiny. He had previously thought of her as a friendly soul but now, standing with folded arms, four square before him as though guarding the door, her attitude was distinctly hostile.

'Elizabeth has no wish to see anybody,' affirmed Ann Butler. 'She isn't well.' Since Mary's fall from grace, she was protective of her daughters, especially where the Oaks sons were concerned.

George was aghast. Had she fallen more badly in the trap than he'd thought, he wondered. Perhaps the restive pony had thrown her out after he had left her. 'Nay,' he thought to himself. 'Yon foppish chap was offering to see her home when I left 'em.'

He looked up to meet the implacable gaze, unaware of the emotions which had been mirrored in his open face. 'It isn't owt Aah've done, is it?' he blurted out.

He was amazed at Mrs Butler's response. She seized his shoulders and shook him. 'What have you done to her? What have you done?' she demanded.

George was unable to understand her reaction. As soon as she released him, he stepped back out of her reach, warily noting her heightened colour and the flash of her eyes.

'It wasn't all my fault,' he remonstrated. 'T'sheep got a bit ahead of mi – that was all. Aah didn't think as 'ow she was hurt.'

Ann Butler shook her head in disbelief. 'Whatever are you talking about? Who said anything about sheep?' She was completely bewildered.

George explained about the sheep milling around the pony's legs and how Elizabeth had been thrown on the floor of the trap.

'She got up and seemed all right,' he concluded. He did not mention having caught more than a glimpse of Elizabeth's undergarments. Discretion told him that it was better for her mother not to know. Neither did he say that he had left Elizabeth in the company of a young man. The simple reason was that it just did not seem important.

Mrs Butler seemed embarrassed at the way she had reacted. 'It's all right, George. Her indisposition has nothing to do with what happened with the sheep,' she assured him. She half-turned away, but hesitated, and took a breath, as though to say more. However, she appeared to think better of it and stood indecisively.

'It's nowt serious, is it?' George was concerned for Elizabeth and yet puzzled by her mother's attitude.

'No, no, she's just resting for a while. It's nowt to worry about.' As she spoke, her eyes slid away from his uneasily. Again she opened her mouth as though to add to what she had already said, but once again thought the better of it.

'Right then. Aah'll be off.' George was reluctant to leave, but realised that he would learn nothing more from Elizabeth's mother. He was confused by the paradox of her manner. One moment she was her normal self and the next, she was almost hostile. She now made no effort to hide her relief at his departure, and turned to go back into the house.

George collected his dogs and began to hurry back home. 'That's a rum do and no mistake,' he reflected. He was bewildered by his reception at the Butlers' farm. Elizabeth had been her usual sparkling, fiery self that morning and yet, by the afternoon, was confined to her bed with some mysterious malady.

Perhaps, he considered, he would ask Joseph for more details of Elizabeth's illness when he saw him at chapel the following Sunday. He turned the idea over in his mind as he made his way home, but then decided against it. He felt self-conscious about his feelings for Elizabeth and had no wish for them to be discussed among his family. In any case, he pondered, looking back, Joseph had not confided in him about his affair with Mary. His mind was in a turmoil as he reflected on the events of the day. He thought with humiliation of his encounter with Elizabeth in the pony-trap and reflected gloomily on how willingly she had accepted the offer of escort from the young blood.

'She'd rather be wi' him than me,' he told himself, tormented by jealousy. 'Aah'd've been better off if Aah'd stopped at home and worked, instead of coming up ti Kirkby; at least none of that would have happened and she wouldn't have turned against me.'

As he trudged down the hill into Sleightholme-dale, he reflected how safe and peaceful it seemed compared with the outside world.

CHAPTER NINE

The year, which had opened so dramatically –
indeed, in Jonadab's eyes, so tragically – blossomed
into the best since he had taken over the running of
the farm from old Joseph, his father. The promise
held out by the early spring was fulfilled by a long,
hot summer.

The little valley of Sleightholmedale was sheltered
on all sides and the four farms clustered in the valley
bottom were always in advance of those on the higher
ground round about. In this perfect year, however,
all hopes and expectations were exceeded.

The only lightening breeze came with the dawn,
while they were busy with the horses. With sunrise,
the breeze dropped and the whole valley shimmered
in the scorching heat. Day after burning day, the
heat sucked up the water, until the beck became a
shallow trickle, moving sluggishly over its stones.
The moor, which rose beyond the beck, had lost the
sable hues of winter and now swept in fresh green
ridges against the blueness of the sky.

George had little time now to dwell on either Elizabeth Butler's fascinations or his brother Joseph's
mysterious problems. He had tried to sound out Joe
but, as far as he could discover, the only thing wrong
with his brother's life was that it was spent 'up t'tops'
among the Butlers, rather than down in the dale with
his own family.

George mentally shrugged. There was nothing to
be done about Joe's inability to accept his new life.
Things could be a lot worse for him, he considered.
As the year progressed, Mary carried the baby tidily,

showing little sign of her advancing pregnancy. There was none of the ungainly heaviness and leaning-back waddle which seemed to overtake most expectant mothers. A slight thickening of the waist and a radiant bloom on her face were the only telltale signs, so that a delightfully vague reticence as to exactly how far advanced she was effectively satisfied inquisitive neighbours.

Sundays apart, every day was work-filled from sun-up to sun-down. No sooner was the land tilled and the crops in, than lambing-time was upon them. Jonadab did not employ a shepherd, considering that on a mixed farm such as his, there were not enough sheep to warrant the expense. This meant that when the lambing season arrived, jobs on the farm were shuffled round, leaving Jonadab and his brother George to concentrate on the ewes.

This year, however, the routine had been altered.

'Noo then, George,' his father had observed one morning, 'Aah want you ti tek turns wi' your Uncle ti see t'ewes.'

Annie Oaks saw how exhausted George looked of late: his round, rosy face was paler and more fine-drawn than usual.

'Yon lad's working too hard, Jonadab,' she remonstrated with her husband, later.

'Nay, he's at the prime of his life. A bit of work never hurt anybody,' he replied. 'Besides, it's time he grew up. We want no namby-pambies here,' he added.

Annie smiled. Namby-pamby was scarcely the label to fix on any of her lads, she considered. 'Go gather me some nettle-tops to make nettle-beer,' she instructed the two youngest girls. 'Take a clean sack from the dairy to put 'em in.'

Their faces fell. 'Oh, Mam! Let our Tamar go,' they pleaded.

'No, thank you,' put in Tamar sharply. 'I've the butter to weigh up.'

'But Mam, we get our fingers nettled,' wailed Martha.

'Nonsense. Grab each one as tight as you can, and just nip off the tip,' answered Annie briskly.

'That's enough noise, girls,' ordered Jonadab. 'A nettle's like life. If you grasp it tightly, you won't get hurt. Off you go now. Your mother wants those nettles today, not next week, or the beer won't be ready for harvest.'

As they went out of the kitchen, George entered, carrying two orphan lambs. 'Feed these, Tamar, please, and then put them in t'fold with t'others,' he requested, handing them over.

'How's things going, lad?' demanded his father.

'Good, Faither. No trouble up to now,' answered George. 'Most are good lambs an'all,' he added, 'and not a bad number of twins – in fact, not many single ones at all.'

'I'll come with you and have a look.' Jonadab did not want George to feel that he was being supervised, but the lambs were an important cash crop and he was anxious to look them over.

As father and son walked out in companionable silence, Jonadab looked sharply down the road. 'Where do those two think they're going?' he demanded, at the sight of Martha and Maria running down the road as fast as their little legs would carry them.

Upon hearing the sound of a coach and pair, George knew very well what his sisters were about.

At the far end of the valley was a spring of healing water, over which a bath-house had been built. When the gentry came through the valley to bathe, or take the waters, Martha and Maria would often stand by the gate which barred the road between

107

them and the neighbouring farms. When they held open the gate for horsemen or coaches to pass through, they would scramble for coppers tossed to them by the grateful travellers.

Jonadab had forbidden them to do it, but their greed overcame even the fear of their father's anger. Now, upon hearing the coach coming down the hill, and little knowing that their father had followed them out of the house, the girls had run to open the gate.

'I'll have no childer o' mine begging,' spluttered Jonadab, as he broke into a run.

George ran after him, alarmed at the way the veins stood out on his father's neck as his face turned crimson with rage. Hearing the hooves close behind them, George grabbed his father's arm and drew him towards the hedge, out of the way of a fine pair of chestnuts.

Seeing that the gate ahead was being held wide open by the girls, the coachman made no hesitation but guided his charges at full gallop through the gateway, tossing a couple of coppers to the children as the coach swept by.

Unaware of their father's approach, Maria and Martha picked up the coins and swung the gate shut, riding on the bottom bar. Their laughter was suddenly silenced, however, as their father's powerful voice cut through the air.

'I'll tan your backsides when I get to you!' he bellowed.

With a gasp of dismay, they jumped off the gate and turned to face the irate figure which bore down on them.

Little Martha began to cry and ran to George. 'Oh, George, is Faither going to hit us?' she wailed.

George picked up the seven year old and held her close, patting her back to comfort her. 'Now, now,

Martha, don't take on so,' he said. 'You know how Faither feels about you begging.'

She subsided into hiccoughing sobs, and glanced sideways at her father from the safety of her brother's arms. 'Are t'farm lads beggin', Faither, when thoo pays 'em at t'year-end?' she enquired.

'Of course not,' answered Jonadab testily. 'It's their wages due to them, for work done.'

The little minx eyed him triumphantly. 'Well, our two farthings was pay for work done,' she announced. 'They pay us for holding t'gate, Faither.'

Jonadab's face was a study. He could not believe that this little chit had not only answered him back, but had got the better of him.

Maria and George stood transfixed at Martha's temerity in standing up to their father. Suddenly, what her sister had said sank into Maria's brain.

'Is it all right then, Faither?' she asked eagerly. 'We are being paid for doing work and some days we get as much as tuppence each,' she finished, as a further inducement for their father's approval.

Jonadab shook his head as if to clear it, and passed a hand across his brow. He found it hard to believe that these two, the youngest of his children, were daring to question his authority. 'No! It is not all right to grovel before t'gentry,' he declared. 'You're Oaks, and we're as good as any folk hereabouts.' His gaze softened as he looked at the two little girls, now standing hand in hand, their eyes downcast and boots scraping in the dust.

'Some jobs is too lowly for my childer,' he admonished, 'and that's that.' Upon which he turned away.

'Come on, George, we'll look over the sheep.' He strode away so purposefully, that the stocky George had to hurry to keep pace with his father's long, rangy strides.

Jonadab was torn between annoyance at what he

considered to be Martha's impudence and a grudging admiration for the logic shown by such a young child. He recounted the episode to his wife at bedtime, the only few minutes of privacy they ever had. 'She has an old head on her shoulders, that one,' he commented. 'There's not so many at her age as could have figured that out.'

Annie realised how amazed and disgruntled he must have felt, to have his youngest child not only dare to argue with him but, apparently, win that argument. She could see, however, that he was impressed by Martha's intelligence.

'Poor Jonadab,' she thought, as she held out her arms to welcome him into the soft folds of the featherbed. She sensed that his world was changing and that he was troubled by the changes. First Joseph, and now little Martha had kicked over the traces, leaving their father bewildered and upset.

Jonadab prided himself upon being an upright man. He set his feet rigidly in what he considered to be the Lord's ways. Throughout their lives, he had exhorted his children to pull together for the good of the family. He had never, in his life, challenged his own father's authority even when he took over the running of the farm from old Joseph. Neither could he ever recollect a time when his brother George had questioned one of his, or his father's decisions. To his deep disturbance, Jonadab had to face the fact that some of his children were straying from the standards he had set.

Not even Annie, his wife, could fully understand his sense of devastation when Joseph and Mary Butler had sinned. He always sensed, too, that beneath Tamar's apparently lighthearted exterior lay a rebelliousness waiting to rise to the surface – and now little Martha had tried to best him. Jonadab felt that his tight-knit world was crumbling around him.

As Annie smoothed away the frown lines on her husband's forehead, she sighed. For Jonadab there were no grey areas in life. Everything was black or white and he could not tolerate those who fell below his own strict standards.

He too, drifted off to sleep on a sigh. How could his children ever deviate from the strict rules he had laid down to guide them, when he knew that he was right?

The good lambing season was a foretaste of what the summer held in store. The weather was hot and dry and the crops were the best that even old grandfather Joseph could remember – and all his seventy-four years had been spent on the farm.

The hay in the meadows was ready early. It stood waist-high in the fields and pollen hung like a pale gold cloud above the heads of the grasses, which rose from a thick mat of white clover. The air was heavy with the murmurous drone of the bees, moving almost lazily among the meadow grasses and hedge-row flowers. So pulsating were the long golden days that the Oaks longed for the luxury of a shower, yet knew that rain would hold up the crucial haymaking.

This was one of the favourite times of the year for the whole family. The men went into the fields first, all working together. They swung the long scythes almost in unison, and the hay fell beneath the blades in fragrant swathes.

Annie and her daughters were occupied in the kitchen, baking and preparing huge amounts of food, not only to be taken out to their menfolk for their allowance, or "lowance' as it was called, but also extra pies and pasties to be eaten when they, too, went out to work in the fields.

After days of gruelling work with the scythes, the men were joined by the women and girls, including Dorcas Weald, the hind's wife. Their gowns were covered by huge calico aprons and their heads and necks were protected by sunbonnets.

Methodically, they moved along the field, using huge wooden rakes to make windrows. These were long ridges of the cut hay, raked together, running the length of the field. Maria and Martha laughed and shouted gleefully, enjoying the work among the sweet-smelling crop. Annie smiled indulgently as she looked proudly at her family. 'Eeh, it's grand to see 'em all pulling together,' she thought. The only cloud on her horizon was the absence of her eldest son, Joseph.

'His place is here,' she had said to Jonadab on more than one occasion.

'He's made his bed, he mun lie on it,' he would answer dourly.

She knew, however, that her husband felt Joseph's absence as keenly as she did. Neither of them ever discussed the subject except in the privacy of their own bedroom. They understood only too well how sensitive their daughter Ann and her husband felt about the situation. It was, after all, their presence in the farmhouse which was keeping Joseph from his rightful place.

Whenever Joseph and Mary were mentioned, Annie saw the tightening of her eldest daughter's face. She would turn her eyes downwards and take no further part in the conversation. John Waind, too, felt deeply about the situation. Never a talkative man, he became even more taciturn if he was unwittingly reminded that his parents-in-law missed Joseph's presence on the farm.

The crop was a good one and the weather remained calm and dry. The windrows were tedded and turned and the hay was forked into haycocks, which stood in rows across the fields.

'There!' exclaimed Jonadab, as he straightened his

112

back now and leaned on his fork. He glanced at the cloudless sky, whose blue was streaked and flushed with colour from the setting sun.

'We'll pray, tonight, that the good Lord'll keep the weather as perfect for the next few days. They're good-sized haycocks,' he added. 'They'll turn a shower, but we want nowt heavier.'

As they turned to fasten the field gate, George surveyed the haycocks. 'By, they're close together. It looks ti be a grand crop, Faither,' he remarked.

'It does that, lad,' agreed Jonadab. 'It'll see us through t'winter, mek no mistake.'

Jonadab's heartfelt prayers were answered, and the weather continued to be kind. The whole family worked together to load the hay crop on to the high waggons. Some drawn by horses and some by oxen, they trundled their way from the fields to the haylofts above the stables. Here, the hay was forked up to Bert Weald, who stowed it away carefully, filling the lofts. This hay would be used first, forked down into the stables for winter feed.

When the lofts were packed, the rest of the crop was stacked in the field. This was the first time that George had forked up to his father, who was on the stack. Jonadab took each forkful from him and placed it carefully, making sure that the stack was built up evenly, and that the hay would lie so as to turn the rain.

Although they seldom exchanged a word, George felt closer to his father than ever before in his life. They worked well together, each seeming to anticipate the other's next move or requirement. He realised that his work since Joseph's departure from the farm had met with his father's approval and he felt a deep satisfaction that his Dad was pleased with him.

He was fully aware that, since Joseph's lapse from

grace, their father had come to regard George as the eldest son, and the heir to the land. Although, on the one hand, it saddened him to oust his elder brother, on the other, he found himself regarding the farm with an almost proprietorial air. Thus the bumper hay crop gave George as much pride and pleasure as it did his father.

So, when the hay was all safely stowed away, father and son exchanged a smile of satisfaction. Jonadab looked deep into George's eyes, the startling blue ones boring into the dark brown ones, which looked back steadily and openly.

'Thoo'll do, lad,' Jonadab murmured, as he turned for the house. George followed, brimming over with happiness. He had never thought to hear such praise from his father, and thought that this must be the high-point of his life, eclipsing even the wedding feast, with Elizabeth as his partner. He could not imagine anything ever happening to surpass the feelings which overwhelmed him on this day.

CHAPTER TEN

Between haytime and harvest came the most tedious part of the farming year. Although the work with the stock still brought interest and rewards, most of the toil in the fields consisted of hoeing the root crop, and what was known as 'luking corn'.

While the women had the interest of sitting broody hens and rearing chicks and goslings, the menfolk spent hour after hour hoeing the corn and pulling up docks. These were thrust into sacking bags, which hung from the waist. When the bag was full, the docks were tipped out and burnt in a convenient hedgebottom.

One bright day in late July, George and the other men were engaged in this work. Jonadab had ridden off, early in the morning, on business. This was the only information he ever vouchsafed, even to his wife. Where he went or what business he transacted remained a closed book to his family.

In his absence, the men were working rather unenthusiastically at their humdrum task. Bert Weald did his best to chivvy them, but he had not the gaffer's authority and even George, who could normally be expected to work to his full capacity, was slow and obviously dreaming.

Over at the house, Annie and her girls were busy putting the finishing touches to the midday meal. She glanced out of the kitchen window into the garden.

'Now, where are those two little imps?' she muttered anxiously. 'I do hope they aren't playing by Hodge Beck.'

She knew that in their father's absence, her two

youngest children had no compunction in disobeying the strict rules which he laid down for them, and Hodge Beck could be dangerous.

'Tamar, tell Gran and Grandad that dinner's ready,' she instructed, as she and Ann set the table. 'Beth, slip to t'valley gate and see if they're there. They know your faither doesn't like 'em opening t'gate for t'gentry.'

Beth removed her apron and left the kitchen, to set off down the road at a run. As the gate came into view, she saw Maria and Martha sitting on the grass verge, making daisy chains. 'Come on, girls,' she called. 'Dinner's ready.'

The two little girls jumped up but did not run towards her as she had expected. Instead, they hesitated, looking beyond her and she heard horses galloping down the road. Could it be their father, returning early? 'Oh, no!' she prayed. 'Don't let it be Faither.' She breathed a sigh of relief as she saw a light carriage, drawn by two straining horses, racing towards her.

The driver was standing up, flicking the team with his whip and laughing to his companion, who was seated alongside. 'Get on, my beauties!' he shouted. 'Did you ever see such a pair, William?'

As Martha and Maria swung open the gate, Beth stepped on to the verge, pressing her back against the hedge, out of the way of the speeding horses. But instead of passing her and charging through the gate, held open by her sisters, the horses were checked.

'*Whoa!*' shouted the passenger, grasping the driver's arm. 'Stop, James!' he commanded.

The driver exerted all his strength to halt his team in full gallop. 'What is it, Forster?' he queried.

To Beth's surprise, the young man jumped down from the carriage and approached her. To the girl, who rarely went as far as the nearest little market town, he was so finely dressed in his jacket of plum-coloured velvet and cream breeches as to seem like someone from another world. As he strode towards her, she noted the way he eyed her in open admiration.

'Hello, young lady,' he smiled as he drew near. 'You're a pretty girl to be tucked away in a place like this.'

Beth was the shyest of Annie Oaks' daughters, and was unsure how to react to this flattery. She felt disturbed as the gentleman approached her. Glancing from side to side she could see no way of escape. Her feeling of unease grew stronger as he came closer.

'Come along, William! Don't be a fool!' called his companion.

By now, Beth's heart was beating so strongly that she was sure it must be audible, and her throat ached with tension. Maria and Martha had let the gate swing shut and were standing hand in hand, eyes rounded with puzzlement. What could the gentleman want with their Beth?

What William Forster wanted was no more than an exchange of pleasantries with a pretty girl. He had an insatiable weakness for the female sex and rarely missed an opportunity to shine in their company. Moreover, he was intrigued by Beth's apparent fear of him.

'Come now,' he said pleasantly. 'There's no need to be afraid! I'm not going to hurt you.'

Beth half-breathed a sigh of relief but as he took a step forwards, his eyes gleaming, she took a step backwards – only to feel the thorns of the hedge digging into her back.

'I've come to take my sisters home to dinner, sir,' she tried to say, but the words came out croakily.

'Mi Mam's waiting and she'll send somebody to fetch us if we're not back soon.'

'What I have in mind won't take long,' he laughed, reaching towards her.

Beth was trapped. The farm was out of sight round a bend in the road, and few people came down the valley. She felt the sweat running down her back and between her breasts as she began to shiver uncontrollably. She tried one last, desperate ploy. 'Go fetch Faither,' she called to the girls.

'Nay, you know he's away for t'day,' answered Maria in surprise. Beth's heart dropped. She could feel the determination emanating from the man, almost like a physical threat.

'That's enough, William. What are you thinking of, man? These people are my father's tenants,' James Sturdy protested uneasily.

In his vanity, William was now resolved to win a smile from Beth before riding on. Looking deep into her eyes, a technique he employed with women of all ages, he reached out to pat her shoulder. She, however, misread his intentions and was convinced that he meant to attack her. If she had been more worldly-wise, she would have realised that he was hardly likely to do her harm, in front of James Sturdy and her sisters. Seeing his hand coming towards her, she panicked and shoved against his chest to force him away.

Caught off-balance and surprised by her action, William teetered for a moment and then grabbed out at her in a vain effort to stop himself from falling. As his fingers caught at her bodice, there was a tearing sound and the material ripped to the waist, exposing her breasts.

William Forster stared at the weeping girl in horror. What had started out as a piece of harmless

118

fun on his part had developed into something far more ugly.

'It was only a bit of sport', he said sulkily, getting to his feet and adding with exasperation: 'How was I to know the fool would take it amiss?'

Martha and Maria had stood in silence while the little drama was taking place, but now they began to cry.

The driver of the carriage groaned out loud. 'My God, William, you've gone too far!' he expostulated, 'Father will take a very poor view of this – and what about Rowena!'

Just at that moment, George Oaks appeared in the lane, having heard the commotion on his way back to the farm. His incredulous gaze took in the tableau. Martha and Maria stood by the gate, clutching each other and looking in horror at the richly-dressed stranger who confronted their sister.

Forster faced Beth, his immaculate breeches stained with grass and his face stiff with rage. 'You bitch!' he snarled, and raised his hand to strike her.

As she flinched away, clutching the torn bodice to try to hide her body, George gave a strangled shout. *'Keep thi hands off her!'* he bellowed and threw himself forward, eyes blazing and fists clenched. Before he could launch a blow, however, the driver, who was standing in the carriage loosely holding the reins, snatched his whip out of its holder at his side. As George hurled himself at his sister's attacker, the whiplash snaked out and flicked his cheek, just below the eye.

George stopped dead in his tracks, raising his hand to his face. Seeing the blood on his fingers, he was momentarily nonplussed, not realising what had occurred.

'Get in, man,' directed the driver, as he gathered up the reins. 'Open that gate, you stupid child,' he

119

flung at Martha who, after a moment's hesitation, ran to do his bidding. His companion was up beside him in a flash and, with a crack of the whip, the horses were urged forward, through the gate and away down the valley.

The four stood in silence for a moment or two, unable to grasp that it was over. Beth was still sobbing.

'Oh, George, thank goodness you came when you did,' she gasped. 'I dread to think what would have happened.'

'It's all right, lass.' George was uncomfortably aware of her torn dress. 'It's yon chap again. Aah wonder why he's always round here.'

'He must be staying at the Towers with t'Sturdys,' answered his sister, beginning to recover from her ordeal.

'Whatever's Faither going to say?' George wondered aloud, still shaking with rage. 'Come on, you two.' He pulled himself together and addressed his younger sisters. 'You know Faither said you'd not to come down here and open t'gate. It's all your fault.'

At this, their sobbing grew louder.

'Please don't tell him, George,' gulped Martha, while Maria tugged Beth's arm.

'Oh, Beth, don't tell on us!' she pleaded.

'Don't be silly. He'll have to know. How can we explain George's face and my dress?' she responded wearily.

George realised that his face was smarting and sore where the whip had lashed him. He groaned inwardly at the thought of his father's wrath.

As the sorry group trudged back home, he kept his eyes averted from Beth, whose hands were grasping her bodice, striving to keep it pulled together.

George was acutely embarrassed at having seen

120

her breasts exposed, not only to a stranger's gaze but also to his own. He'd still been a child when his mother had nursed the two youngest as babies, and this had been done circumspectly, with her clothing disarranged only sufficiently to allow the baby to nuzzle the nipple.

Never before in his life had he set eyes on a girl's body and the sight of Beth's firm young breasts showing creamily against the tan of her face and neck had brought a sensitive realisation of how she must have felt to be thus exposed.

When they trailed into the farmhouse kitchen, their mother was already serving out the potatoes. Her eyes widened in shock and she hurriedly replaced the big, black iron pan on the range at the sight of them.

'The good Lord have mercy on us!' she gasped. 'Whatever's amiss?'

Beth was a tall, straight girl with plenty of spirit, but now she threw herself, weeping, into her mother's outstretched arms. 'Oh, Mam, Mam!' she sobbed, and the rest was just babbled incoherently.

'What's happened, George?' demanded Annie, rocking and patting the sobbing girl. 'You can't have been scrapping, surely, at your ages?'

'Nay, Mam,' he answered, flushing.

'How did thi face get scratched?' asked young Jonadab.

In their father's absence, Grandad Oaks took charge with a firmness which belied his seventy-odd years. 'Tek yon lass upstairs and get her properly clad, Ann,' he instructed his eldest granddaughter. 'Wash your hands, girls, and get your dinner,' to Martha and Maria. 'See to George's face, Mother,' he told his daughter-in-law, 'and the rest of you get on with your food. We'll hear what's befallen 'em,

121

never fear,' he added firmly, as he retook his seat at the table.

When Annie had gently washed his wound and dressed it with homemade salve, he placed a finger over her lips.

'Our Beth'll tell you all t'tale, Mam,' he said. 'Aah just want to slip out for a minute.'

Knowing that the two young bloods had not yet returned from the healing spring down the valley, George was determined that they would not get away scot free from what they, no doubt, regarded as just an escapade.

'Shame my sister, would they?' he muttered, as he ran as fast as his heavy boots would allow, past the pond and towards Cauldron Mill. Will Baldwin the miller's son was, he knew, rather partial towards Beth, and he hoped Will would help in his plan.

As luck would have it, Will was just coming out of the mill, having remained behind at dinnertime to finish off a job.

'Will! Will!' called George. ''Ere a minute, quick! Aah wants thoo ti gi' me a hand.'

'Whativver's up, George,' asked Will at the sight of his panting friend.

'Our Beth's been shamed by two toffs, an' Aah wants ti teach 'em a lesson,' George told him urgently.

'Shamed?' gasped Will. 'You mean –?'

'No! No!' interrupted George. 'Nowt 'appened, but only because Aah got there in time.'

The whole incident was exaggerated in George's mind by now. He had really only seen the end of the little drama, but was convinced that his intervention alone had saved Beth from a worse fate. He quickly explained what had occurred and what he intended to do.

'Come back wi' me and we'll push oor rulley across t'road, just round t'corner,' he stated.

''Ang on a bit, George.' Will was reluctant, now that he knew that Beth was not really harmed. 'Don't forget that one of 'em's Dad's our landlord, same as yours.'

'There'll be no trouble, nivver fear.' George was an Oaks and had blind faith in his father's ability to sort out any difficulties. Will was reassured and together, they set off on the road back. When they reached the Oaks' farm buildings, they strained and pushed to get the four-wheeled dray moving into the road and there, with much heaving and grunting, they manoeuvred it into position, sideways on, filling the narrow road almost from side to side.

'There, that'll stop 'em!' grinned George with satisfaction, as he passed his shirt-sleeve across his dripping brow. 'Get back ti t'mill, if thoo wants,' he said kindly, seeing the look of apprehension on his companion's face, as the sound of horses came to their ears from down the valley.

'Nay – Aah'll see it through,' Will answered staunchly.

'Good lad! Come to t'back of t'wall, then,' said George and pulled him out of sight.

They could now hear the carriage wheels rattling along the stony road. As the hoofbeats grew louder, the laughter of the two young men mingled with the crack of the driver's whip as he urged his horses on. 'Surely he'll stop in time,' prayed George, under his breath. As they rounded the bend, horses and passengers spotted the obstruction simultaneously. 'Whoa! Whoa!' called both men, though without need – as the horses reared and whinnied in their eagerness to come to a halt.

'What the devil is this?' cried the driver.

'Some damned yokel with no sense,' answered his

companion. 'It must have been left there by some stupid farmworker.'

'No, sir, it wasn't.' George sauntered out from behind the wall, his nonchalant attitude belying his racing heart. 'It was put there for a purpose, for us ti have a word.' With this, Will joined him beside the carriage, and the two sturdy young countrymen presented a formidable sight as they stood side by side. Their rolled sleeves showed powerful arms folded across solid, muscular chests.

The driver half-raised his whip, but George lifted a hand in warning. 'There'll be none of that this time, sir,' he said grimly. 'All Aah wants is a word wi' thi friend.'

Turning to the other dandy, he went on, 'We're respectable folk hereabouts, and don't take kindly to our womenfolk being insulted. You've frightened and shamed my sister and it'll be better for you if you don't come down into this dale again.'

The face which glared down into his flushed with rage and the light blue eyes turned cold. 'Damn you! My God, James, does your father allow his tenants to speak to you like this? Give him another twitch and put a civil tongue in his head!' he spluttered.

George stood his ground and looked at James Sturdy fearlessly. 'Mr Sturdy, sir. Your father knows my father, Jonadab Oaks, and would not take kindly to one of his girls being threatened. Will and me will move yon rulley and Aah'd be obliged if you'd take your friend out of our valley.' He turned his back on the pair and put his shoulder to the cart, alongside Will. As they got the vehicle moving and rolled it out of the way, the pair in the carriage could not hide their amazement that these two brawny men could move the dray without the aid of a horse.

'Strong in the back and weak in the head,' sneered

William Forster, as James clicked his tongue and ordered his horses to walk on.

'Not so weak in t'head as Aah couldn't stop thee,' called George, laughing as they disappeared up the lane. His good humour was completely restored now that he felt he had done something to avenge Beth's distressing encounter. 'Thanks, Will,' he continued, clapping his friend on the back. 'It'll be all right. There'll be no trouble, nivver fear.'

With that, he set off to run back home for his belated dinner.

His entrance was greeted by congratulations from his mother. 'Thank goodness you heard the commotion and turned back,' she said tremulously. Suddenly, the valley which she had always regarded as a haven of peace seemed threatened.

'When they found yon spring and built that bath-house, I didn't like it,' she said. 'All sorts of folks come down into t'dale now.'

'Nay, Mam,' George answered. 'Sir Francis Sturdy owns t'valley and Mr James can come when he wants. We don't know what sort of friends he has and can't do owt about it. Anyroad,' he added gleefully, 'yon other chap isn't likely ti come again!'

'Whatever do you mean?' his mother demanded, 'Oh, George, you haven't done owt foolish, have you?' She was terrified that, even after three generations, they might lose their tenancy.

'No, Mam, don't worry,' was all that George would say.

Upon Jonadab's return, he received everyone's version of the story and his expression became sterner at every telling. Martha and Maria had been sent by their mother to stand facing the wall in opposite corners of the kitchen, awaiting his homecoming.

He sank heavily into his Windsor chair and called

them over to him. 'What is the fifth Commandment, Martha?'

'*Honour thy father and thy mother*,' she answered in a whisper.

'You two have not honoured me!' His voice rose until, at the final word, it thundered through the kitchen. Jonadab rose to his feet and slowly took off his belt. 'Aah nivver thought it would come to this,' he said sadly.

Seeing the two little figures cowering in front of him, however, his heart softened. 'Go and feed the hens, girls, and never disobey me again,' he admonished.

'Yes, Faither,' they chorused as they ran from the room, thankful for their reprieve. Annie smiled to herself. She knew that, for all his sternness, Jonadab would never lift a finger to any of his children.

George had told no one else about the culmination of the afternoon's events but, after a momentary hesitation, he decided that his father should know in case the landowner, Sir Francis Sturdy, followed up the matter. As he poured out the story of how he and Will had stopped the carriage and warned off Beth's accoster, a sardonic smile lightened his father's face.

'Well done, lad! Don't worry. Next market day, I shall go down ti t'Towers and have a word with our landlord. He is a fair man and won't be too pleased to hear of his guest's behaviour!'

The incident was never mentioned again, but the next time George went to Kirkbymoorside, he met the Honourable James Sturdy in the street and felt a quiet satisfaction when the young man inclined his head slightly. 'Good afternoon, Oaks,' he said graciously.

'Good day, sir,' George answered, recognising Sturdy's respect.

CHAPTER ELEVEN

Now that Mary Oaks' time was drawing near, she
and Joseph had stopped their visits to Sleightholmedale. Although Annie and Jonadab still saw their son
on Sunday evenings at chapel and afterwards strolled
back to the Butlers' farm with him, he became more
morose and withdrawn. Even George, who had
always been the closest to his brother could no longer
draw him into the old banter and chat, no matter
how hard he tried.

These Sunday evening walks, in the company of
the Butler family, became the highspot of George's
life. He fell more and more in love with Elizabeth
Butler. Although the unending labour of his working
week gave him little time for dreaming, his Sundays
were spent thinking of her and turning over in his
mind witty remarks and clever phrases to impress
her.

Poor George! The very sight of her sent them
flying out of his mind. In chapel, he sang the hymns
mechanically, not really knowing what words were
coming, while he gazed across at the curve of her
neck or the line of her cheek. Often, his tardiness
in standing up or sitting down earned him a glower
from his father or a nudge from one of his sisters.

On the walk back from the chapel at Gillamoor to
the farm at Fadmoor, Elizabeth frequently chose to
walk beside him. The younger girls' chatter and
giggles irritated her and, though she sometimes
strolled and talked to his sister, Ann, more often
than not she would fall into step at George's side.

This caused him a mixture of delight and embarrassment. To be in her company brought a heady glow to his tanned cheeks, but he remained awkward and tongue-tied. The remarks that had been so carefully prepared refused to pass his lips and he suspected that Elizabeth was secretly laughing at him. 'A real lummox she must think I am,' he often thought miserably.

He still had no idea why Elizabeth had refused to see him on the day that his lambs had upset her pony. Each time he tried to pluck up the courage to ask, his heart failed him. He was only too delighted that she chose his company, and had no desire to upset her.

Elizabeth did not really know what her feelings were for George Oaks. She was undoubtedly fond of him, even though he was six years her junior and nothing could ever come of it. His openness and straightforward nature appealed to her, and she recognised in him an intelligence which his meagre schooling could not hide. 'He could really make something of himself if he wasn't dominated by that martinet of a father,' she often thought, gazing with dislike at Jonadab's ramrod-straight back, as he strode ahead with her father.

Jonadab would survey the land at each side of the road with satisfaction. The bleak upland fields were a good couple of weeks behind his, down in the valley.

'Not ready for harvest yet, John?' he remarked with deceptive casualness, one Sunday early in August.

'No,' answered John Butler. 'Another couple of weeks yet. What about you?'

'Another couple of days, if this weather keeps up,' replied Jondab, with quiet satisfaction.

George had overheard this exchange and excitement conquered his shyness of Elizabeth. 'Aah'll be

128

glad when harvest's here. It's my favourite time,' he burst out, eyes shining.

Elizabeth smiled. The vivacity which she hadn't seen in him since Mary's wedding transformed him. 'Why, George, I do believe you're handsome,' she teased, in a low voice which no one else could hear.

'Now thoo's poking fun at me,' he retorted, flushing with pleasure all the same.

He walked on with his thoughts in a daze. Could Elizabeth really like him, he wondered and then ruefully decided that such bliss was beyond the bounds of possibility. He had told himself a thousand times: a sophisticated young lady of twenty-four would not be interested in a seventeen year old lad like him.

As the party approached the Butlers' farmhouse, he determined to speak out, to end his agony. Looking at her shyly out of the corner of his eye he half-whispered, 'Elizabeth, you do like me a bit, don't you?' and glanced around to see that none of the others could hear.

'You know that I do,' she answered quietly.

'Sometimes I think you do, but then again, there's times that you're, well . . .' George fumbled for the word. 'You're, well, *cool*,' he finished.

Elizabeth bit her lip. It was true. She knew that at times she did withdraw from George. The difference in their ages made her unsure of herself.

'Don't play fast and loose with me, Elizabeth,' he pleaded now. 'If I've no chance, say so straight out.'

She did not immediately reply and, as they caught up with the others, he was still left in doubt as to what her true feelings could be. Jonadab's voice brought him back down to earth. ''Appen I was exaggerating a bit when I said a couple of days,' he remarked, 'but t'fields is coming on nicely and we should be starting on t'long field by next week.'

Sure enough, the harvesters began to descend on to the farm by the end of the week. When he was a child, this had seemed almost magical to George. His father only had to rub an ear of corn between his hands, test the released grain with his teeth, and an army of workers appeared as if by magic.

No doubt, Martha and Maria still thought of it in this way, but George knew the amount of planning and negotiating which his father put into the venture.

The family and their own farmworkers managed to cope with the haymaking but a larger workforce was needed for harvest-time. Some of these were local families who eked out a mere subsistence by keeping a couple of pigs, a cow and a few hens, and growing their own vegetables. When local farmers needed casual labour, these whole families would turn out to earn a little money. The rest of the workforce came from further afield, many of them having already finished harvesting up on the wolds.

Young Jonadab, albeit tall for his twelve years, was not yet up to using a scythe. As he gatherd up the sheaves, standing them ten together to form a stook, he was envious of George who strode out with the other men, wielding his scythe.

George soon established a rhythm and felt almost hypnotised by the swish of the blade as it cut through the stalks. Just as soon, however, he realised that the work was telling on muscles which had not been used since hay-time. When they stopped for mid-morning 'lowance, George's back felt as though it had been whipped. He leaned painfully against a stook with his meat pasty and tea, and thought of the minister's sermon on the previous Sunday. The preacher's voice had echoed round the room which was used as a makeshift chapel. 'I will whip you with scorpions!' he had thundered.

'Aye. That's what it feels like,' George reflected ruefully. 'As though Aah've been whipped wi' scorpions.' He wasn't quite sure what it meant, but it seemed to be a graphic description of the agony of his back and shoulder muscles.

Young Jonadab threw himself down beside his brother, holding the sleeves of his shirt away from his arms.

'There's not many thistles,' remonstrated George. 'This field has been well luked.' Jonadab rolled up his sleeves, to show scratched arms, red and swollen.

'Thoo envies me, doesn't thoo?' George demanded.

'Aye, Aah does an' all! Aah'd rather be doing anything than stooking.'

George put a piece of straw between his lips and chewed it reflectively before answering. 'At least thoo's summat to show for thi pain. Every bone in my back's red hot and there's nowt ti see at all. Scything's nowt it's cracked up to be – at least, not on t'first day,' he added, trying to be fair. He knew that he wouldn't really choose to step back into his recently-left childhood and change places with his brother.

After the first day and night, when he didn't know how to lie in bed to find comfort for his aching back and shoulders, George's muscles eased into the new routine until he felt as though he'd been scything in the cornfields all his life.

At the end of the shimmeringly hot summer, the harvest exceeded even Jonadab's expectations. Each night, at dusk, he surveyed the close-packed stooks with pride and then looked anxiously at the pearly-pink sky and dancing midges. He knew that the weather would hold, but dare not voice his confidence. 'I hope it 'olds,' he would murmur, as if to placate his Lord by showing his fears.

'It'll 'old, Jonadab,' Annie would reply firmly.

'Nay, nay, we mustn't be over-sure,' was his grudging response. 'How long must it stand before it's led, girls?' he asked the young ones.

'Till it's heard three church bells, Faither,' chorused Martha and Maria.

'Aye, that's right – then, God willing, we'll be leading afore t'weather breaks,' he prayed fervently.

The glorious summer did not let him down and when the last load was led, topped by a corn dolly, it completed the best harvest that Jonadab had ever known.

'Come in, friends,' he called to all those who had helped. 'My missus and the girls have prepared t'Mell Supper and Bert Weald's tuned his concertina,' he added, with a rare smile. 'We'll celebrate this harvest in true fashion.'

Even though this was the traditional culmination of the harvest, it was always greeted with surprised gratitude by the workers. As they shuffled into the kitchen in embarrassed silence, the corn dolly was propped up in a corner to survey the celebrations. Tomorrow she would be put in one of the barns to replace last year's, which would be burnt. If a corn dolly lasted until the next harvest, intact and uneaten by the rats and mice, it augured well for the farm during the following year.

Extra tables had been brought in from the parlour and the hind's house until the kitchen was filled. 'Breathe in,' one laughed to another, and the ice was broken, as they jostled and shuffled to find a place. The company exclaimed at the quality of the ham, pork pies and beef laid out on the tables, along with apple and blackberry pies.

It was a matter of pride among the farmers' wives to supply plenty of good food for their workers, both for 'lowance and dinner during the weeks of work, and especially so at the Harvest, or Mell Supper, with which the end of harvest was celebrated on each farm.

Everybody tucked in and in addition to the mountains of food, there was ale for those who wanted it and fruit cordial or tea for the rest. Shyness was forgotten now as tales of other harvests were exchanged, and each tried to outdo the other in amounts scythed in a day, by legendary uncles or fathers.

The party was in full swing when there came a sudden knocking on the door. The whole company fell silent as Jonadab looked up.

'I can't manage to get out. Would you answer t'door, Bert?' he asked the hind, who was seated at the end of the table. As he pushed his chair back and took the one step to the door, every eye was on Weald. He reached out his hand to the latch and swung the door inwards.

There, on the step stood a boy of about twelve. He was turning his cap in his hand, obviously abashed by the dozens of eyes turned towards him.

'M-Mr Oaks, sir?' he spluttered, taking a half-step inside the doorway.

'Yes, lad?' Jonadab spoke encouragingly.

'P-please, sir, Mr Butler's sent me. Their Mary – your Joe's missus, has come early.'

'Come early?' Jonadab's brow was furrowed with perplexity. 'Come early to where, lad?'

The boy took another step inside the door, overcome with mortification at not making himself clear before all these strangers. 'N-nowhere,' he answered, 'leastways, that is – to bed. She's had a bairn,' he finished triumphantly.

'Oh! Oh!' Annie was on her feet, hands clasped. 'The Lord be praised.'

'Amen to that,' responded her husband.

'What is it, lad? Are they both well?' She could

hardly get the words out, shaking as she was with excitement.

'It's a lad and nobody said they wasn't all right, so Aah 'specs they are,' he answered.

'Come in, come in! Here, have some pie.' Annie was so overcome that she could have kissed the young messenger, as he was manhandled into the kitchen and a place squeezed for him on one of the overcrowded benches.

George caught sight of his sister Ann's face. A faint shadow seemed to pass over it, as she smoothed a hand over her flat stomach but before he could be sure, she and her husband were as carefree and excited as the rest.

This news was the crowning glory of the Harvest-Home evening. George was as thrilled as the rest. *It was a lad!* He wondered if Joseph would remember his promise to name his son after his brother, just as their own father had done with him and Uncle George. Would indeed, Mary and the other Butlers allow the bairn to be called George? He didn't really know much about the Butlers, apart from Elizabeth, but Joseph certainly didn't seem at all happy living with them.

George knew that both his parents were concerned about Joseph. At first, their eldest son had seemed to brighten up during their Sunday evening walks back from chapel, but of late he took little part in the general conversation between the two families. He seemed preoccupied and depressed.

'Maybe 'e's been worried about Mary,' George thought. 'Yes, that'll be it. He'll buck up now t' bairn's safely here.'

When the harvest meal was finished, Bert Weald took out his concertina and everyone joined in the songs.

134

'Away to bed, girls,' Jonadab had instructed Martha and Maria, when the tables were cleared.

'Oh, Faither, please let us stay up a bit for the singing,' pleaded Maria.

'After all, we're aunties now,' put in Martha triumphantly.

Jonadab was forced to join in the laughter at the seven year old's statement. 'Oh, so you want to stay up, do you, Auntie Martha?' he teased. Martha's lip began to quiver, as she thought she was being ridiculed before all these people. 'Now, now, let's have no tears. You can stay up a bit, if you sing the first song,' he decided.

Her face was illuminated by a brilliant smile. 'Thank you, thank you! Our Maria'll sing one with me,' she bubbled.

As the girls began to sing, George reflected. He was now Uncle George, just as his father's brother was their Uncle George. Had Uncle George felt as curious and proud about him, as he did about his nephew, he mused.

The next morning, when his parents were ready to go up to visit their grandson, George approached rather pleadingly. 'Does thoo think Aah could come an' all, Mother?' he pressed. 'Aah won't stop in t'house long, but I did stand for them at t'wedding . . .' His voice trailed away as his father turned his steely gaze towards him.

Annie looked fondly at the spaniel-brown eyes, turned so beseechingly in her direction. They were so like her father's. 'Aye, Aah don't see why not, do you, Faither?' she asked Jonadab, so sweeping the ground from beneath his feet.

He half-frowned, not believing in being what he thought of as weak with his children. However, he would not gainsay Annie in front of any of them.

'Just one look at the babby and then you can come home and see to things.' He gave ground grudgingly.

Mary looked as radiant as on her wedding day when Joseph led them up into the bedroom. Mrs Butler followed the group and, sweeping Joseph aside, bent over the cradle which stood by the bed. 'There, look what a fine boy he is,' she crooned, picking up the baby and unwrapping the shawl in which he was swathed. 'There, now. Who's Grandma's little man?' she added.

'Could this Grandma hold him a bit?' Annie Oaks held out her arms for the baby, much to her hostess's discomfiture.

'Why, of course.' She reluctantly passed over the little bundle for the Oaks grandparents to study. 'We haven't thought of a name yet,' she volunteered, 'though I do fancy John.'

Joseph stiffened, glanced at Mary and drew himself up. 'His name is George,' he announced firmly.

George's heart raced. They hadn't forgotten! Mary half-smiled as she saw the pride and pleasure in her brother-in-law's face.

Her mother, however, did not try to hide her chagrin. 'George? We've never had any Georges in the Butlers',' she stated huffily.

'It's an Oaks' name for an Oaks' bairn,' said Jonadab with satisfaction.

Joseph crossed to the bed and put his hand on Mary's shoulder. 'We decided at the start – Elizabeth for a girl and George for a boy,' he stated. 'And they'll be his godparents – our George and your Lizzie.'

George walked down the stairs and into the Butlers' kitchen without even realising that he had done so. Once there, he did not even notice the other girls. He only had eyes for Elizabeth.

'We're going to be his godparents,' he told her.

136

'Yes, I know. He seems a good, strong boy to bear a good, strong name,' she answered, and put a mug of tea on the table in front of him.

As the rest of the girls resumed their tasks and talk in the kitchen, she seated herself on the settle beside him. 'Something else we're going to do together, George,' she teased in a whisper. 'Another thing we shall share.'

George did not answer. He just sat sipping his tea, his thoughts a confused mixture. 'She's like a witch,' he decided. 'Not an ugly, evil witch but a beautiful, clever witch, who knows all my thoughts and laughs at them.'

When he had finished his tea, he stood up. 'Aah've ti get back 'ome,' he told her.

'I'll see you to the gate,' Elizabeth offered as she opened the door. The other girls exchanged significant glances as they passed through the door together.

At the gate, George turned. 'Aah'm glad we're to be his godparents,' he confided in a whisper. 'What Aah means is – me and you. Us two, together, if you know what Aah means.'

'Yes, George. I do know what you mean, and I'm pleased too,' she murmured. As he turned away, she added quietly, 'Grow up soon, George. I'm getting on, you know.'

He whirled back. 'Nonsense, Lizzie Butler, you're beautiful! Young and beautiful,' he added. Watching her glow under the influence of his last remark, George decided to ask the question he had been worrying about for months. His mouth was suddenly dry and he licked his lips. 'Elizabeth,' he stammered, 'there's summat I've been meaning to ask. It's been bothering me for weeks. You know when t'sheep upset you and t'pony? Well, I came to see if you

137

were all right, but your Mam said you weren't well. Was it because of me?'

Elizabeth hesitated. 'No, it was nothing *you'd* done. It was . . .' she appeared to reconsider. 'It was something I don't want to talk about.' She had obviously decided not to confide in him.

George frowned. 'Was it owt to do with that fancy chap?' he demanded. 'Aah didn't like you going off wi' him, and I'd never have let you, if I'd known what a blackguard t'fellow is – but there was nowt Aah could do, with having t'sheep ti see to.'

Elizabeth was silent for a moment, but seeing his troubled look, she gazed deeply into George's eyes. 'Someday I'll tell you,' she promised. 'But I can't talk about it yet.'

'Well, at least that sounds as though you'll still be talking to me,' he said with relief, as he set off down the road at a run.

Elizabeth watched him go with a faint frown. What did she want of him, she wondered. She looked back in her mind at the chances she had turned down from men richer, older and more polished than this callow youth. None of them had roused in her the feelings which she had for George Oaks.

Although she had been vaguely aware of his existence ever since his childhood, it was only when he had acted as Joseph's best man that she had really noticed George. Though she could look with pleasure at the velvety brown eyes and the thick springiness of his chestnut hair, it was not his physical appearance that had first drawn her to George. He possessed a transparent honesty and an air of trusting innocence unusual in a grown man. He had at first appealed to her as a puppy might, hoping for affection. As their friendship deepened, however, she grew to appreciate the innate kindness and immense compassion which raised him above the other men of her aquaintance.

Even today she had experienced his concern for her and his protective attitude. 'If only he were older,' she thought ruefully. 'Or I were younger,' she added, with a smile at herself.

She turned back into the house, still unsure of what she really wanted of George.

CHAPTER TWELVE

The hot dry summer was followed by a mild damp winter. Mists lingered in the valley, clinging to the moist ground in smoky drifts, veiling the trees, which rose through it, wraith-like, with outstretched fingers.

Annie Oaks fussed over her family. 'It's a sickness-breeder,' she confided to her eldest daughter, as she assiduously rubbed the girls' chests with goose-grease each bedtime.

Martha and Maria had almost grown out of their red-flannel petticoats, but she decided that they must squeeze into them for another year. Annie pinned great faith on red flannel to ward off ills and chills. 'Aah hopes they don't shoot up too much this year, and then Aah can put off making new ones till next year,' she sighed.

While realising that the year's hay and corn crops had been bumper ones, she considered that it was up to her to run the domestic side of life as frugally as possible. That was her countrywoman's heritage, passed on from her mother and her mother's mother, back into the past. This she, in turn, was passing on to her girls to hand on to their daughters.

On the whole, life was uncomplicated for Annie and her girls. As season succeeded season, their tasks varied only slightly against the ever-present background of housework. Cooking, baking and dairy work were constant, as were washing, ironing and needlework. Each time of the year brought variety in the making of different jams, jellies and preserves, as each crop of the orchard and hedgerows was succeeded by another.

From spring to autumn, the tiers of shelves which lined the dairy and pantry were gradually filled with stone jars, their contents ranging in colour from amber through deepest ruby red to the rich blue-black of bramble jam. No sooner were they filled to Annie's satisfaction than winter began its inexorable drain on her store. As preserves followed pickles on to the table, she felt a mixture of pride that so much had been provided and reluctance that they were being depleted.

Although baby George was growing, Joseph and Mary lacked the spark which all new young parents should have. It was obvious to all who knew them that they were still devoted to each other and that the child's coming had completed their circle of love, but yet there was something missing . . . No matter how often Annie and Jonadab discussed the problem, before drifting off to sleep, they could think of no reason for this cloud which seemed to overshadow Joseph and Mary. George's tentative probing had met with no success at all so once again he put it down to the responsibilities brought about by married life.

In due course, Rosie and Violet foaled, each producing a filly. Though not identical, the two were very well-matched. Young Jonadab was delighted. 'By – Aah'm fair capped,' he confided to George. 'How does thoo fancy Bonnie and Bluebell for names?'

George feigned enthusiasm. 'Oh, aye. They're right grand names,' he answered. This conversation brought home to him how great a change had taken place in him since the previous spring. Looking back to his excitement when the two greys had been served, he could scarcely believe his lack of interest in their progeny. He still regarded the mothers as his own horses and spent all his spare time grooming them and confiding in them. He had, however, lost his interest in the foals, once he knew that they were to pass into his brother's charge.

George felt shamefaced and rather unworthy because of these feelings. He was pleased when both mares were safely delivered of fillies, of course. The better the stock, the better it was for the farm, as he appreciated. The two grey mares were, however, special to him and he could not regard his brother's charges with the same affection. As it transpired, the fact that Jonadab had been given the care of the new foals brought nothing but good. When the young horses matured, each boy tried to outdo the other in the grooming and care of his team, and the result was two pairs of gleaming, immaculate greys who always did credit to their grooms.

The back of Aumery Park Farm was towards the road, and the front garden looked on to a meadow, beyond which the dale was bounded by a sweep of heather-clad moorland, rising quite steeply. Between the meadow and the moor meandered a stream known as Hodge Beck. Although the beck was shallow, rippling over a stony bed, after a heavy storm the level was liable to rise quickly in a flash-flood.

On the far side of the stream was an established heronry, which the Oaks family regarded with a somewhat proprietorial air. Each spring they waited for 'their' herons to arrive, feeling superstitiously that if ever the birds failed to come, it would augur ill for their household.

As this dank and dreary winter moved into an equally dismal new spring, each member of the family began to glance over the beck at odd times of the day.

'Them herons is late, this year,' Jonadab brooded uneasily.

'They'll come, never fear,' answered his wife. Despite her apparent confidence, however, Annie found herself at the front of the house scanning the skies at least once a day.

One palely sunny day, Martha came running into the house from where she had been skipping by the pond.

'They're 'ere, Mam,' she shouted excitedly.

'Who are, lovey?' asked Annie.

'T'erons – t'birds!' She was triumphant at being the first to spot them. 'There's two, just flew over!'

Annie felt a surge of relief – another lucky year! Then she mentally chided herself for her superstition. 'Of course they're 'ere. Did you ever doubt it? This is their summer home!' She was reassuring herself, as well as her child.

With the comimg of the herons, the hearts of the whole family lifted. The steady good weather of the previous spring was, alas, not repeated. May followed April, lit only rarely by a fitful sun, whose weak rays were a pale mockery of last year's blazing gold.

With the coming of June, however, the weather picked up. The sun at last gained power and the flowers of spring put in a late appearance. The woods leading down to the valley were carpeted with a profusion of primroses, violets and rich, dark purple bluebells, all blooming together, so that their combined fragrances hung heavy among the trees.

Martha and Maria gathered great untidy masses of blooms, crushing them into jars and any other containers until the whole house was thick with their scent. Annie welcomed all the flowers except May blossom. This, she was convinced, was unlucky and would not allow it in the house. 'On the windowsill outside,' she would insist, if the dainty flowers ever tempted the girls to tear branches from the hedgerow.

'Nay, lass. How can anything created by the Lord be unlucky?' Her husband would chide, but she was not to be moved. Knowing that Jonadab sometimes grew impatient with her superstitions, considering that they showed a lack of trust in the Lord, she had twinges of guilt about them, but they were a part of her family-lore, ingrained from generations back and, try as she might, she could not cast them off.

So Annie continued to search the heavens when the new moon was due, to avoid the misfortune of 'viewing it through glass'. One solitary magpie sent her eye scanning the skies for another, to avoid seeing 'one for sorrow' and each one she encountered was greeted, albeit under her breath, with: 'Good morning, Mr Magpie,' so avoiding an unlucky day.

One golden, late June day, Maria and Martha decided to pick flowers in the front meadow, now that the blossoms of spring were fading in the woods. They wandered through the flower-spangled grass, Martha tugging at buttercups and ferreting among the grass for daisies and creeping blue speedwell. Maria, on the other hand, was more discriminating. She quartered the meadow, selecting a variety of tall, nodding grasses with which she arranged spikes of foxglove and campion – both red and white.

When they reached the beck, they sat on the grass and trailed their warm, moist hands in the water. The flowers were laid aside while they lay on their stomachs, grasping for tiddlers with no success.

'I know!' Martha rolled on to her back. 'Let's cross t'stepping stones and look for t'herons.'

Maria considered, allowing her gaze to rake the opposite bank. 'No,' she replied, 'we might frighten 'em off. If we did, our Dad would be vexed.'

As her eye wandered idly up and down the length of the bank, she spotted a clump of vivid pink flowers tucked into an inlet.

'Ooh! Ragged Robins!' She pointed, drawing Martha's attention to the blooms. 'By – they'd look grand in t'parlour,' she added.

'Let's go and pick some for our Mam,' urged Martha.

'We'll leave t'other flowers 'ere till we come back!' Maria was already on her feet and running along the bank towards the stepping-stones.

The chuckling beck was only ankle-deep and they would have loved to paddle across it. To have removed their boots and knitted stockings, however, would give rise to their father's anger. Ever since they had been caught opening the gate, the pair were certain that, like God, Jonadab would find out and would descend in wrath if they contravened his laws.

The stepping-stones had probably been in position even before the house. They marked a route taken by medieval shepherds moving their flocks between the valley bottom and the high moor at different seasons. Solid and moss-cushioned, the stones spanned Hodge Beck, leading to a single track on the opposite side which snaked between the heather to the ridge of the moor.

Maria took a wide stride on to the first stone and then moved easily on to the next, to make room for her sister to follow. When she reached the third stepping-stone, she realised that Martha was lagging behind. On turning round, she saw that Martha was still hesitating on the bank. 'Come on, slowcoach,' she called. The younger girl still hung back. Always before, she had been swung over the first big gap, on to the security of the stone by an older brother or sister. Now she faltered at the thought of venturing unaided.

145

Martha was not afraid of the water – only reluctant to get her boots and stockings wet. Thrift was so instilled into Jonadab's family that the thought of such a calamity filled her with dread.

In most things, although two years younger than Maria, she was the leader, possessing a more adventurous spirit than the older girl. She now knew, in her heart, that she just could not stride that gap unaided. 'Aah daren't,' she called out, flushing, ashamed to be found lacking.

'Huh! It's easy.' Maria waved her arms above her head and leapt to the fourth stone. As she landed, her boots slipped on the damp moss. She teetered for a second, grabbed at the air and then, arms flailing wildly, plunged forward into the beck, crashing face-down in the water.

Martha gasped and stared unbelievingly. 'Ooh, Maria! Get up! Your clothes is all wet. Faither'll kill thee!'

Maria was unmoving, the waters of the streamlet eddying round her body, strangely still and silent.

'Maria? Maria!' There was a note of uncertainty now in Martha's voice. 'Don't tease,' she pleaded. 'Get up. You'll get into bother.' Like a flash of piercing light came the overwhelming certainty that something was badly wrong. She turned and began to run wildly towards home.

'Mamma! Mamma!' she shrieked, blundering unseeing through the grass over which she had dawdled so happily such a short time before. Annie, busy bustling in the kitchen with the older girls, heard nothing.

Jonadab was working with Bert Weald in Blackgate field, which sloped up from the road at the other side of the valley. From time to time, out of years of habit, his gaze wandered round to survey and check all his farm – land, stock and buildings. So it was he who first saw Martha's stumbling progress across the field.

Thinking at first that she was playing some childish game, he looked behind her for Maria. Then the straining urgency of the little figure and the way she weaved her way forward, blinded by exhaustion, brought a premonition of catastrophe.

Jonadab dropped his hoe and his long legs covered the ground at top speed as he ran down the hill and across the road, towards his youngest child. As he grew nearer, his certainty of disaster was heightened. Her dark eyes bulged wildly from a chalk-white face and her breath came in choking sobs. When they met, he grabbed her by the arms and lifted her so that her face was level with his.

'What is it? What is it?' He shook her slightly. She was, however, too spent to answer. There was a rasping in her throat, as she fought for breath and tears rolled down her cheeks. Jonadab set her down, to continue her way back to the house while he, once more, began to run towards the stream, following her route as shown by the flattened grass.

'Oh, dear God, no!' he muttered, when he came into view of the beck and saw the little figure crumpled in the shallow swirls. He knew, however, that his prayer was in vain. His child's spirit had gone from her body, which lay as lifeless as a rag doll.

For an instant, Jonadab's life appeared to stop. His heart filled his throat with a thunderous, pulsating throb; his ears were filled with a deafening roar and a red mist covered his eyes. For a wild moment, he thought that he was going to fall down unconscious, but gathered himself together and rushed into the water to scoop up the child's body.

Her head had struck a large stone on the stream's bed and, shallow though it was, the water was deep enough to cover her face.

Jonadab and Annie had, for the first time, lost a child.

He turned and made his way heavily back towards the farmhouse, shoulders bowed and head bent over the limp body, as his lips moved in silent prayer.

For Jonadab Oaks, the heat of the sun froze, all birdsong ceased and the myriads of insects stopped their chittering, as his leaden feet dragged their way back through the field with his daughter's body clutched to his chest.

By the time she had reached the kitchen, Martha was incoherent. She could not speak; her breath came in gasps and hiccoughs and she began to shake uncontrollably.

With a deepening feeling of unease, Annie Oaks rushed from the house, closely followed by Ann and Tamar. Beth remained behind to try to calm and comfort the distraught Martha.

Bert Weald had come slowly down the hill in Jonadab's wake and now stood by the meadow gate. Having seen Jonadas's wild rush across the field he witnessed his stumbling return, bearing his pathetic bundle.

When the three figures emerged from the kitchen and looked anxiously up and down the road to find the cause of Martha's distress, he called, 'Here, Mrs Oaks,' and motioned Annie towards the gate. There was such compassion in his voice that she instinctively knew that whatever had occurred must be a fearful tragedy. As they rounded the corner of the house, Jonadab was close enough for them to see the grief and despair on his face and they realised immediately that the child in his arms was dead.

This was the scene that greeted George and young Jonna, as they rounded the corner on their way home to dinner.

'What's up?' asked Jonna, as they saw their

mother, ashen-faced and supported by Ann and Tamar. Bert Weald stood hesitantly by the gate, undecided as to whether he should go to his master, and yet unwilling to push himself forward into his grief.

George took in the situation at a glance and, shouldering Weald out of the way, hurled himself through the gate towards the grief-torn man and his grim burden.

'Give her to me, Faither,' he whispered, holding out his arms.

Jonadab clutched his child protectively to his chest. 'Nay, nay, lad,' he murmured brokenly. 'Saddle up Topper and ride into Kirkby and fetch t'doctor. There's nowt can be done, though,' he added, gazing tenderly down.

One thing that George had inherited from Jonadab was the ability to act decisively in a crisis. He turned on his heels and ran to the stable. By the time he rode past the house, the sad little procession had gone inside.

Maria was buried in the churchyard at Gillamoor, only a few months before her Grandmother Oaks drifted away in her sleep and followed her. There were not many families which had not lost at least one child, but Jonadab was fiercely proud of the strength and sturdiness of his children and had great faith in the pure water of the spring in which, in his view, they all owed their health.

To have had the joy of Maria for ten years and then to have her life snatched away in full health was a cataclysmic blow to him. He searched his conscience to see what he could have done, for God to punish him so harshly. He became even more rigid and strict towards the rest of his family.

'We must walk in the Lord's ways,' he cautioned them with great regularity.

Annie Oaks was devastated by the loss. After the first torrent of grief, she became morose, given to spells of melancholy – of staring, unseeing, into space. The three elder girls set themselves to watch out for these depressions, when they would ask her advice or remind her of some task which needed her expertise.

Martha, of course, was the most affected by Maria's death. She had never in all her eight years known life without Maria as a constant companion and playmate. Now she withdrew within herself. Her bubbly spirit was quenched and, instead of playing outside, she took to sitting on the hearth, staring into the fire, oblivious to the efforts of the rest of the family to cajole a smile from her.

The death of his mother, following so closely as it did upon the death of his child, was a shattering blow to Jonadab's self-confidence. His family had seemed inviolate and now he had suffered the loss of two members of it in such a short space of time. Both he and Annie slept only fitfully, even though their daily work was long and exhausting. One night, she wakened to face one of her usual periods of tossing and turning, mourning over the little lost child and stretching out her hand to clasp Jonadab's, she found his side of the bed empty and cold. Where could he be?

As she slid out of the high bed, Annie saw the light of flames reflected on the walls. Rushing to the window, she could see that there was indeed a fire somewhere down the road towards the buildings.

Snatching her cloak from its peg at the back of the door, she ran down the stairs, still in her bare feet. Sure enough, there was a fire, but it appeared to be in the lane, rather than in one of the buildings. As she drew closer, Annie saw Jonadab with a hayfork in his hands, moving round the bonfire, keeping it contained in the middle of the road.

Whatever was he burning, she wondered. Upon reaching him, she was disturbed, even horrified, to see that he had brought the corn dolly out of the barn and set it alight. Now, with tears running down his cheeks, he tended the fire, determined that every last ear and straw should be consumed by the flames.

'Oh, Jonadab, no!' she exclaimed.

He whirled round, his face suffused with grief and anger. 'What luck has it brought us?' he demanded. ' 'Tis a pagan symbol, woman, and I'll have no more on my farm.'

Although deeply religious Annie, like most country folk, still clung tenaciously to the old superstitions. Now faced with the casting aside of the lore of her forebears, she was filled with disquiet. She stood beside her husband in silence as the flames died down. The small pile of soft ash in the road bore little relationship to the enormity of his act, in her eyes.

What was done was done, but Annie was left with a sense of foreboding and unease. Like most of the farming class, she believed in playing safe. Although a deeply devout Christian, she still held on to the old beliefs. Not for the first time, she reflected that there were depths in her husband that she still did not understand.

Stumbling back to the house, she winced as her feet encountered pebbles which had gone unnoticed before.

'Thoo silly lass,' Jonadab chided in a more gentle voice than he had used for some time. With that, he swung her up in his arms and carried her back into the house and up to bed. The incident was never mentioned by either of them again.

A few weeks after Grandma Oaks' death, Ann Waind took on a luminosity which was accounted for when she confided to her mother that she was pregnant. This brought about the first step in Annie Oaks' recovery. The news that there would be a baby in the house once more eased the burden of Annie Oaks' grief and gave her a new interest in life.

George's solace came from Elizabeth Butler on one of their walks from chapel. Her comforting words brought him acceptance and inner peace.

'Look George,' she said gently, 'try not to dwell too much on Maria's death. She had ten happy years on this earth and, although it's not a great deal of consolation, at least she didn't suffer.'

George himself began Martha's climb back into the world. After a word with his parents, he came in one day carrying the prettiest of a litter of kittens which he had come across in the barn.

'Here you are, Martha,' he said, dropping the appealing little scrap on to her knee. 'Can you look after him?'

As the kitten thrust its head into her hands to be caressed, her face lit up and she smiled for the first time in months.

'Oh, thank you, George.' Gratitude made her face radiant. 'Can Aah keep him, Faither?'

Jonadab disapproved of cats in houses. Their place was in the buildings, keeping down the vermin. However, he would agree to anything which would bring Martha back to her normal, happy self.

'Aye. As long as he earns his keep and grows into a good mouser,' he replied, apparently grudgingly.

Thus, although there would always be a shadow in their lives, the family picked up the threads and outwardly resumed their usual routine. Each tried to make an effort for the sake of the rest of the family. Living as they did in such an isolated backwater, however, had forged them into a close-knit group and life after the loss of Maria could never be the same. It was almost as if the harder they tried to return to normal the more Maria's death haunted their minds. Annie, in particular, never really regained her former liveliness. She felt that to outlive one's child must be the most dreadful thing that could happen and her eyes often lingered on the place at the table, which had been Maria's.

CHAPTER THIRTEEN

In due course, Ann Waind was delivered of a baby
girl. The winter months had occupied the womenfolk with the making of the layette and the refurbish-
ment of the family crib. This had held Annie Oaks
in infancy, and all her children after her: and probably her mother before her, but about this she could
not be certain. John Waind had filled a cotton bag
with chaff from the threshing-floor and this was
placed in the bottom of the cradle to serve as a
mattress.

Ann's pregnancy had bloomed into quiet fulfil-
ment. She felt, at last, that she was a real woman
and was completing her role as a wife. John, her
husband, had become livelier and more talkative as
the months of her waiting progressed and it became
obvious that she was brimming with good health.

The labour too, had been uncomplicated, and the
baby was delivered by her mother, with no need to
send for the village midwife.

To Martha's delight, Ann and John decided to call
the baby Mary. That she was named after John's
mother, who made the journey from Bransdale to
see her grandchild, made not a scrap of difference
to young Martha's happiness. Martha and Mary were
linked in the Bible, she knew, and she regarded the
baby as special. She spent hours leaning over the
cradle, crooning and talking to the baby, whom she
regarded, in some way, as her own property. Indeed,
she decided that she loved baby Molly, as she became
known, even more than Blackie, now a fullgrown
cat, who followed her everywhere. Jonadab and

154

Annie felt that life was regaining its even tempo. The void left in their hearts by Maria's death could never be filled and, indeed, each Sunday after chapel, they stood by her grave and uttered a silent prayer. They were, however, comforted by their simple faith which convinced them that the child had gone to a better life.

'It's selfish of us to mourn, because God has taken her,' Jonadab often admonished Annie, but both knew that the pain would remain.

The only other cloud on Annie Oaks' horizon was George's relationship with Elizabeth Butler. She was bewildered by the unexplained but obvious bond which so clearly existed between them.

'It's not as if they're courting,' she fretted to Jonadab. 'After all, our George is only nineteen and she's an old maid.'

'You can hardly call her an old maid,' he protested. 'She's a fine-looking woman.'

'Aye, well, it's not right. He's making a fool of himself, casting sheep's eyes at her.' Annie could not understand the relationship and was, therefore, unhappy with it.

Whenever there was a gathering between the two families, it disturbed her to see the way that George and Elizabeth were drawn to each other and would remain together, often unspeaking, but always content, each obviously enjoying the company of the other.

Jonadab made a point of watching the two and, although it was clear to him that George was, or thought he was, head over heels in love with Elizabeth, he could not reach any conclusion about what she felt for George. She treated him lightly but affectionately and yet, not as she treated her own younger brother, Jack. 'It's a rum do,' Jonadab told himself. He did not like to be faced with a situation which he could not understand. George had grown into a responsible and dependable man, so Jonadab quietened his wife's nagging and left things to take their course.

'He's got his head screwed on right,' he maintained. 'He'll meet a lass more his own age afore long and then you'll be moaning because he wants to be wed.'

This time had already come for their own Beth. Will Baldwin had failed to make a declaration, and she was being courted by John Smithson, the son of a farmer in Gillamoor. He had already approached Jonadab for her hand, and now all the girls were busy helping to sew her trousseau.

Like her sisters, Beth had begun to collect her 'bottom drawer' from the age of twelve and, by now, had enough bed and table-linen stitched and some even embroidered, to last her for years. Now, however, a stock of clothing must be laid up. The wedding outfit itself would be created by a dressmaker in Kirkbymoorside, but the shifts, petticoats, blouses, skirts and stockings would be made over the coming year, or even longer. Engagements were not short and Beth was young enough yet.

In the period between the haytime and the harvest of 1851 the Oaks were surprised one evening to receive a visit from Joseph. When he pushed open the door and entered the kitchen, his mother glanced behind him, expecting to see Mary and George.

'Haven't you brought Mary and t'lad?' she enquired.

'Nay, Mam. Aah've come on mi own.' Her eldest son appeared to be embarrassed and uneasy. 'Where's Faither?' he asked, looking round the kitchen.

'Somewhere in t'buildings with George and Jonna.' Annie's curiosity was aroused by something in his manner. 'Is summat up, lad?' she asked anxiously. 'T'bairn's all right?' Her protective instinct was aroused. She would have liked her grandson down in the valley in his proper place, where she could keep an eagle eye on him.

'Aye, they're both all right, Mam, never fear.' Joseph turned and made his way to the buildings to search for his father. He found Jonadab and his two brothers in the byre, inspecting one of the cows who had torn her udder, probably by stepping on it as she rose to her feet.

'I'll come back and put some salve on her.' Jonadab indicated the cow with a flick of the head. 'Best come into t'house, lad. Thi mother'll have t'kettle on,' he instructed Joseph.

As Annie made the tea, she looked round the kitchen. Ann Waind sat in the rocking chair beside the fire, nursing her baby. Martha occupied a little stool by her feet. Beth and Tamar were by the small table in the window, sewing. Young Jonna was settled at one end of the table, reading, while his father sat at the other end with the other two sons and John Waind, gossiping about farms and farming.

Annie passed round the mugs of tea with a sense of peace in her heart. It was the first time since his marriage that Joseph had been alone with the family, unaccompanied even by his wife.

Silence fell in the room as they all sat drinking the hot tea. The pause was broken by Joseph nervously clearing his throat.

George looked up swiftly and saw Joseph's anxious glance from his mother to his father. His heart sank and he felt a constriction in his throat. He knew with a dreadful certainty that Joseph's visit had some purpose behind it.

'Aah've come to tell you,' he spoke with a kind

157

of pleading desperation, 'that me and Mary's going away.'

'Going away?' echoed his mother. 'Have you got chance of a farm to rent, then?'

'Nay, we're going a long way.' He paused and looked from face to face. 'To the Canadas.'

His family sat stunned.

To have moved out of the valley was bad enough, but out of Ryedale, out of Yorkshire, out of England, even, was beyond the realms of their understanding. Jonadab passed a hand over his forehead as though trying to straighten out his thoughts.

'The Canadas?' His incredulity would have been comical had the situation not been so serious.

'What's the Canadas?' asked Martha, but her question went unanswered as the adults exchanged disbelieving glances.

Jonadab's chair scraped on the flagged floor, as he pushed it back and began to pace back and forth across the kitchen. He ran his hands through his hair until it stood almost on end, giving a semblance of wildness to his whole appearance. It was obvious that he was working hard to control an uprush of temper, so that he could speak to Joseph with more reasonableness than he considered the occasion warranted.

No one else dared speak but Annie ventured: 'Nay, lad. Put this silly fancy away from you.'

'It's no silly fancy, Mother. It's been thought about long and hard. Me and Mary has both decided.' This latter statement was added with a frightening finality.

Jonadab retook his chair at the head of the table. 'Thoo'd best begin at t'beginning, lad,' he said.

George marvelled at his father's control. He knew what Aumery Park Farm meant to him.

Although Jonadab, in his heart, still regarded his

158

son as a sinner he had, since the marriage and more especially the birth of young Georgie, softened the harshness of his attitude to Joseph. He now regarded him as a strayed sheep; one whom he was ready to take back into the fold should the opportunity ever arise. His own father was failing and the half-formed thought which had recently come into his mind was that when his father eventually died, Joseph and Mary could come down to live in Joseph's rightful home.

Joseph really did not know where to begin. When he came to put them into words, his feelings seemed so petty and unreasonable. 'It's t'Butlers!' he burst out.

'What about 'em?' asked Jonadab. 'Aah should think you'd be grateful to 'em. They've given you a good home and a job – that seems a good exchange for getting their lass into trouble.'

Joseph's face was suffused by a flush. Time had dulled the memory of the circumstances of his marriage to Mary and to be reminded of it now, when it had been an effort to screw up his courage to face his family with his decision, was like a blow beneath the belt.

He bit his bottom lip, took a deep breath and continued more steadily. 'Their ways isn't our ways.'

'No-o,' Jonadab drawled the word. 'No doubt John feels like that, with us,' and he raised a sardonic eyebrow at John Waind, who shook his head with a deprecating smile.

George could see that Jonadab's patience was stretched to breaking-point. He could not understand their father's attitude. Was he playing for time, or was he perhaps trying to minimise whatever it was that was driving Joseph away? He placed a restraining hand on Joseph's arm.

'Tell us exactly what's wrong, Joe,' he said quietly.

'Well, it wasn't too bad when we were first married though, of course, it was strange. Mary was t'only one Aah really knew very well.' He paused there, expecting a retort from his father to this unfortunate remark but Jonadab had achieved the purpose of his baiting, which was to make Joseph assemble his thoughts into some sort of order and state his complaints against his in-laws in a fashion which they could all examine and discuss. 'Mrs Butler's too bossy. We get no privacy, either.'

'Well,' his mother glanced at Ann and John Waind, 'our Ann and John live in with us.' It had never occurred to her that they might feel any resentment over the situation. She had lived all her married life with her in-laws and had expected no other way. It was the custom of their class.

'When they shuts their bedroom door, it's their own little world, isn't it? You don't walk in there, do you?' he appealed to his mother.

There was silence in the kitchen as each digested this piece of information.

'Do you mean that she comes into the room when you are both in bed?' Jonadab could not hide his shock and amazement.

The whole story then came tumbling out. Mrs Butler had cooled towards Joseph when he continued to call her 'Mrs Butler' after the wedding. To her suggestion that he should call her 'Mother' he had replied that he already had one mother and could not think of anybody else in that way.

It was not often that John Waind took a part in family discussions unless they concerned the farm but now, to everyone's surprise, he spoke up. 'Nay, Joe. Couldn't you call her "Ma"? I've got my own

160

mother, but I calls yourn "Ma" to make a bit of difference,' he said.

Joe had never thought of this solution to the problem. 'Anyroad, we set off on t'wrong foot,' he said miserably. He seemed to get on well with his father-in-law and the rest of the family. Indeed, he and young Jack Butler, Mary's brother, had become close friends. Life, it appeared, had not been too bad for him until the birth of the baby. 'She turned right bossy then,' Joe told them. 'Mary has no say over Georgie and if he cries in the night, she walks into our bedroom and picks him up.'

'Well!' Annie Oaks was speechless. Surely folks could expect to be private in the marriage bed.

'Mary's fed up an' all.' Joseph was by now in full spate. 'Her Mam runs our lives. She even chooses what our Georgie wears every day. We never go anywhere or do anything 'less she organises it.'

George sat back. So this was the reason for Joseph's heaviness of spirit. Jonadab sat in thought for a minute or so.

'Now, I'm sure we can come to some arrangement fairly soon. Don't do anything hasty and I'll have a quiet word with John Butler.' He patted Joseph's shoulder, all anger gone. The lad had had enough to put up with to make him contemplate such desperate measures.

'It's too late, Faither. We've booked a passage.'

In the stunned silence which followed this announcement, Ann Waind rose with the sleeping baby in her arms and, motioning to her sister Martha, went through the parlour door to go upstairs. Martha's highly nervous state after Maria's death had only just settled back into normality and Ann did not want the child to witness the inevitable arguments and upset which would follow.

As she lay the baby in the cradle and Martha

tenderly tucked the patchwork quilt over her, she heard the thunderous roar of her father's voice.

'What?' he bellowed. 'You've done WHAT?' Seeing his wife's stricken face, he took a deep breath and lowered his voice to a furious hiss. 'Hasn't your mother had enough sorrow of late?' he demanded. 'We've lost one child – must we lose another? And a grandchild as well?'

Joseph was torn but could not be moved. Although normally undemonstrative, he went from the table and put his arm round his mother and kissed her. 'You know we don't want to leave you, Mam, but it's the land of opportunity.'

'Huh!' came from his father.

When they settled down to more reasoned discussion, they found that, on a rare visit to Kirkbymoorside, Joseph had seen in one of the shops a poster advertising passages, both to Canada and New Zealand. He and Mary had talked it over in bed, night after long night and eventually reached the joint conclusion that this must be their future. They had chosen Canada because the journey to New Zealand took six months and it seemed so much further away from home. Also, of course, the journey was far more expensive.

'We could have gone steerage for thirty shillings but, with having Georgie, we've paid six pounds each for a cabin,' he said. 'I've added a bit to our wedding money when I could and with it being in the bank, they've put some to it, like you said they would, Faither.'

Annie heaved a great sigh of resignation upon discovering that not only was the passage booked, but paid for. 'When do you go?' she hardly dared ask.

Joseph looked guilty. 'We've been lucky. We managed to get on a ship sailing from Whitby in two weeks' time.'

This last blow was too much for his mother, who began to cry quietly.

'Look, Mam,' Joseph tried to reassure her, 'we've promised each other that we shan't break into our fare home. If we haven't made our fortune when we've nearly got down to that, we shall use it to come back. Anyway, if we do make our fortune, you can be sure we'll be back,' he comforted.

Young Jonna had been staring at his brother with eyes popping. 'There's Red Indians in the Canadas,' was his contribution to the conversation.

Annie's sobs rose into a wail. 'Oh-oh! don't let them get little Georgie!'

'Nay, Mam, they're friendly in the part we'll be in.' Joseph was not quite sure of the truth of this statement, but hoped that it would prove to be so.

It was fortunate that both families had had so little warning of the impending parting that their sorrow before the voyage, at least, was curtailed. Indeed, the next two weeks seemed to fly by. The evening before the sailing, Joseph and Mary came down to bid farewell to those who were not going to Whitby to see them off.

Joseph knew that he would never see his Grandad Joseph again and was tearful at the parting. The old man had aged pitifully after the death of his wife. His Uncle George pressed a golden guinea into his hand, as they shook hands. 'I haven't much, lad, but here thoo is,' he muttered emotionally. Joseph's sister Ann could not go because of the baby and John, her husband, was staying to look after the stock with Uncle George, Bert Weald and the lads.

The following morning, the Oaks set off at dawn. Jonadab and Annie were in the pony-trap, with George in a cart behind driving Rosie. Violet was attached at the rear, as both horses were needed to relieve each other on the long journey across the rugged moorland roads. The girls sat on a huge wooden crate, into which Annie had stowed as much non-perishable food as possible, to save Joe and Mary's money on the journey. As well as a whole ham and a large joint of salted beef, there were jars of preserves, cheeses and even slabs of butter wrapped in layers of cheesecloth.

When they reached the village, the Butlers were waiting with a similar box of provisions and a large tin trunk containing clothes and personal possessions. Joseph and Mary were seated on the Butlers' wagon with Mary's sisters but, to George's proud surprise, Elizabeth Butler chose to climb up and sit between him and Jonna on their cart.

The journey was a revelation: the Oaks, in particular, found the great sweeps of heather-clad moors breathtaking. The moors round their dale were covered with heather in late summer but, from their vantage point on the cart, the Whitby moors seemed to go on forever. From horizon to horizon, the whole world seemed to consist of undulations of purple.

The road was dotted with weeping families accompanying emigrants to the ship, many of them on foot. One couple with two small children, walking dejectedly with no one going to see them off, were picked up and given a lift on the cart by George.

Their first glimpse of the sea was met with awe. Jonadab had signalled George to stop above the town, while he cautioned him about the steepness of the hill down into the port. They had all seen pictures of ships at sea, but were completely unprepared for the vastness. 'Where does it end?' Martha whispered.

'It doesn't, love,' George answered. 'It goes on forever.'

Martha had no time to digest this information as they began the long, sharp descent. Their view of Whitby from the clifftop had impressed them with its size. The streets, winding down to the harbour and the hundreds of redroofed cottages clinging to the cliffs at each side of the river seemed endless.

'By, it must be as big as London,' breathed young Jonna.

'Aah don't think it is,' George answered, although he wasn't sure. After that, all his attention was concentrated on guiding the big horse down the steep hill.

Of his passengers, only Elizabeth Butler had been to Whitby before, and that just the once. To the rest, the impact on their senses of the sights, sounds and smells of the town was overwhelming.

Over all hung a pervading smell, the like of which they had never before encountered. The greasy, fatty odour was so thick as they approached the quay, that it blotted out both the smell of the sea and of fish. George was later to discover that it came from the sheds where the blubber of whales was rendered down. Whitby was a famous whaling port and the smell of whale-oil clung to the whole town.

The closer they drew to the quayside, the thicker were the jostling crowds. It made even Kirkby on market day look sleepy, thought George.

The culmination of all the new experiences was the sight of the boats in the harbour. There were laden ferryboats, low in the water, being rowed backwards and forwards from one side to the other. There were fishing cobles riding cheek by jowl with sailing ketches but, by far the most impressive were the tallmasted sailing ships – schooners, barques and whalers.

Realising that there was no room for unnecessary vehicles on the quay, George pulled into an inn-yard and he and Jonna helped the girls down. He then realised that he was in a quandary. It would take him and Jonna all their time to carry one of the crates to the ship and he dare not leave the other two boxes in the inn-yard unattended; nor could he leave any of the females of the party to keep an eye on them. He had already noticed the glances they had drawn from many of the men who thronged the pier.

Such a place as Whitby, he was sure, was full of thieves and vagabonds waiting to rob honest country-folk. His dilemma was solved, however, when an ostler came out of the inn-door.

'Which ship are you bound for, sir?' he asked.

Never having previously been so addressed, George was slow in answering.

'The *Pandora*,' answered Elizabeth, who was the most composed of them all.

The ostler put two fingers to his mouth and let out a shrill whistle. 'Don't let him charge you more than threepence,' he said out of the corner of his mouth as a man with a donkey-cart came into the yard.

The two brothers helped the man to load his cart, and then they all fell in alongside him down the cobbled pier. 'The *Pandora*, is it?' he asked.

'Aye,' answered George, gazing around him at the bewildering bustle. He was trying to take it all in, to tell those left at home when he returned. It was, however, impossible. There was so many people and so much happening, that the little group bunched together for security, hurrying to keep up with the luggage-porter.

Round the ship, everything was in ordered confusion. Sailors were up and down the gangplank carrying crates, boxes and barrels with which they

166

disappeared below, while others were busy with ropes and lines.

The ship was spotless, with gleaming paintwork and scrubbed decks, in contrast to many of the shabby vessels nearby. The captain stood at the top of the gangplank greeting passengers, and George noticed the curt way he had greeted the poor family who had ridden with them, directing them into the steerage. Joseph, however, received a handshake and a sailor was despatched to lead the party to their cabin.

Not even their mothers could find any fault with the quarters. True, the cabin was small, too small for them all to inspect at once, but it was a model of cleanliness and neatness.

It was only now that the full impact of the step they had taken seemed to strike Joseph and Mary. Mary began to cry and went to her mother and sisters, hugging and kissing them, while Joseph constantly cleared his throat and moved among his own family, taking his leave.

It seemed no time at all before, from the deck, they heard the cry: '*All ashore that's going ashore!*'

There was a scramble to the deck and the emigrants lined the rails as their families jostled on the quayside, shouting their goodbyes. The seamen heaved on the capstan as the anchor was raised; ropes were cast off and hauled aboard and sailors swarmed aloft, unlashing sails and pulling on lines.

Jonadab cupped his hands to his mouth and his voice rang out in the true Yorkshireman's advice to his son: 'Look after thi brass, lad!'

Joseph waved and nodded, to show that he'd heard, while Mary held little Georgie aloft for a final wave to the families.

The *Pandora* was towed out of the harbour by two large boats, rowed by muscular sailors. Once through the entrance, the sails filled and billowed, as the ship turned to catch the breeze.

The Oaks and Butlers, silent and united in grief, made their way sadly back to the inn-yard. When the horses were harnessed and they trudged beside them to the clifftop, the ship already looked like a toy in the distance.

'She's a grand sight,' murmured George huskily, swallowing hard to stop the quaver in his voice.

'Shall we see 'em again, Mam?' whispered little Sarah Butler.

'Aah don't know, love,' her mother answered, and suddenly turned away in tears.

'Come on, Mother. Into the trap with you.' John Butler spoke gruffly as he took her arm and helped her up.

It was a desolate group which took the road across the moors back to their farms. They had never envisaged such an event occurring in their tight-knit families. Other people's children emigrated to the Canadas, or even New Zealand, but not those of the Oaks and the Butlers.

Annie Oaks was devastated. Her life had been torn apart by the death of Maria and now, the loss of her eldest son had the finality of death. She never expected to see him or his child again.

Even George and Elizabeth exchanged no words on the journey home. She twisted and wrenched her handkerchief between her hands as she sat, white-faced, staring straight ahead. George thought back over his life and could not imagine the future without Joseph. 'Mebbe he'll mek his fortune and come back rich,' was the only comforting thought he could find, as the two families parted and the Oaks made their way back down into the dale.

CHAPTER FOURTEEN

The departure of Joseph, Mary and little Georgie was a great blow to the two families, but Annie Oaks was worst affected. She plunged once more into the melancholia which had overtaken her after Maria's death. Leaving her daughters to organise the household tasks and the dairy work, she would sit for hours, staring into the fire.

The crisis came on the first Wednesday after the trip to Whitby. Beth and Tamar gathered together what they had prepared for the market, and loaded up the trap. Even though they bustled about, their actions evoked no response from their mother, who sat still and silent in her chair beside the fire.

'Come on, Mam, it's time to set off,' ventured Tamar uncertainly.

'Which of us is going with you, or do you want to go on your own?' Beth put in.

To their consternation, their mother did not reply. Still staring into the fire, she merely shook her head.

'Go and fetch Faither,' instructed Beth, 'while I slip upstairs for our Ann.' Annie had now begun to rock backwards and forwards, her knuckles pressed against her teeth.

Ann Waind and Beth came through the parlour door, as Jonadab hurried into the kitchen from outside, closely followed by Tamar.

'Now then, Annie, what's up?' he said in a falsely cheerful tone, as he approached his wife. His expression altered, however, as he took in the glazed eyes and the rhythmic rocking. Annie's body was, by now, racked with dry sobs and she seemed oblivious to their presence.

Jonadab relied on his Bible to guide his life, but it had no way of preparing him for the situation that faced him now.

His look of bewilderment changed to one of decisiveness, as he became aware that three of his daughters were looking to him for guidance.

'Ann, make your mother a pot of tea and keep an eye on 'er,' he instructed. 'Come on, lasses,' to the other two, 'get thi cloaks and go and stand t'market. When Aah've saddled mi 'oss, Aah'll catch up. No doubt Aah'll find summat ti keep me busy in Kirkby until you're finished.'

So it was that Beth and Tamar began to take their mother's place in the Wednesday market. Annie gradually climbed back from the pit of despair into which she had fallen, but although she resumed her place as the organiser of the household tasks, she could not bring herself to face the other farmers' wives in the market.

No matter how the family urged her during the week, when it came to Wednesday she flinched from contact with outsiders.

'Nay, Jonadab. Aah can't face folks yet,' she would remonstrate, when he tried to persuade her to take up the threads of her full life again. 'Aah'm afeared they'll ask about Joe, and Aah can't stand questions, yet.'

As Jonadab would not allow the girls to go unaccompanied to Kirkby, it meant that he or George must, of necessity, give up work on a Wednesday to go with them. This was especially important as they returned home with their takings from the market. Two postboys had recently been stopped and robbed, one on the road from Whitby, and one riding from York, and Jonadab Oaks was too protective of his daughters to risk their safety.

One Wednesday, Jonadab remarked at the breakfast table: 'Aah've a chap coming ti 'ave a look at some foals, so you must go with t'girls, George.'

'Aye, all right, Faither.' Although George was quite happy to take a day off from the arduous work of the farm, he knew that his labour was needed. However, he would be given plenty of errands to occupy him during the day and they would return home as soon as the girls had sold up. There was no wandering round the shops, nowadays.

George saw his sisters settled in Kirkby with their goods and then made a start on the shopping list given him by his mother.

While George was doing his shopping, William Forster strolled up the market place. He was making one of his periodic trips up from Leicestershire to stay at the Towers and continue his assiduous courtship of Rowena Sturdy. To escape from his amorous duties for a while, he had accompanied James Sturdy into Kirkby, where his friend had an appointment at the Estate office. They had arranged to meet later for a meal at the Black Swan, but William had decided against waiting at the inn, which would, doubtless, be crowded on a market day.

It was high noon, on a cloudless August day, so he decided to amble through the market, which straggled up each side of the steeply-rising main street of the little town and then, crossing over at the end of the stalls, to come down the other side. He reckoned that the stroll would just about fill his time and, also, give him an appetite for lunch.

As he made his leisurely way up the street, his height gave him a good view of all that was going on around him. The market place was bustling with shoppers, haggling and joking with the stallholders.

The town appeared to shimmer in the baking heat and William suddenly realised how uncomfortably hot he was. Instead of going on, he would turn back and wait for James in the cool, semi-darkness of the inn, over a cold drink, he decided.

As he swung on his heel to retrace his steps, he heard a burst of laughter from the section where the farmwomen sold their produce. Looking across, he saw a lovely, strangely familiar face. William's weakness for a pretty girl had not diminished with his pursuit of Rowena Sturdy, and he found himself crossing the street towards Tamar, drawn almost irresistibly to her side.

Beth was unaware of his approach, being busily engaged in serving a customer, but Tamar could see him coming towards them and her heart began to race as she recalled the rider's open admiration when they had met at the spring.

As Sir William drew closer, he found himself looking again into her distinctive amber eyes, lit with flecks of gold. Tamar was an innocent in the ways of the world, having met few men besides her own brothers and their friends. Jonadab had ruled his family with a rod of iron ever since what he regarded as Joseph's fall from grace. She was, however, fully aware that men found her attractive and flaunted her sexuality in a provocative manner, while remaining unconscious of the risks involved.

Now her eyes met Forster's boldly and her lips curved in a slow, self-satisfied smile. She knew that he was coming over to speak to her.

'My God! This little minx could take London by storm, given the right clothes,' he told himself, as his eyes took in the trim figure and flawless features.

He stood before her and raised his hat, giving her a slight bow. The sun glinted on his golden hair and

Tamar thought that he was even more handsome than before.

'Good morning, young lady.' As he drawled the words, his eyes moved over her from head to toe.

'Good morning, sir.' Although her dark lashes quickly swept downwards, veiling her eyes with apparent demureness, her tone held a touch of spirit.

He glanced at the baskets spread at her feet, seeking an excuse for coming to talk to her.

'May I buy one of your cheeses?' he asked. 'They look delicious.' He had no idea what he would do with the cheese, but it gave him the opportunity to study the girl. He felt that he had seen her before, but was certain that he would have remembered.

Tamar suddenly heard Beth gasp, and turning round, saw that her sister had gone very pale; her eyes were fixed on Sir William, as though mesmerised.

'Have nowt ti do with him, Tamar,' she urged, in desperation.

'What on earth are you talking about, our Beth?' Tamar was at a loss to understand her sister's attitude, unaware that this was the man who had torn Beth's bodice. All she knew was that this was the man who had made his admiration obvious when she was only sixteen. That he still thought her desirable gave her confidence.

'Please excuse my sister, sir. She's not well.' Tamar smiled deep into his eyes as she spoke.

With a shock, William recognised Beth and decided to make his escape as quickly as possible, before any trouble arose.

'How much is the cheese?' he asked, taking out his purse.

Tamar, realising that his interest was waning, gave him a dazzling smile as she replied, 'One and sixpence, please, sir.' As she held out her hand for the money, their hands met and their fingers seemed to curl together of their own volition.

It was this scene which met George's eyes as he pushed his way through the crowds towards his sisters. Beth was pale and tense, standing behind her chair, both hands gripping the back. When he saw Sir William Forster, apparently caressing Tamar's hand and smiling down into her eager, upturned face he was overcome with blind fury.

He covered the ground between them at a run and, seizing Forster's arm, swung him round.

'Leave my sisters alone! We've had enough of you.' He hurled the words like missiles.

William's eyes narrowed and his face whitened with rage. He dashed George's hand from his arm with such force as to send him staggering.

'Get your hands off me!' He almost spat the words. 'My God! It's you again! Do I have to bump into you every time I set foot in this area?'

George recovered his balance and faced his antagonist once more.

'I've told you once and I'll say it again! Keep away from our family.' He uttered the words quietly, but the warning was clear.

'Don't threaten me or I'll give you the thrashing you deserve,' spluttered William, giving George a violent push on the shoulder and following it up with a punch, which only brushed the side of George's face as he had seen it coming and dodged aside.

By now, a crowd had gathered, eager to witness the confrontation but unaware of its cause. George knew nothing about prize-fighting, but Forster had underestimated the speed and strength of a man who worked to physical capacity, from dawn to dusk. Seeing the other man's fists raised, he smashed through his guard and landed a blow on the point of the jaw, which knocked Forster to the ground, half-dazed.

A shocked murmur ran through the crowd of onlookers just as the town constable pushed his way through.

'What's going on here?' he demanded, looking from George to William Forster. The latter rose groggily to his feet, rubbing his jaw.

'Arrest that man!' he commanded, pointing a finger at the hapless George, who stood appalled at what he had done. Beth was now sobbing aloud, while Tamar blanched. 'Oh, no, sir,' she begged, but he ignored her pleas. The constable looked uneasily from one to the other. He knew that the Oaks' were a respectable, God-fearing family and that George was a hardworking and law-abiding citizen. However, it was clear that he had struck a blow against a member of the nobility and the constable could see no way out.

'You'll have to come, lad,' he said to the wretched George who, by now, bitterly regretted allowing his hatred of Sir William to overcome his normally placid nature.

Forster was seething with rage: he had been made to appear a figure of fun and the sympathies of most of the bystanders were obviously with George. As James Sturdy appeared and came forward to help brush him down, he shook with rage.

'I'll teach the little pipsqueak a lesson,' he muttered through clenched teeth, as James led him across to the hostelry, where a table was booked for lunch.

'Come on, Beth.' Tamar bustled about, repacking their unsold produce, as the crowd began to drift away. 'We must get back and tell Faither what's happened. He'll sort it out.' Such was their faith in

Jonadab that they could envisage no predicament which he could not solve.

As they made their way gloomily back to Aumery Park Farm without George, Beth explained that Sir William Forster was the man who had accosted her in the lane. Although this explained George's reaction, Tamar flattered herself that, in similar circumstances, she could have handled him. Although she was fond of Beth, she considered her to be timid and self-effacing.

'She can't stand up for herself,' Tamar thought, as she regarded her sister's tearstained face. 'She doesn't know how to use her looks.' She herself was determined not to end up as a farmer's wife in the Dales though, as yet, she was unsure how this was to be accomplished.

When the constable had taken George by the elbow and led him off to the cell which adjoined the police-house, the news swept like a forest fire through the little market town. By nightfall, it was known in almost every moorland and dales farm and cottage that George Oaks was in prison. Those who knew him expressed their doubts, but there were too many witnesses for those doubts to be sustained.

When the news reached the Butlers, Elizabeth was disbelieving. 'No! No! George is too kind and gentle ever to attack anyone!' she insisted.

Her father frowned. 'There's bad blood in that family,' he stated. 'You've only to look at the way their Joseph took advantage of our Mary, to see that.'

Elizabeth shook her head, but before she could reply, her brother Jack chimed in. 'Nay, Joseph's a good lad. Let's face it, Faither, it takes two to make a bargain. Our Mary wasn't blameless.'

John Butler looked round his family. 'We don't

176

see much of the Oaks since our Mary and the bairn were taken away and we'll see less from now on,' he instructed, choosing to ignore the fact that both Elizabeth and Jack looked mutinous at his ultimatum.

The constable, meanwhile, felt in a cleft stick. He knew there were plenty of witnesses to the fact that George had attacked the visitor, who was a frequent guest at the Towers and, indeed, he had personally seen the gentleman sprawled on the ground. Although he had known George since his youth and knew the family's reputation, he had no alternative but to lock him up.

George had not uttered a word since his arrest but, as the cell door clanged shut with a sound of utter finality, he looked through the bars.

'What'll happen to me, Mr Bannister?' His tone was hopeless and his face mirrored the black despair that was in his heart.

The policeman could give him no word of comfort. 'Nay, lad! It's not for me to say. It all depends on the decision of the court.' He spoke with compassion and, as he turned away from the grille in the door, George knew with certainty that he would be found guilty and that Constable Bannister expected the law to demand the ultimate penalty.

He slumped on the bench, his head in his hands, his thoughts in a turmoil. How bitterly he regretted the rash impetuosity which had led him to strike Sir William Forster. He realised that his actions had been in self-defence – a natural response to the other man's raised fists. However, this reasoning would carry no weight with the magistrates, who would regard his action as an attack on one of their own class.

As the day drew to a close, George contemplated his bleak future. He was confident that he could survive life in prison, or even transportation to Australia, but was worried as to how the family would manage without him.

Throughout the long night, which seemed like an eternity, George's thoughts covered every facet of his life. He thought long and deep about his relationship with Elizabeth Butler. He was certain that he loved her and yet her attitude towards him was a constant puzzle. Although, after the wedding she had seemed to be drawn to him, ever since the day that his sheep had upset her in the trap, her behaviour had been inconsistent. He wondered whether he would ever see her again, to try to iron out their relationship or, indeed, whether she would want to see him again – if and when he returned to the free world.

He agonised over how his parents had taken the news of his arrest when his sisters arrived home. The sorrows of the recent past had taken their toll of his mother and he wondered how she would endure this latest blow and still retain her sanity.

He knew that his father was fiercely proud of the family name and could imagine the horror with which he would greet George's disgrace.

What George was unaware of during the tormented hours in the cell, was that his father had ridden up to the police-house as soon as the girls arrived home with their news.

The customer had bought the foals and Jonadab was walking towards the house from the stables when he heard the pony-trap approaching the farm. As he shaded his eyes to peer along the road, he felt disquiet when he saw Beth and Tamar returning early and without the protection of George.

'Rob!' he shouted to the farm lad who had been helping in the stables, 'see ti t'pony and t'trap.'

As Tamar pulled the pony to a halt by the door,

their father looked from Beth's tear-puffed face to Tamar's set expression and compressed lips.

'What's up? Where's George?' he demanded.

Beth immediately dissolved into tears and, although she tried to answer, her words were drowned in hiccoughing sobs. Their father turned to Tamar for an explanation. Although as shaken as Beth, she was cast in a firmer mould. 'George is in jail!' She felt there was no roundabout way in which she could break the news.

Jonadab was incredulous. He looked from one daughter to the other and realised that something was certainly very much amiss. As Beth made for the door, he caught her arm and held her back. 'No! Don't go in yet. Your mother's had as much as she can stand of late.'

Gradually, he got the whole story from them or as much of it as Tamar felt should be revealed. The man who had accosted Beth had approached her again in the market, causing her distress. George had come upon the scene, whereon Sir William had raised his fists to attack George.

Jonadab could understand his son's feelings and approved of George's physical defence of his sisters, but was aghast at the outcome. 'Be careful 'ow you tell your mother. Be gentle,' he instructed, as he turned back towards the stables. 'Aah'll go up ti Kirkby meanwhile and see what's ti be done.'

When he arrived at the police-house, however, it was to discover that there was nothing to be done.

'I'm sorry, Mr Oaks, but charges will be laid in the morning,' said the policeman. 'I can't let you see George. No doubt you'll come to the magistrates' court in the morning.'

'Shall we need a lawyer?' Jonadab was out of his depth and resented the feeling. He was used to directing, not only his own life but the lives of his family, and it seemed to him that there were more and more occasions in the last year or two when this power had been taken away from him.

Bannister could not help him, however. 'I don't know about the magistrates' court, but you will if it goes to a higher court,' he replied.

Jonadab Oaks rode home, sad and apprehensive. There were many who would see George's conduct as shameful, bringing dishonour to his family's name, but Jonadab knew his son and realised that he must have been provoked into uncharacteristic behaviour. However, this would not help his son to overcome the deep trouble which he was now facing.

The family prayers that night were even more fervent and heartfelt than usual. Despite his dire dilemma, Jonadab could not plead with his God. His prayers for George were more of a challenge to God – to prove that He could and would help his son. Although most of the household eventually slept through sheer misery and exhaustion, Jonadab lay awake, staring into the darkness, his mind whirling in a confusion of possibilities and probabilities; to no avail. He could find no solution.

The next morning saw the work of the farm start as usual. No matter what calamities befell them, there were cows to be milked and animals to be fed. When they had been back for breakfast, which few could manage to eat, Jonadab went upstairs to change ready to go to the magistrates' court.

While Ann Waind and Beth attended to the dairying, Annie called the other girls to help her upstairs. Thursday was Bedroom Day, when the bedrooms were swept, rugs beaten in the open air and furniture polished.

Far from dealing a final blow to Annie Oaks, George's situation seemed to have stiffened her resolve and brought about a transformation in her demeanour. Although she felt waves of sickness sweep over her when she thought about George's state, she bustled her daughters around in a flurry of hard work, determined to keep them and herself occupied.

As Jonadab came downstairs ready to set off, there was a knock on the back door. When he first opened it, he only took in the tall shape of a stranger silhouetted against the sunlight.

'Yes?' he queried, as he stepped outside.

'Mr Oaks?' asked the visitor.

Jonadab took in his appearance, from the gleaming boots to the well-cut riding jacket. When the steely deep blue eyes stared into the translucent pale blue ones, Jonadab knew instinctively that this was the man who had caused his son's imprisonment.

'Who wants him?' he asked with an uncompromising glare.

The man inclined his head, slightly. 'Sir William Forster. I have come to tell you that my host, Sir Francis Sturdy, has persuaded me not to press charges against your son. Sir Francis is your landlord, I believe, and in deference to his wishes, your son will escape the punishment he deserves for his vicious and needless attack upon me.'

Within himself, Jonadab was repeating: 'Thank you, Lord! Thank you!' but, externally, he displayed no sign of emotion at the news. He was determined not to give this man the satisfaction of knowing the relief which flooded through him. He merely gave a slight nod and said, 'That's very kind of Sir Francis,' turned on his heel and shut the door in Sir William's face.

As he was left standing there, an upsurge of rage brought the blood rushing to William Forster's face. The pale eyes narrowed in fury as he swung round and remounted his horse. Upon passing the paddock which ran alongside the house, he saw Tamar vigorously beating the clip rugs which she had tossed across the hedge.

'I'll teach that peasant to respect his betters,' he muttered between clenched teeth as he reined in the horse. By the time Tamar looked up and caught sight of him, he had slipped a mask of good humour over his ill-temper. Smilingly, he beckoned her towards him. Tamar was intrigued, although her better judgement warned that she was playing with fire.

'Your brother will, by now, be free. I could not bring sadness to that lovely face,' he murmured in a caressing tone.

Tamar's face shone. 'Oh, thank you! Thank you, sir,' she gasped.

'I shall wait in the quarry on the hillside next Friday afternoon. Try to meet me there.' With that he clicked his tongue and spurred his horse into a canter.

Tamar went about her work in a dream for the rest of the day. Her mirror told her that she was pretty, but never in her wildest dreams had she hoped to be courted by a nobleman . . .

Her restless spirit had always found life in the little valley tedious and stifling. She longed for excitement and was determined that, if at all possible, she would not end up as a local farmer's wife, bound by what she considered to be the dreary drudgery which engulfed her mother. Now, for the first time, a way out presented itself. She could not see beyond Sir William's open admiration, which she accepted at face value. Her fertile mind considered and discarded various ploys to escape from the farm and meet her admirer. She was adamant that nothing would prevent her from keeping the tryst, but realised that it must be done deviously. She dare not defy her father openly, especially after the scene in the market place.

In the end, the plan she decided on had the virtue of simplicity. No matter what the season of the year, her mother needed blossoms, berries and herbs for the making of cordials and remedies. Tamar had always grumbled at the requests for her to search the woods to gather whatever was in season.

Now, however, she saw with blinding clarity that she was presented with a twofold gift. Her forays in search of woodland produce would not only give her the opportunity to meet Sir William, but would improve her standing in her parents' eyes.

She realised that her mother despaired of her slip-shod ways in the house, but had the feeling that her father could see into her soul and realised how much she resented life on the family farm. Now, however, she told herself, if she played her cards properly, not only would she escape into the wider world, but she would become a lady.

Sir William rode away from the farm, feeling well pleased with himself. He knew from her response that Tamar would meet him in the quarry, if humanly possible. His lips curled in a triumphant smile. He had other fish to fry and when his plans came to fruition, he could return to his London townhouse with his rich, eminently suitable wife and need not visit this bleak and dreary, Godforsaken northern land again, except on rare occasions. He felt a little dalliance with the beautiful and vivacious girl from the valley farm would not only add spice to the time he was forced to spend in Yorkshire courting his chaste young bride-to-be, but would also be a means of avenging himself on her brother and father.

'I'll teach that oaf to attack me,' he gloated, as he followed the road out of the valley. 'And I'll give the old man something to think about. How dare he slam the door in my face? I'll teach them to know that they can't treat me in that fashion.'

As William Forster rode up the hill, George was riding down it. Recognising his enemy, George looked straight ahead with a set face and the two men passed, with no sign of recognition.

CHAPTER FIFTEEN

A wedge had appeared between the Oaks and the Butlers. The marriage of Joseph and Mary had originally drawn the two families together and, now that the link had gone, they were no longer on visiting terms. There was no open hostility – the families still spoke – but the strolls together after Sunday meeting had stopped.

Each felt a hidden resentment that the other's offspring was responsible for the loss of their own. Joseph had made it only too clear to his family that their decision was the result of his mother-in-law's dominating attitude and the Butlers were convinced that it was Joseph who had persuaded Mary to emigrate.

This rift meant that George had no more opportunities to be alone with Elizabeth or even to talk to her at any length. When they did meet, she was almost cool. George was left wondering if it was his night in prison which had affected her attitude towards him.

Bereft of her company, he grew more morose, and though his mother was relieved that his calf-love, as she called it to herself, was finally over, she was concerned at the change in him. From an uncomplicated, outgoing youth, George developed into a solemn and brooding man.

The year which followed the departure of Joseph and Mary was not a good one for the farmers of the North Yorkshire dales and moorlands. Heavy rain and gales throughout the summer battered both the hay and cornfields, making the crops difficult to cut and shaking out the grain from the ears. Some of the corn stood so long in the stooks that the grain began to sprout on the stalk. This meant that the stooks had to be pulled apart and the sheaves strewn out to dry again, before being reassembled.

The hay and corn harvests ran into each other and dragged on for so long and the labour was so exhausting that the usual enjoyment of these periods was totally lacking. Jonadab Oaks saw the depleted profits of the harvest being swallowed up by the wages of the migrant workers, who had to be kept on for twice the usual length of time. The meagre crop of hay would not feed his stock for the whole winter and he knew that he must enquire far afield to supplement it, as none of the farmers in the area would have any to sell.

To add to the family's gloom, there was no communication from Joseph and Mary. More than a year had passed since their departure, and it was accepted by most that they had died.

Many of their acquaintances whose families had emigrated had never heard a word from them again. Both Joseph and his wife, however, were capable of writing and, to their families, the lack of a letter was ominous.

Annie had determined in her mind that death had been their fate and, like Maria, they were lost to her. Although she applied herself diligently to her work, she was thinner, more finely-drawn and laughed less than she used to.

Many a time in the evening, Jonadab would glance up from his seat at the table, where he sat reading the *Malton Messenger*, to find that his wife's eyes were fixed upon him reproachfully.

'She blames it all on me, because I burnt that corn dolly,' he often told himself. The incident, however, was never mentioned since the night it had taken place.

Beth married John Smithson at the end of harvest and left the dale to take her place at his parents' farm in Gillamoor. Annie missed her daughter's help with the dairywork, which was now taken over by Tamar. Whereas Beth had been thoughtful with a painstaking attitude to her tasks, Tamar was more vivacious and tended to be rather slapdash, so that she needed more supervision. Poor Annie often thought with a sigh that little Martha could have managed better, but felt it was her duty to see that Tamar was well-grounded in the work of a farmwife, as well as that of a housewife. She was still ignorant of Tamar's secret ambition to escape this fate.

Early in the December of 1853, Annie began her preparations for the Christmas livestock and poultry show at Kirkbymoorside.

The cockerels from the spring hatchings of chicken had been fattened up all year and were to be crated up and taken in the trap. All the geese, apart from the breeding stock and a couple of extra plump ones which would be killed and dressed for their own Christmas Dinner, had to be driven to the market.

The day before, they were kept fastened up until the men had time to help the womenfolk. Then the geese were driven through a passage made of sheep bars, which narrowed towards a trough of tar, so that they were funnelled through it. This was followed by a trough of sand, which stuck to the tar, giving their feet a protective coating, ready for the walk to Kirkbymoorside.

Tamar and Martha were to accompany their mother, and each was provided with a pig's bladder, blown up and tied to a stick. With these, they could hit any recalcitrant goose without hurting it, or bruising the flesh.

Martha had not walked into Kirkby before. Her few previous visits had been in the trap with her mother and this seemed like a great adventure to the girl.

'Eeh! Won't it be grand in Kirkby?' she asked her sister, time and time again.

'We've ti get there first,' answered Tamar grumpily. She had driven geese on previous occasions and knew what a slow and frustrating job it was.

They were ready and well-wrapped up in good time next morning. It was imperative to set off at first light, as the journey would take a long time. Annie was determined to arrive at the show before the poulterers from the big towns had bought all they required. Her geese were extra plump this year and she needed to obtain a good price. As the harvest had been so poor, the geese had been turned into the stubble-fields to feed on the grain which had been lost. This had fleshed them out and given them an extra sleekness.

The crates of cockerels were stacked in the trap, leaving little room for Annie. Then the flock of geese started off, with Tamar and Martha helped by Jess and Shep, the dogs.

Although they were only required to perform this task once a year, the two dogs soon adjusted their technique and kept the geese more or less under control, helped by the two girls who were quick to give a light thwack with a bladder, if needed.

Before they started out, Jonadab spoke earnestly to his wife. 'Aah don't have to tell thoo how important it is to get t'best price possible. Things are nobbut dowly just at present and we must mek a bit where we can,' he impressed upon her.

'Aye, Aah knows, love,' she replied.

'Gooing into t'heavy horses hasn't begun to pay off yet, and they took a good bit of mi capital.' He had never admitted before what she had recognised herself. Things were difficult in farming and many of those known to them were struggling; some, indeed, had gone under.

'It'll be all right, Jonadab. We s'll pull through,' she reassured him.

'It wasn't just buying Rosie and Violet that took t'brass.' He was in full flow now and found it difficult to stop, having begun to confide his worries to her. 'There was all t'new tack for 'em from t'saddler and extra food for them and t'foals.' He was silent for a moment, reflecting. 'Anyroad,' he went on, 'they'll prove a worthwhile investment. They're good breeders and there's more and more demand for heavy horses.'

She put a hand on his arm. 'Don't worry, Jonadab. This lot should fetch a good price,' she promised firmly.

''Oo's worrying? Aah'm certainly not,' he asserted stoutly, as he turned away.

The journey passed without incident, though driving the geese was a slow and energetic job. About half a mile outside the town, Annie passed the girls with their flock and drove down into the town, where she had pens for geese already ordered and paid for.

After stabling the pony at the inn, she hired her chair and paid a boy a halfpenny to help her with the crates of cockerels.

When she saw her daughters driving the geese down the market place, she swung open the gates of the two pens and helped to pen the flock, thinking how well they looked as she did so. Quite a lot of the cockerels had already been sold so the girls first had something to eat and then carried the empty poultry crates back to the inn-yard, stacking them up to be loaded into the trap later for the journey home.

By mid-afternoon, Annie had successfully sold all her stock and helped the girls to stack the rest of the crates near the trap.

Having set off before it was really light that morning, she had hoped to reach home before darkness fell. However, the two girls were tired and cold so she said cheerfully: 'Now, lasses, let's have a look in one or two shop windows. It'll soon be Christmas and perhaps we can see something cheap for little Molly's stocking.'

Only the small children hung up their stockings and received a present. Many girls of Martha Oaks' age were by now out at work as servants or nursemaids.

As they passed the Post Office in Red Lion Square, Robert Cooper, the postmaster, came out to put up the shutters at the shop window.

'Oh, Mrs Oaks, a letter has come for you!' he exclaimed. The three stopped in their tracks.

'A letter?' Annie was astounded: she had never received a letter before, although Jonadab now and again wrote and collected business letters.

'Yes. Just a moment.' He hurried inside and came out carrying not one, but two letters. 'There's one for John Butler, at Fadmoor. Will you be seeing him?' he asked, as he handed over one of the letters.

'No, but he is in town. If I see him again, I'll tell him. No! Give it to me – I'll take it!' She was so excited that she did not really know what she was saying. She stood fingering the letter which was addressed to both her and Jonadab. The two girls pressed round her, anxious to see the letter. As Annie turned it over in her fingers, she turned pale. 'Tamar – Aah think Aah'm going to faint,' she whispered.

As she swayed, Tamar supported her to the pavement edge. 'Sit down, Mam. What is it?' she asked

'Nay, nay! Aah can't sit there. What'll folk think?' Annie remonstrated as she tried to pull herself together. Tamar looked round, but the streets were clearing and she could see no one else she knew.

'Sit down, Mam,' she instructed. Turning aside to her sister, she whispered, 'Oor Martha – run to t'pub, tell 'em who you are and fetch a noggin of brandy for Mam. Tell 'em she's poorly and we'll come in and pay when she's better.'

Martha sped away. She felt rather apprehensive at approaching an alehouse, much less going into one. If Tamar had not been so upset by her mother's collapse, she would never have sent her sister on such an errand. The girl pushed open the inn door and hesitated in the doorway, peering through the smoke-filled room. Behind a counter, at the end, she was relieved to see a woman. Running forward, past the settles and tables of what she could only think of as Satan's home, she began to cry.

'Lord bless us! What's wrong with the child?' exclaimed the landlady.

'It's me Mam. She's been took bad and oor Tamar says can I have a noggin of brandy?' she gulped. 'Oh, Aah forgot! Aah'm Martha Oaks from Sleightholmedale, and we'll pay later.'

One or two of the customers knew Jonadab Oaks and could not understand how the child of a man they regarded as straitlaced and puritanical could be in such a place.

'Job!' the woman shouted. 'Take over t'bar for a minute.'

She took a bottle from the shelf behind her and poured some of the spirit into a small glass. 'Come along, love.' She came round the bar and took Martha's hand. 'Where's your Ma, then?'

191

Together they hurried outside and ran to where Annie was rising from her seat on the ground, leaning on Tamar for support.

'Drink this, missus,' the woman urged, as she raised the glass to Annie's lips.

Annie tossed it back and then gasped and began to cough and splutter. 'Whatever is it?' she asked.

'A tonic. It'll do you good,' answered the landlady. Tamar took charge of her mother's purse and paid the landlady who, once she saw that the neat brandy had revived Annie, returned to the bar, smiling to herself at the woman's naïvety.

The girls knew that if once they managed to get their mother into the trap, they could get her home. With one at each side, she made her way somewhat unsteadily back to the Black Swan yard.

'That letter's from Joseph,' she told the girls. 'It's from the Canadas! They're alive!'

Tamar and Martha were delirious with joy at the news.

'Are you sure, Mam?' Martha asked anxiously.

'Yes. Their name's on t'back – Mr and Mrs Joseph Oaks. That's what made me come over queer,' she replied, quaveringly.

'Praise the Lord,' said Tamar. 'I never thought we'd see this day.'

Dusk was falling and the journey home would only be at walking pace, as the trap was loaded with the empty crates. Tamar, however, showed that despite what her father regarded as her slapdash ways, she was a born organiser. She still had the purse, so went to pay Joseph Jackson, the landlord, for the stabling and harnessed up the pony and yoked it to the trap.

'Now, young Martha, get atop yon crates as far forward as you can,' she ordered.

Martha obliged. She was only too thankful not to

have to face the walk home after a long day. Tamar looked at her mother and sister.

'Now then, you two. Oor Dad's not to know about the brandy.'

'Brandy?' gasped Annie. 'What brandy?'

'That "tonic" the landlady of the pub gave you was brandy.'

Annie almost fainted again at the thought that the Devil's brew had passed her lips. 'How could it be? It made me feel better,' she protested.

'Well, it was,' answered Tamar grimly. 'You'd had a shock and we had to get you over it, somehow. Don't ever tell Faither, though, or he'll skelp the hide off me, even if I am twenty.' So saying, she mounted the step at the back of the trap, hanging on to the woodwork. 'Keep well forward, oor Martha, to balance me,' she enjoined, as they made their way home.

Down at the farm, Jonadab and the rest of the men of the family had come in for tea. He frowned to see only Ann Waind in the kitchen. 'Mother and the lasses not back yet?' he said, looking at the grandfather clock.

'No, Faither!' she replied, a faint shadow echoing his frown.

'They should have been back by now.' Just as they spoke, they heard the pony's hooves and the sound of voices outside. 'Good! Mash t'tea,' he exclaimed.

Suddenly, the back door was flung open and his wife rushed into the room. To the surprise of those inside the kitchen, Annie was transformed. She seemed to have shed ten years since her departure that morning, so great was the change. With shining eyes and arms outstretched, she ran to her husband, waving the letter.

'It's from Joe!' she announced breathlessly. 'They're alive!'

There was a brief moment of silence in the kitchen, and then everyone began to talk at once.

Jonadab looked at his wife. 'What about Topper?' he demanded.

George thought that no matter what happened, the stock came first with his father.

'It's all right. Bert was coming out of t'stable as we drew up, and he's seeing to t'pony and trap,' Annie hastened to reassure him.

Jonadab turned the letter over. 'You haven't opened it, Mother.' It was inconceivable to him that she had brought it home unopened.

'Nay, Jonadab. It's wrote to us both and I thought it best that you should be the one,' she stammered, hoping that he could not smell the brandy.

Martha spoke up. 'It made oor Mam feel poorly, so – ' she caught Tamar's glare, 'so we got her back as quick as we could,' she finished, with a smirk at her sister.

'What does he say, Faither?' asked young Jonna, speaking for them all.

Jonadab drew his Windsor chair up to the table and moved the oil-lamp so that it shone on the letter. He slowly broke the seal while the rest of the family took their places round the table.

George looked at his father and noticed the slight tremor of his hands as they held the letter. Even though their father had kept a tight rein on his emotions, George realised that he had felt the loss of Joseph and his family as much as the rest of them.

When Jonadab began to read, his voice held a slight huskiness, but soon resumed its usual strength.

' *"Dear All"* ,' he read, ' *"This is to let you know that we arrived here safe. Mam and Mary's mam packed*

*us so much food that we sold some to other people on the
ship, as the Pandora's food was not too good. You said to
look after my brass and we landed with more than we set
off with. This is a wonderful land. I am a foreman on a
big farm, over two thousand acres . . ."'*

Here Jonadab paused. Two thousand acres!
Neither he nor his listeners could imagine such a
farm. He looked back down at the letter on the table
before him and read on: ' *"We are saving all we can,
to buy our own farm. Mary and Georgie are well. He
is a big boy for three and can milk. We have told him
all about you and next time we go to town, we will have
one of those new pictures took and send you one."* '

Nobody really knew how photographs were taken,
although they had heard of such things.

' *"I will write again as soon as I have time and hope
that you will write to us. Your affectionate son and
brother, Joseph."* '

As Jonadab put the letter down a sigh rippled
round the table. Then they all began to speak at
once, delight and relief reflected in each face.

'Whoa! Just a minute! It's like t'tower of Babel!'
protested Jonadab.

'They sound to be doing well, don't they, Faither?' said Ann Waind tremulously. She had always
felt guilty about Joseph's emigration. If she and John
had not been at the farm, Joseph would never have
left England. Now, however, it seemed as though it
had been a fortunate move.

George looked at his parents. 'Somebody should
go and tell t'Butlers,' he suggested.

Annie clapped her hands to her mouth. 'Oh! I
forgot! Mr Cooper at t'Post Office gave me a letter
for the Butlers. I thought I might see Mr Butler
again in Kirkby, but I didn't feel well, so we came
back home.'

'As soon as we've finished oor tea, I'll ride up with their letter,' George ventured.

'Right. We'd better have another pot made, Ann.' Jonadab motioned to his eldest daughter.

'Do you think I should take oor letter for them to read?' asked George, as the family settled down to the meal. His mother looked anxious. She felt that she could not bear to part with the precious letter. Jonadab, however, was pleased with his son's thoughtfulness and knew that the Butlers would appreciate the gesture.

'Aye, do that. It's all right, Mother,' he comforted his wife, 'he'll bring it back, safe and sound. Thoo can read it till t'writing falls off.' That he should joke with her was an indication of his own relief at the arrival of the letter.

George finished his tea as quickly as possible, without appearing to bolt it. At least he hoped to get the chance of a word with Elizabeth when he took the letters up to the Butlers later that evening.

CHAPTER SIXTEEN

When tea was over, George had a good wash at the kitchen sink. He would really have liked to change his clothes, but didn't wish to give his brother and sisters anything to snigger about.

His mother, however, came to his rescue. 'Put thi clean shirt on, lad,' she instructed, as he combed his hair before the mirror. George did not need to be told twice. He shot up to the bedroom and changed his shirt.

When he went out to saddle up Topper, the moon was almost full and it was a bright frosty evening. 'Aah'll not be long,' he said, upon leaving the house.

'Nay, lad. There's no hurry. Tek thi time,' his father had replied affably. The letter had certainly mellowed him, George thought.

As he rode towards Fadmoor, he pondered about Elizabeth Butler's changed attitude towards him. 'When I was a lad,' he thought ruefully, 'she more or less encouraged me. Now I'm twenty-one, and a man, she wants nowt to do wi' me.'

He had heard that women were supposed to be changeable and not as steady as men, but he knew little of women, apart from his own sisters and Elizabeth herself. He had still found no satisfactory reason for her behaviour when he eventually arrived at the farm. The back door was opened to his knock by Jack, the Butlers' son.

'Now then, George! Come in,' said Jack in a friendly greeting, opening the door wider to usher him inside.

John Butler and his wife were seated one at each

side of the fire, he in a Windsor chair, with a pipe between his teeth and she in a rocking chair, knitting as she rocked gently. The rest of the family, as in his own home, sat round the kitchen table, busy with needlework or reading.

They were obviously surprised and embarrassed to see him and George detected a coolness in the parents' manner.

'Good evening, all,' George addressed the whole company.

There was an uneasy silence, before John Butler spoke. His tone was steady, almost hostile. 'Now, George, what can I do for you?' George noticed that he was not invited to sit.

'We've had a letter from Joe, and Mr Cooper gave mi mother one for you an' all. It's from Mary!' George felt proud to be the bearer of such momentous news and handed both letters to his host.

'The Lord be praised!' exclaimed Mrs Butler, jumping to her feet. 'Thank you for turning out with it tonight.' She could say no more, for tears.

John Butler held out his hand and took both letters.

'Sit thissen down, lad,' he instructed, as he held up his hand to quieten his family. 'Now, hold your hush till I've finished,' he commanded, and began to read aloud.

Mary's letter was very much like Joseph's, except that it contained a description of the house: ' *"They are all made of wood, with only the chimneys made of stone,"* ' she had written.

'I don't like the sound of that. Surely it's draughty!' interrupted her mother.

'Na, then! Wait till I've done and then you can all have your say.' John Butler continued to read until both letters were finished.

In vain did George try to catch Elizabeth's eye as

198

the Oaks' letter was being read, for she kept her gaze fixed on her father.

All were impressed, as his own family had been, with the optimistic tone of the letters. The young couple's enjoyment of their new life and faith in their future was only too clear.

'Oh, what a relief!' exclaimed Mrs Butler, as she rocked back and forth, fanning her face with a newspaper.

'Thank the Lord that they were taught to write,' said Elizabeth fervently. 'We might never have heard from them again.'

'Aye, we can sleep easy,' answered her father, 'now that we know they're safe and well.'

When the discussion about the letters seemed to be exhausted, George retrieved his parents' letter and rose to his feet.

'Well, Aah'll be off, then,' he announced, hoping beyond hope that Elizabeth would offer to accompany him to the gate, as she had so often before. She made no move, however, apart from joining in the general goodnights.

'Aah'll be seeing you, then,' as he turned towards the door.

Suddenly, the clear voice of Sarah, the youngest girl, rang out. 'Thoo won't be seeing oor 'Lizabeth. She's going to live in Leeds!' she declared defiantly, as Elizabeth's hand flashed out to stop her.

George felt stunned. He stopped dead in his tracks and turned slowly back to face the room. Each face mirrored a different emotion, from curiosity as to how he would take the devastating news, to triumph on fourteen year old Sarah's face at the effect her announcement had caused. 'Oor 'Lizabeth's to have nowt to do with a jailbird.'

Elizabeth was embarrassed and full of contrition as she saw George's stricken look. She rose hastily to

199

her feet and moved towards him. George, however, swung away and groped blindly for the latch. He was outside and the door had banged behind him before she reached it. She swiftly opened the door and followed him into the night.

'George! George! Please come back. Let me explain!' she pleaded.

'There's nowt to explain.' He would not face her though she had, by now, reached him.

'Please, George. Hear what I have to say,' she begged, taking him by the arm.

Angrily, he shook her hand off. 'Aah knows what Aah heard and thoo can't say owt to change that!' He almost snarled the words. 'Is it to be wed, then, that thoo's going ti Leeds!' His local accent was strong now, in his distress. He normally tried to please Elizabeth by attempting to correct his dialect.

Elizabeth caught her breath. 'Of course not! I'm going to keep house for my Uncle Nathan. He's Mother's brother, whose wife died. He's had one or two housekeepers who've robbed him, so he's asked for one of us to go.'

The explanation did nothing to placate George who felt deceived and let down.

'Aye, an' if Aah hadn't come up tonight, you'd have gone without me knowing,' he challenged.

'No, of course not. I meant to tell you, George but not before I was ready to go. It's hard enough to leave, without you working on me to persuade me to stay.'

George digested this information. Could it mean what he thought, he wondered. 'You've been avoiding me lately,' he accused.

'Oh, my dear! I'm twenty-eight and you're twenty one. I only want to give you the chance to get to know younger girls!' She looked up at him in the clear moonlight. 'Take no notice of what Sarah said. She's only a child.'

'Aye, but she repeats what others have said,' he answered bitterly. 'Don't worry, there's many a body avoids me, now. I see 'em whispering when I pass 'em in t'street.'

George poured out the whole story of what had led to his night in prison, and how he had merely been protecting his sisters.

Elizabeth hesitated. 'Do you remember when you uptipped me in the trap, with your sheep?' she asked. 'You came up later, to see how I was and my mother said I was ill.'

'Yes, love. You've never told me what was wrong. Was it through me?'

She smiled. 'No, George. It was really my own fault, and Sir William Forster's.' She must choose her words carefully, she thought. George already hated Forster and she had no wish for more fuel to be added to his ire.

'He was actually very kind,' she continued. 'He removed a stone from Bella's hoof, but when I tripped and fell against him he thought I was trying to flirt with him.' What she had no intention of telling George was that she had found Sir William quite attractive at the beginning.

George was outraged. 'That's typical of him – the conceited brute. He just can't leave decent women alone.'

'Anyway,' she said, 'to cut a long story short, I lost my temper with him and got myself in such a tantrum that by the time I reached home, my head was splitting and I felt quite ill.'

'So that was why you were poorly! It was through that swine, and I thought it was summat I'd done.'

Elizabeth looked deep into the faithful brown eyes. 'Never, George. You could never do anything to hurt me. Of that, I'm sure.' She saw with a sudden clarity what it was she wanted of George. The age difference was of no consequence. She loved this faithful, devoted man and wanted to spend her life with him.

As she looked up at him, she shivered and he could see the glint of tears on her cheeks. George tenderly enveloped her in his arms.

'I love you, Lizzie Butler,' he whispered, as he gently wiped away her tears with the back of his finger. 'I've loved you ever since Joseph and Mary's wedding. You must know how I feel. Don't leave me, love. Stay here, and we'll be wed.'

As she snuggled against him, feeling his strength and enveloped in the warmth of him, Elizabeth was tempted.

She sighed. 'No, George, dear. I've given my word to Uncle Nathan and I must keep it. I will, however, make a bargain with you. I want you to feel free to look for a girl more your age and if you find one, marry her. There'll be no recriminations from me. I will stay in Leeds for two years and then, if you still want me, I'll come home and we'll be married.'

As she gave the promise, George was overwhelmed. 'How can I wait two more years for you? I've already waited four. I'm a man now, Elizabeth. I want you for my wife and I'll still want you in two years' time. I can't wait and I won't wait.' So saying, he rained kisses upon her upturned face. His arms tightened and his lips hungrily found hers.

Elizabeth was shaken not only by the intensity of his passion, but by her own response to it. As they clung together, she was thankful that they were at the gate on a cold night, rather than lying in a barn or a meadow. In any other circumstances, she could not have controlled their passion.

Shakily, she pushed him gently away. 'No,

George. Please, we must be sensible! I'd hate us to marry in haste and for you to regret it.'

'In haste? What are you talking about, woman? I've been courting you these last four years.' George's response made her laugh.

'Courting me, is it? I can't remember us really being alone together for more than a couple of minutes!' she teased. 'I must go back to the house, George. They'll wonder what's going on.'

George held on to her hand. 'If you won't change your mind, can we have an understanding?' he beseeched. 'Can we be betrothed?'

She considered a moment. 'We shall not tell anyone of our bargain, but if you want to consider that we have an understanding, then so be it. Remember, George, you are not bound in any way. You are free to choose someone else, if you wish.'

'Aye, and so are you,' he declared stoutly.

She sighed. George Oaks was the one for her. It was only the fact that she loved him so much that forced her now to give him the chance to look round.

'I must go,' she protested. 'If you can get into Kirkby on Wednesday, I'll meet you at Mrs Sleightholme's tea-house at two o'clock. I have to go to the Black Swan to book my seat on Saturday's coach to York.'

'I'll get there, don't worry. I shan't ask mi faither. I s'll *tell* him.'

So saying, George left Elizabeth to return to the house, to the inquisitive but unsatisfied eyes of her family.

As he rode home, George reflected on the day. First there had been the news that Joseph was alive and doing well, and now his own understanding with Elizabeth. George had no intention of ever looking at anyone else. Elizabeth had captivated his heart when he was a youth of seventeen, and he was determined to have her for his wife.

He savoured the feel of her in his arms – her softness and femininity. He relived their passionate kisses and glowed with heat, even though the night was bitter.

'Oh, Elizabeth,' he murmured to himself, as the pony descended the hill into Sleightholmedale. She was the first woman he had ever held or kissed, for Jonadab Oaks' children did not indulge in dalliance, after Joseph's escapade. He could only hope that his father's keen eye would not detect any change in his appearance and guess that he had been kissing and embracing Elizabeth.

He need not have worried. His mother's relief at the receipt of news from Canada had wrought such a change, bringing back the glow of her old cheerfulness, that the alteration in George was attributed to the same cause.

In bed that night, Annie confided in her husband, 'Eeh, Jonadab. I'm that relieved, I feel a new woman.'

'Aye, lass, and I'm glad.' Her husband patted her hand in a rare show of affection. 'I've worried a lot about thi,' he admitted.

'Our George has cheered up a lot an' all,' she observed. 'That's what's been up with him. 'E's been worried about Joseph and Mary.'

'Aye, so it seems.' Jonadab was not so sure. The transformation in George had come, it seemed to his father, not with his brother's letter, but after his trip up to the Butlers.

Jonadab, however, kept his own counsel. The arrival of Joseph's letter was like the lifting of a heavy weight from his mind, and he was quite content to know that they were safe and seemed to be building a good future. As far as he was concerned, George was a steady and dependable man who could be trusted to run his own life.

George's statement that he intended to go to Kirkbymoorside on market day caused no surprise. For some time, he had been breeding pigs in a couple of sties lent for his use by his father. He had opened a bank account in his own name.

Now and again, he went into the little market town to make deposits or withdrawals at the York Union Bank, where Mr Frank greeted him in a businesslike fashion, giving no indication that he remembered the first time they had met.

So it was that he came to be sitting in the teahouse the next Wednesday, opposite Elizabeth. He felt out of place and clumsy in the elegant surroundings, holding a tiny china cup, but was so overjoyed to be in her company that he didn't care.

'Now George, we haven't long, and there's a lot to discuss,' Elizabeth began briskly.

'You will write to me, won't you, love?' George's eyes across the table were spaniel-like in their devotion.

She clicked her tongue impatiently. 'That goes without saying. We haven't time for chit-chat. There's a lot to settle.'

She told him that she was to take Saturday's stage to Spurriergate in York, where she would spend the night at the George Inn. The next day, her Uncle would come from Leeds in his carriage and take her to his home.

'Has he got his own carriage?' asked George, in amazement.

'Yes. He's a rich man. He has a large draper's shop in Briggate, the main street,' she answered.

George's face fell. Would Elizabeth wish to live down in Sleightholmedale in the farmhouse as his wife, after two years as housekeeper in a rich man's home?

'Look, George. You mustn't have silly ideas. We have come to an understanding and I shall remain steadfast. I just don't want you – ' she paused and then, with more emphasis, ' – I don't want you to feel constrained in any way.'

'I shall remain true to you, never fear, Elizabeth,' George protested hoarsely, seizing her hand across the table. He covered her hand with his. 'Oh! I've just had a thought! You'll be gone by Christmas!' He looked so crestfallen that she felt sad that this would be their last meeting for some time.

'We shall have many Christmases together, George,' she promised, 'and many stockings to fill, God-willing,' she added, almost in prayer.

'I've money in the bank. Let me buy you a betrothal ring before you leave me.'

'No, my darling,' she whispered, glancing round to see that none of the other clients could hear. 'Save your money, George, and I shall save mine. My Uncle will pay me for my services and we must both save as much as we can. Some day, we shall have our own farm, I am determined on that score. Meanwhile, our promise to each other shall remain our own secret.'

George gazed at her in adoration. 'Oh, love, I could take you in my arms right here and smother you with kisses. How can I wait two years?' He sounded desperate.

She gave his hand a squeeze. 'I shall come home now and again for the weekend and hope to see you then,' she promised.

George looked panic-stricken. 'I must kiss you goodbye,' he whispered. 'Please wait for me on the road home.'

While he paid the bill, she left the tea-house to

yoke up the pony and trap. George went to the bank and then had a word with his mother in the market place. 'I'm off now, Mam. I've done all I came to do,' he said.

'All right, son,' she answered. She was enjoying her day at the market, recounting to all the other farmers' wives how well her son in the Canadas was doing.

George went to the inn-yard, saddled his horse and rode up the hill and out of the town. When he reached the turn-off to Sleightholmedale, it was to find that Elizabeth had turned her pony-trap off the main road to Fadmoor and was awaiting him in the avenue of trees which led to his home.

As soon as he reached where she was standing by the pony's head, he leapt from his horse and swept her into his arms.

'Oh, my little love,' he whispered. 'How can I live without you?' She returned his kisses with heartfelt passion for a moment or two, but then she placed her hands on his shoulders to widen the gap between them.

'If we remain faithful, the time will soon pass,' she promised, 'but swear to me, George, that if you find someone else, you will write and tell me straight-away. Don't make a fool of me, my darling.'

'You are all I've ever wanted,' he said huskily, as he took her into his arms once more. 'I shall be true, don't worry.' As he stroked her hair, he kissed her tenderly – first her eyes, then the tip of her nose, and then his lips fastened upon hers in a long, passionate meeting.

Elizabeth was shaken by the wild longing which his caresses aroused in her. She reluctantly disengaged herself from his arms.

'I must go, my dearest one. We can't meet again before I go to Leeds, but I shall think of you constantly, and write to you as soon as I arrive at my Uncle's. Goodbye.' She reached up and gave him one last lingering kiss, before entering the trap and turning for home.

George's emotions were in turmoil as he watched her drive away from him. At the corner, as the pony turned, she looked back and raised her whip in a farewell gesture – she was too far away for him to see the tears streaming down her cheeks.

While he was delighted that the desire he felt for Elizabeth was reciprocated, he was devastated to be losing her for so long, just as their mutual love had been declared.

'I wish I'd spoken out before. We could have had some time together before she'd gone. In fact, she might not have gone at all if she'd known how I felt,' he told himself.

Little did he realise that every member of their two families had known how he felt about Elizabeth since he had first got to know her. What they could not have guessed was that she returned his love . . .

As his horse picked its way delicately down the steep drop into the dale, George had time to compose his thoughts before facing those at home. He was determined to take a long-term view and look towards the day that Elizabeth would return, rather than dwell upon her absence. This decision so cheered him that he was whistling as he unharnessed the horse and rubbed him down.

Jonadab put his head round the stable door, as George was putting some oats in the manger. 'You're sounding more cheerful.'

There was a question in his voice and George hesitated. Should he tell his father about Elizabeth? Then he thought better of it. 'Aye. It's been a big relief to hear from our Joe and Mary,' he answered, as he rubbed down the horse. Glancing up, he caught his father's eyes studying his face and felt that it was turning scarlet.

'It has an' all,' was all Jonadab said as he turned out of the stable.

George was left with the uneasy feeling that his father knew full well the nature of the errand which had taken him into Kirkby, but he was determined to keep his and Elizabeth's secret and fill the coming two years with hard work and saving.

'After all,' he thought to himself, 'look how long Jacob worked and waited for Rachel, in the Bible. Well, I shall be just as patient.'

CHAPTER SEVENTEEN

When Annie Oaks heard of Elizabeth Butler's departure, she watched George anxiously. To her relief, he seemed utterly unmoved at the news.

'Whatever he thought he felt for her, he seems to have got over it,' she remarked to Jonadab. 'I thought he might have moped when he heard she'd gone, but he hasn't turned a hair.'

Jonadab was not at all sure that she was right, but had no foundation for his suspicions that George was still 'keen on Butlers' lass', as he put it to himself. Certainly, George was his old cheerful self and worked hard from morning until night. He and his brother Jonna had more in common, now the gap between them seemed smaller and they chatted in the evenings as they groomed the big greys.

Early in the spring, old Grandad Joseph developed a severe cold which he seemed unable to shake off. Since his wife Jane's death, he had become both physically frail and confused in his mind. When it became obvious that his condition was deteriorating, Annie tried to keep him in bed, but he took to wandering round the house in his nightshirt, calling plaintively for his wife. This hung like a cloak of depression over the whole family, but the time soon came when the old man was too weak to get out of bed.

On his next trip to Kirkbymoorside, Jonadab called at the doctor's house and described his father's symptoms.

'I'm afraid it sounds as though he's not long for this world, but I'll come down and examine him in a day or two.' So saying, the doctor gave Jonadab a draught to keep the old man sedated.

After tea that evening, Jonadab looked round at the family. 'I'm afraid your Grandad's longest time is only short, so mek his last days as peaceful as possible. Try to keep t'bairn as quiet as you can,' with a glance at little Molly Waind, 'and see that he's comfortable.'

It was only a day or two after this that old Joseph Oaks died in the bed in which he had been born. Although the event was tinged with sadness, his death also brought a guilty feeling of relief to the women of the house, on whom the burden of his illness had fallen.

Ann Waind was pregnant with her second child, but was not enjoying this pregnancy as she had the first. She was frequently sick and often dragged herself about her household tasks with a hand pressed to her aching back. Although she realised that it placed a heavier burden on her mother, Tamar and Martha, there were many days when she was so ill that she could not get out of bed in the morning.

'It'll be all right, won't it, Mam?' she tentatively asked, one day, when she was feeling particularly ill.

'Bless you, lass! Aah was just the same with oor Tamar,' said Annie, and gave her daughter a pat. 'Nine months of purgatory, and then she slipped out with no trouble at all.'

When Grandad's bed had been stripped and the room cleaned by Tamar, George spoke to his mother. 'Aah knows you've much to do, you and t'lasses,' he said, 'what with Ann being badly. If you like, Aah'll limewash Grandad's room before we get too busy outside.'

Annie was touched by his proposal. She and the girls never seemed to stop working and she was grateful.

George had not been into his grandparents' bedroom very often and he looked round now with curiosity when he went up to limewash the walls. It was larger than he had thought, and he surveyed it with approval. This was the only empty bedroom in the house and this was the room he would share with his bride when he and Elizabeth were married.

Crossing to the window, he stooped to look out. The thatched roof swept low over the house at the front and the window was almost at floor level. The view however, was impressive.

In front of the house, the meadow lay spread out before him. Now that it was shorn of the hay which had clothed it, it was dotted with sheep, placidly grazing. They had been brought down from the moors, to run with the rams in the fields close to the farm. Beyond the meadow lay the straggle of willows, which marked the meandering progress of the beck. Although now, they stooped over the water, with grey, bare branches, George could already see in his mind Elizabeth looking out across this view in the height of summer, when the meadow would be spangled with flowers and the now-bare willows a mass of verdant greenery, veiling the stream.

Immediately before the farm, dense woodland swept upwards, filling the view but northwards, nearer to Cherry Tree Farm and their neighbour James Waring, the trees gave way to open moorland. On this grey, December day, the moors seemed menacing, reaching skywards in sweep after sweep of sombre folds, but with the coming of spring their drabness would give way almost overnight to fresh green. Later, they would be again transformed, as the heather took on shades of purple.

George sighed with satisfaction. 'Aye. This'll suit us nicely,' he thought, as he turned back into the bedroom and began to whiten the walls.

Early in June of the following year, another letter arrived from Joseph. To everyone's delight, it contained a picture of Joseph and Mary with, not only Georgie, who had grown into a sturdy little boy, but also a baby cradled in Mary's arms.

'Eeh! We didn't even know there was one on t'way,' breathed Annie, taking the photograph to the window to study it more closely.

'It's all in t'letter, if thoo'll sit thissen down and listen,' Jonadab chided.

Joseph's letter was still full of praise for his new country and the opportunities there. Although he missed his home and his family, it was clear that the couple had no regrets about their decision to make a new life in a new land. The baby, he said, was fair-haired and pretty, the image of her mother.

'Her name's Jean-ette,' Jonadab concluded with a frown.

'Jean-ette? Does he mean Janet?' asked Annie.

'No. He says there's a lot of French folks round where they live, and it's a French name.' His voice rose on a note of incredulity. 'A French name? An Oaks, with a French name? Them foreign parts has addled his brain!'

Jonadab was so incensed that, after this outburst, he was speechless for a few moments. Even thousands of miles away, Joseph was still defying him. So it was that baby Jean-ette came to be known as Jean to her relatives in England. Jean-ette was a mouthful, so Jean it was.

Whenever George went to Kirkbymoorside he called at the Post Office, where there was usually at least one letter from Elizabeth waiting for him. He would, for his part, despatch one to her, which he had laboriously penned over several evenings at the kitchen table. If anyone wondered why he now wrote so much, or to whom, no one ever asked. He hoped that the family thought that he was writing to Joseph.

George usually stopped to read Elizabeth's letters on his way home, but after that, they were an embarrassment to him. He was at his wits' end to know where to keep them. He still shared what was known as the lads' room with his brother Jonna and Uncle George. His mother and sisters regularly went into his chest of drawers to put away clean clothes and even under the mattress was not a safe place, as the featherbeds were well-shaken daily and turned over every week.

George had started out by slipping the letters on to one of the beams in the bedroom, close to the thatch. However, as he received more, the bundle of letters grew too big to remain hidden there. His dilemma was solved, however, when he spotted in a hardware shop a selection of cash-boxes.

'By gum! They're just the job!' he thought to himself with glee.

His mind was more at ease when the letters were transferred to the box, which he could leave in his top drawer, safely locked. He was still in two minds whether or not to confide in his parents about his and Elizabeth's plans, but had decided to keep the news to himself at least for the time being.

Although his pig business was doing nicely, there was really no way in which George could expand. He still only had the two pigsties which his father had allowed him to use, rent-free, and he puzzled and speculated as to how he could earn more money to build up a nest-egg for the future. All daylight hours were spent on farmwork apart from the occasional trip to market and he could think of nothing he could do to add to his capital.

One day, however, when he and his Uncle George were busy with lambing, his problem was solved.

Sheep! Apart from rounding them up for washing and salving in October and then at lambing-time in the spring, they would take up very little of his time. Of course, he must not forget shearing in June, the biggest job of all. However, he was sure that he could manage.

'Uncle George,' he began, as he paused among the ewes.

'Aye, lad?' came back the laconic reply.

'Faither doesn't tek up all his rough grazing up on t'moor, does he?'

'Nay, we use very little of it. We've enough grazing down in t'valley for most of t'flock.'

That evening, as they sat in the lamplight, he put his proposition to his father. 'Aah'm thinking of going into sheep, Faither,' he said.

'Oh, aye?' Jonadab evinced little encouragement.

'Well, we don't take up all oor grazing rights on t'moor, do we?'

'*I* don't,' Jonadab emphasised the pronoun. Although he liked his sons to take an interest in the family farm, he was determined to leave them in no doubt as to who was in charge.

George paused a moment before pursuing the subject. 'When you come to sell t'lambs, Aah'd like to buy about a dozen. Aah'll give you t'market price,' he stated, getting it out in a rush before he could be interrupted.

Jonadab cogitated on this for a few minutes. 'If Aah agrees and Aah haven't, yet, Aah'll certainly expect t'market price. Have no fears on that score,' he commented. ''Ow about t'grazing? Am Aah expected ti provide that free?' he quizzed, with a straight face.

George was speechless. 'Nay, Faither! It's going to waste! Thoo doesn't graze a tenth of what thoo's allowed.' His father could see that George, who was normally even-tempered, was growing annoyed. Deep down, he was only too pleased for his sons to show business acumen and had merely appeared to challenge George from force of habit.

'Anyroad,' he continued, 'it'll suit me not ti have ti get 'em ti market.' He smiled sardonically at George as he added, 'nor pay t'auctioneer's fees!'

George bit his lip in vexation. He should have thought of that, before offering the full market price. He could have got a discount. 'Thoo'll give me a bit of luck,' he challenged.

Luck money, as it was called, was usually demanded by the buyer after the sale of any animals and the seller often put a bit on the price, to allow for what he would be expected to give back 'for luck'.

'Aye, Aah expect Aah shall.' Jonadab looked across the table at George. 'As well as a bit of luck, Aah'll give thi a bit of advice. Thoo can buy thi sheep off me this time, but in future, never do business with friends, relatives nor neighbours. It's t'road to no spot but Troubletown.'

George was satisfied. His little flock would multiply and he could write and tell Elizabeth that he was laying the foundations of their savings.

No sooner was lambing finished, than news came back which was to reduce the workforce on the farm. Annie returned from market on Wednesday, carrying a letter for John and Ann Waind. Not only was there now room for them in the Wainds' farm at Bransdale, owing to the marriage of the last of his sisters, but his labour was needed, as two of his brothers had decided not to choose farming for their careers. They were now short-handed and needed John back home, as soon as possible.

This came as a great shock to the Oaks. John Waind had settled well into the family and was a good worker, particularly with the cattle. Jonadab would be unlikely to be able to hire someone in his place until the next Martinmas hirings. Thus, the burden of work would be increased on the rest of them.

Annie Oaks was reluctant to allow her daughter to go before the baby was born. After the wretched pregnancy, she wanted to deliver Ann's baby herself. In vain, however, did she try to persuade Ann, when the two of them were in the kitchen together.

'No, Mother. John's duty is to his family. He must go back as soon as possible,' Ann asserted firmly.

Her mother then suggested that John should go, and Ann stay in Sleightholmedale until after her imminent confinement. She was adamant, however, that her place was with her husband but agreed, not without relief, to leave little Molly until after the new baby was born, and even, perhaps, weaned. Molly was a mischievous little girl and encouraged by her uncles and aunties, was becoming quite a handful. Ann Waind did not feel up to coping with the child in new surroundings, feeling as unwell as she usually did these days. So it was that, when one of John Waind's brothers came down to the farm with a flat cart on which to take their clothes and personal belongings, Molly Waind stood in the road and waved goodbye to her parents, quite happy to remain with her grandparents in the only home she knew.

That evening, as Annie looked round the handful of family sitting in the kitchen, she reflected how their numbers had dwindled since Joseph's marriage. Tamar attracted quite a lot of local lads, although she had not yet made her choice. She was a strikingly beautiful girl, and her mother realised that she could not rely on having her at home for much longer.

How on earth would she manage in the house with only young Martha's help, she wondered.

Jonadab's thoughts had also been running on the same lines. In addition to all the cleaning, baking, washing and ironing, the women were responsible for the poultry and dairywork. As if this was not enough to occupy them for all the hours of daylight, their services were needed in the fields at hay-time and harvest.

He pondered for a few minutes and then reached what was for him, a momentous decision. 'Aah s'll go up t'union house in t'morning and see if they have a lad and a lass, ready for work,' he announced.

The union house, or workhouse, had been built a few years before, a short distance to the north of the town. It was a large, handsome building which, in addition to caring for those too ill, or elderly to work, was responsible for the bringing up of orphans and setting them to a trade when they reached the age of ten.

Annie had never thought to see the day when she would have a maid to help in the house. 'Where shall we put 'em?' she queried, trying to get used to the idea.

'Bert Weald'll put the lad up with t'other two and t'lass can sleep in t'same room as t'bairn. Either they can move into Ann and John's room or Tamar and Martha can.'

'What about us?' young Jonna demanded. 'There's us three grown men in t'loft over kitchen and Grandad's room is empty. Why can't some of us move in there?'

George could see the room which, in his mind, was now reserved for him and Elizabeth, being snatched away. 'Nay! Oor Mam and t'lasses have enough to do without using another room,' he protested.

Jonna, however, was a younger version of his

father, and would not give in easily. 'It seems daft,' he insisted, 'that three of us should share, when there's an empty bedroom.'

George was growing desperate. His face took on a mulish look. 'Right then! Aah'll move in.' He was defiant now, as his family looked at him with curiosity.

'And why should you be so privileged, might I ask?' His father's tone was cutting. 'If anyone moves, it will be your Uncle George.'

'Nay, Jonadab,' Uncle George said deprecatingly, 'Aah'm all right where Aah am.'

'No, thoo's not! Thoo'll move!' It had now become a battle of wills, which Jonadab was determined to win.

There was a moment's silence and Annie sighed. Would Jonadab ever stop this flying off the handle, she wondered. A few moments ago, the scene in the kitchen had been peaceful, but now the atmosphere was explosive. She sensed that George was disturbed, but for the life of her could not imagine why.

George took a deep breath and rose from his chair. His mind went back to over five years ago, when Joseph had dropped his bombshell.

'Grandad's room is for me and my wife, when Aah gets wed,' he declared.

Tamar burst out laughing. 'Get wed?' she mocked. 'Thoo's never looked at a lass, except for Lizzie Butler, so how can thoo get wed?'

George had so wanted to keep his secret, but it was now forced out of him. 'When Elizabeth Butler comes back from Leeds next year, we're to be married,' he announced defiantly.

Annie knew better than to voice any objection. If George had really made his choice, then it would be hers too. Nevertheless, she was disappointed and distressed to hear his declaration.

Young Jonna, however, could not keep silent. 'Marry 'er? She's old!' was his reaction.

George was stung to anger by the thoughtless outburst. His face suffused with rage, he leapt to his feet, ready to fell his brother with a blow. Their father, however, forestalled him.

'Hold thi tongue!' His voice was like a whiplash. 'It's thi brother's business, Jonna, not thine. We'll have no violence. Settle thisselves down.' When they were all seated in an uneasy silence, he resumed.

'Now, George,' turning to the elder son, 'have you spoken to her of it, or is it just what you hope?'

George explained about the understanding which he and Elizabeth had reached. This was the reason for his wanting to set up his own flock of sheep and save as much money as possible.

'Aah knows you want mi to look for a younger lass, but Elizabeth's been the one for me ever since oor Joe's wedding,' he stated flatly. 'If Aah don't marry Elizabeth, Aah s'll stay unwed.'

He turned beseechingly to his mother. 'She's good for me, Mam. She wants me to make summat of missen and for us to have oor own farm one day.' He had no hope of influencing Annie's private opinion, but he was not to know that.

'Anyway,' he finished, triumphantly, 'when t'woman wears the oldest head, the children never want for bread.'

'How could you keep it a secret from us, George?' His mother was tearful.

'Aah was going to tell you, Mam,' he muttered guiltily, 'honest I was.'

Jonadab Oaks was assessing the situation. The Butlers were a well-respected family and they were already connected by marriage. Certainly, George had always been set on the eldest Butler girl, and it seemed that he wouldn't change now. If it hadn't been that she was getting on for thirty, he couldn't have wished for a more suitable daughter-in-law.

'That's settled then, Mother. Oor George'll move into t'spare room.' He astounded his listeners with his about-turn.

George begged his family not to spread the news. 'Let Elizabeth tell her own folks in her own time,' he implored them. 'It wouldn't look right coming from us.' With this they heartily agreed and all gave their word. 'Thoo an' all, oor Jonna,' he admonished, with a glare at his younger brother. 'Aah knows what thoo's like. Thi tongue's tied in t'middle and wags at both ends.'

'Nay, George. That's not fair,' their mother protested. 'T'lad's given his promise.'

With this, George had to be content. He was not sorry that his family were now aware of the situation – he was an open man, who had not liked to deceive them. He was not sure however, how Elizabeth would take the news that the Oaks now knew of their unofficial engagement.

'It isn't my fault they know,' he consoled himself. 'I had to stake mi claim to that room.'

His last thoughts as he fell asleep were, as usual, of Elizabeth and he sleepily vowed that he would write to her the following day.

'She'll have to know,' he decided. He still could hardly believe his good fortune in securing Elizabeth for his promised bride and always, deep down, lay the fear that something would happen to come between them.

CHAPTER EIGHTEEN

True to his word, Jonadab Oaks set out for Kirkby-moorside with the pony and trap the next morning, to apply to the union house for a couple of workers.

During his absence, his wife became quite agitated. 'Aah'm not too sure Aah wants a lass in t'ouse,' she confided to Tamar. 'What if we don't like her?'

'That'll be her bad luck, not oors.' Tamar could be quite hard, her mother reflected. 'Look at it this way, Mam. We're giving her a home and it's up to her to make us like her. If she doesn't suit us, we can always take her back and get another.'

As far as Tamar was concerned, that was how things stood.

Annie continued to worry until she heard the pony's hooves on the road, just before dinnertime. Unwilling to wait until her husband brought the girl in, she opened the door and stood on the step, watching as they dismounted from the trap.

'This 'ere's Tobias. Aah'll just tek him along to Mrs Weald's,' said Jonadab, as he motioned with his head for the boy to follow him. 'And that's Lydia,' as he hooked his thumb towards the girl.

Annie eyed the girl for a moment. She was small and slight with lank brown hair. Her eyes were bright and dark and moved uneasily before Annie's, like a frightened animal.

'Oh, dear,' Annie thought, 'she doesn't look to have much work in her.' However, the child was obviously nervous in the unfamiliar surroundings and Annie's warm heart was touched.

'Come in, Lydia.' She led the way into the kitchen and the child picked up her bundle and trailed behind.

The meal that followed was awkward. No one quite knew how to behave towards the girl, and felt constrained about discussing family business in front of her. Consequently, the conversation was spasmodic and stilted.

When the men had gone back out to work, Tamar ladled water from the side boiler by the fire into the enamel washing-up bowl.

'Just leave it a minute, Tamar,' said her mother. 'Come here and let us have a little talk with Lydia.'

As they all sat round the table, Annie explained who the members of the family were and about Joseph, Beth and Ann who no longer lived at home. She was doing her best to make Lydia feel at ease.

'Now then, and what about you?' she enquired kindly.

Lydia was ten and only just old enough to come out to service. 'Aah knows t'Maister wanted one o' t'bigger lasses, but they're all younger than me an' not old enough to go ti work,' she apologised. 'Aah'm only little but Aah can work, Missus,' she went on. 'Aah've been in t'workhouse since me mam died when Aah was seven, an' we had ti work there.'

'You must call me Mrs Oaks,' corrected Annie, and determined there and then that Lydia would not be sent back if she proved to be anything like suitable.

As it turned out, once she had overcome her initial nervousness, Lydia proved an asset to the household. Though small, she was wiry and was a conscientious worker. Little Molly Waind adored her and a lot of Lydia's time was spent caring for the child. All her untapped source of love was focused on her mistress and she constantly sought ways to save Annie work, by anticipating her needs.

Unfortunately, Tobias proved to be a bad choice. Jonadab had selected him because he was a big lad for his twelve years, but he was slow and clumsy, always needing to be chivvied to get on with his work.

'He never sees a job,' Jonadab often grumbled to anyone within earshot. This was true enough. When one task was completed, Tobias never used his own initiative, but always needed direction. His presence on the farm irritated Jonadab, who often threatened to take him back to the union house; which threat usually galvanised him into action sufficiently to mollify his master, until he slipped back into lethargy.

Although he would never have admitted it, Jonadab, who was now in his mid-fifties, was troubled by rheumatism in his right shoulder. Considering this to be a weakness in a man who was still in his prime, he refused to acknowledge the pain. Gritting his teeth, he worked as he had always done, lifting and forking with the rest of the workforce.

One hot, sultry day in June, he was faced with a dilemma. Walking round the hayfields the previous evening, he had noted that the buttercups had shed their petals. This was a sure sign that the hay was ready for cutting. He realised that his shoulder would never allow him to swing a scythe, and yet he was determined that nobody should know of what, in his mind, he regarded as a temporary inconvenience.

'Thoo'd better start cutting t'Long Meadow today, George,' he announced, as he rose from the breakfast table.

'Won't you be leading t'mowers, Faither?' George was amazed. This was the master's privilege, by tradition, and for his father not to stride out ahead of the rest, setting the pace, seemed unthinkable.

'No. Aah wants ti ride over ti Cherry Tree Farm for a word with James Waring.'

George knew better than to question him, but no matter what his father's business was with their neighbour, it could surely have waited. He glanced at his mother, but she looked as puzzled as he felt, so she obviously was not in her husband's confidence.

'Anyroad,' Jonadab continued, 'it won't hurt thee ti lead 'em out. If thoo intends ti have thi own farm, thoo'd better get practising.'

Since his revelation about his relationship with Elizabeth, none of the family had broached the subject again. Every time he met one of the Butlers, he expected them to remark on the subject but Elizabeth must have kept her own counsel, as her family continued to treat him as coolly as they had done since his night in the cells.

Although he had received many letters from her, Elizabeth had not been back since her departure to Leeds the previous December and this was a source of worry to George. He longed to see her and was tortured by the idea that she had met someone else and could not bring herself to tell him.

Despite his perplexity at Jonadab's decision to be absent from the hay-cutting, George was flattered to be entrusted with the job of being in charge. He smiled wryly to himself as he glanced across at his brother. Jonna had caught him up a year or two ago when he finally swung his scythe with the mowers, but George was now promoted above him again.

When his sons had made their way to Long Meadow with the hired men, Jonadab sat for a few moments in deep thought. He had heard a rumour that things were going badly for his neighbour, Jim Waring. Certainly, farming was becoming less profitable with the influx of cheaper grain from the New World.

Jonadab, however, had great faith in his own farming ability and the hard work of his two sons, feeling sure that he would manage to survive when smaller farms were going under.

'Waring's sixty-four acres would just build my farm up nicely,' he thought to himself. He had confided his plans to no one, not even his wife, but he had already decided that, if Jim Waring intended to relinquish his tenancy next Lady Day, he would approach the landlord in good time with a view to taking it over. If the farm was not paying, it might prove difficult for Sir Francis Sturdy to attract a new tenant. Many moorland farms were already left empty and falling into dereliction, due to the slump in agriculture. Jonadab had diversified, and had confidence in his ability to weather the storm. His venture, the heavy horse breeding, was proving a success, with a constant demand for his young stock.

'You can't have too many irons in the fire,' he often told his sons, and he believed this to be sound advice.

Having settled on an excuse for not swinging a scythe, he strode to the paddock gate and called for Topper. After taking her back to the stable to saddle, he set off down the valley. He often boasted that he would never ask his men to do anything that he himself could not do better, or faster, and he had no intention of being humiliated by the offending shoulder.

'Anyroad,' he thought as he mounted and moved off, 'it'll not hurt to have a word and see how the wind blows at Cherry Tree Farm.'

The day was sultry and as they moved briskly down the road, both Jonadab and the horse were beset by flies. In vain, he swiped at them with his hand as he jogged along. As the oppressive heat caused perspiration to course down his face, the flies

226

became ever more worrisome, buzzing round his head in a constant swarm.

'Get out, drat thi!' he exclaimed, as he wafted ineffectually at them.

The horse too, became restive, flicking her tail and tossing her head to try to rid herself of the cloud of insects.

When they reached the gate which separated his land from Waring's, Jonadab dismounted to open it and lead the horse through. Each time he passed through this gate, his thoughts went to Maria and he was overcome by a wave of grief.

He unfastened the latch with one hand as he held the reins loosely with the other, scanning the sky anxiously, wondering whether the oppressive heat was the sign of a storm. The moment's hesitation cost him dear! The reins were suddenly jerked from his hand as the horse, tormented beyond endurance by the flies, flicked her head and lashed out at them with her back legs.

'Whoa! Whoa!' Jonadab shouted as he lunged forward to retrieve the reins. Topper, however, swung round to try to rid herself of the flies, and her head caught Jonadab on the shoulder, causing him to lose his balance and stumble. As he toppled, the horse's back legs came down, the hooves catching Jonadab across his thigh. He crashed to the ground as the searing pain shot through his leg. For a split second, he thought he was going to vomit, but then blackness engulfed him and he slipped into unconsciousness.

When Jonadab opened his eyes, he could hardly focus them, so sickening were the waves of pain, not only from his broken leg but also from his back which he seemed to have twisted when he fell so awkwardly. With a groan, he tried to move, but the attempt caused such excruciating pain, that he felt faint once more.

'Thank goodness nobody saw me in a swoon,' was his first thought. He then realised that this was the least of his worries. All his neighbours would be busy haymaking and were unlikely to come along the road. Unless some of the townsfolk or gentry rode along to the healing-well, he would lie there until he was missed at home.

Luckily, Topper was nowhere in view, so Jonadab presumed that the horse had galloped home. He could only hope that the horse would be seen either from the house or hayfield, and that someone would come to investigate. Jonadab closed his eyes and began to pray. 'God is my refuge and strength: a very present help in trouble,' he intoned, as he settled down to wait.

As luck would have it, Jonadab's wait was not as long as he feared. Although Topper arrived at the stableyard before the farmhouse, she had to pass the Wealds' cottage on her way to the stable. Fortunately, Weald's wife Dorcas was peeling potatoes at her kitchen sink in front of the window, when the wild-eyed horse galloped past. Dropping the knife, she ran out, to see the horse turn into the yard and, when Dorcas arrived, she was standing, panting, before her stable door. Quickly, Dorcas ran to the Oaks' house where Annie and the girls were busy preparing the midday meal, the kitchen door standing open because of the heat. They turned, startled, as she ran into the kitchen. 'Why, whatever's wrong?' Annie demanded.

'Oh, Mrs Oaks, t'Maister's horse has come back wi'out him,' she gasped, clutching her heaving chest.

For a few seconds, Annie seemed stunned. She then gathered her wits and issued her orders quickly. 'Tamar, go and bring Topper,' she instructed. 'Martha, run to Long Meadow and get our George. Go on! Be quick about it!' she exclaimed. Turning to the little maid, she said, 'Make Mrs Weald a cup of tea, Lydia, and then fill t'kettle up and put it back on t'hob.'

Dorcas Weald was a big woman, 'built for comfort, not speed', as Jonadab often said. Now she sat slumped in a chair, holding her mug of tea with shaking hands clasped round it. It was obvious that the run up the road from her own cottage had been too much for her. 'Aah hopes there's nowt amiss,' she kept repeating.

Annie concentrated on the midday meal, realising that no matter what happened, those who were working must eat. 'I'm afraid Mr Oaks must have taken a tumble,' she answered. She could not understand how this could have happened as, like many farmers, Jonadab had ridden since childhood and was as at home in the saddle as on his own feet.

Tamar brought Topper to the door and tied the halter-shank to the bootscraper. 'What can have happened, Mam?' she asked, as she came in.

Annie was quite short when she answered. 'How do I know?' she demanded. Her imagination was running riot, now that Jonadab had not appeared in Topper's wake. It was with relief that she heard the sound of George and Martha's boots on the road, as they ran towards the house.

'Don't worry, Mam. I'll ride down to Waring's, and see what's happened. Topper maybe just got free and came home,' George said from the doorway. He then freed the horse, mounted and rode off quickly down the valley.

In his heart, he realised that the explanation he had given his mother could not be true, as if his father *had* reached Waring's, the gates across the road would have been fastened behind him. Whatever had happened must be between their buildings and the first gate.

As he approached it, his heart sank as he saw his father's shape huddled in the road. 'Oh, God. Let him be alive,' he whispered to himself, as he approached. He quickly dismounted and bent over the body. Jonadab's eyes were closed, but his lips were moving. 'Faither, Faither,' George said.

Jonadab opened his painfilled eyes, and focused them with difficulty. 'George,' he whispered, 'don't move me, lad. Mi leg's broke.' He winced, and then went on, 'Mi back's bad an' all.' The effort to make these statements was almost too much for him and his eyes closed once more.

George realised that there was nothing he could do alone. 'Don't worry,' he comforted, 'Aah'll be back before you know it.'

He swiftly remounted and went back to the farm. Realising that his brother, Jonna, was the only other capable of riding expertly and quickly, he despatched him to Kirkbymoorside for the doctor. 'Tell him it's urgent. Faither's leg's broke and his back's hurt,' George urged as his brother rode off.

While Bert Weald yoked one of the big greys into a flat rulley, George got the two farm lads to help him to lift a door off its hinges and load it on to the dray.

Tamar ran from the house with two blankets. 'If he's hurt bad, Mam says, pad t'door with one and cover him with t'other,' she puffed as she passed them up on to the rulley.

Tobias hung about, getting in the way, until George felt like shouting. However, realising that the boy only wanted to help, he said, 'Go in and tell Mrs Oaks to put two oven shelves in t'Maister's bed. He must be kept warm, even though it's a hot day.' He realised that his mother would not need to be told, but it was a way of making Tobias feel useful.

After tea, in winter, the oven shelves were

wrapped in pieces of old blanket and placed in the beds to warm them before bedtime. George knew that his mother would do as he asked, no matter how garbled a tale Tobias told.

When they reached Jonadab, the door was placed in the road as close to him as possible. George then organised the men to raise him with as little disturbance as they could, and place him gently on it. The door was then carefully lifted and placed on the rulley.

Throughout this procedure, not a sound escaped Jonadab's gritted teeth, although his face was ashen and sweat stood out on his forehead.

George then coaxed Rosie to move off as smoothly as possible, while the three farmworkers steadied their master, keeping him motionless on the door.

Once home, they soon realised that there was no way the sick man could be carried up the stairs, so the door was placed on the parlour floor. Annie and Tamar painstakingly undid his boots and gaiters, drawing them off with as little movement as possible.

Before long, the doctor arrived. He confirmed that Jonadab's thigh was broken, but his back, fortunately, was merely badly twisted. Turning to Annie, he said, 'Have you a pair of good scissors? I shall have to cut his trousers off.'

Jonadab's eyes opened. 'What?' he demanded weakly. 'These is mi best britches, and Aah'll not have 'em cut!'

'Come along, Oaks. Don't be foolish, man. It will be agonising for you if we pull them off,' remonstrated the doctor.

'Aah'll manage ti bear it. It'll be more agonising if Aah've ti have a new pair o' breeches made,' and with that, he sank back, exhausted.

Annie Oaks was discomfited that her husband should argue with a doctor, but Jonadab was adamant and Annie had to call George to help her remove his father's breeches.

The doctor set the leg and bound it in wooden splints. 'This will be a long job,' he warned. 'The thighbone is the largest bone in the body, and will take some weeks to set.' Turning to Annie, he went on: 'Get your sons to lift him on to the sofa. He must stay here, Mrs Oaks, until I say that he can move.'

He gave Annie a small bottle. 'Put a few drops of Laudanum in water for him, if the pain gets too bad to bear, but be careful. It is very dangerous stuff and must be used sparingly.'

In the kitchen there was consternation. They could not imagine life on the farm, nor within the family, proceeding smoothly without Jonadab's direction. Both his family and the farmworkers were so used to his dominance that they could not imagine what would happen without his presence to oversee their every move.

George was to prove, both now and during his father's enforced idleness, that he was a true son of Jonadab. He took charge quietly, but firmly, and was so capable and appeared so self-assured that his authority was never questioned.

Each evening, after the day's work was done, he went into the parlour and told his father in detail what work had been done that day and his proposals for the next day.

Although Jonadab was sorely frustrated and often became tetchy and short-tempered, he respected George's ability, realising that he had grown into a responsible man and a good farmer.

'A true Oaks, he is,' he often thought to himself. To his wife, he exclaimed with pride: 'A chip of t'owd block, oor George is.'

Annie agreed, but remembered all the times tha

George and Joseph had been condemned by their father for taking after their mother's side. She smiled to herself, but made no comment. Jonadab was difficult enough to cope with, confined as he was to the parlour sofa, without being rubbed up the wrong way.

CHAPTER NINETEEN

A few days after Jonadab's accident, the men were
once again out working in Long Meadow, raking the
dry hay into haycocks. George was anxious that this
should be completed before nightfall, and was driving himself and his workforce as hard as he knew
that they would have been driven, had his father
been in charge. The afternoon 'lowance had already
been taken when he paused and leaned on his
wooden rake to survey the field and calculate how
long it would take them to finish.

As he passed his forearm across his dripping brow,
he glanced towards the road that led through the
dale. For a moment he stood as though transfixed,
unable to believe his eyes. He half-closed his lids to
see more clearly through the heat haze.

'It is!' he murmured out loud. 'It's Elizabeth!'
Dropping his hayrake, he ran across the field to the
gate, reaching it just as Elizabeth did. Looking at
her radiant face, he knew that his fears had been
groundless and that her love for him was as strong
as ever.

'Oh, my little love,' he said, as he seized her hands
across the gate.
'Why didn't you write and tell me that you were
coming?' He was overwhelmed by the strength of
his feelings. He ached to sweep her into his arms
and cover her with kisses. He was, however, only
too conscious of the curious glances of the haymakers
and the grin on his brother's face.

'I was not sure that Uncle Nathan would be able

234

to spare me until the last minute. As it is, I've only come for two days.'

George feasted his eyes on her. Elizabeth was wearing the same apricot-coloured muslin gown which she had worn at Mary's wedding, over four years ago, although he did not realise this. He only knew that she was beautiful and she still loved him.

'Mi faither's had an accident and is laid up,' he said. 'I'm in charge,' he added shyly.

Elizabeth gently disengaged her hands from his strong, brown ones, which were grasping hers so tightly as to be painful.

'Go down to t'house and talk to mi Mam and t'lasses,' he urged. 'Aah'll be back as soon as Aah can and when Aah've done tonight, Aah'll walk thi home.' Poor George! He had been trying so hard, in Elizabeth's absence, to improve his speech, but his excitement at seeing her had driven him back into the strong dales dialect.

'Oh, George,' whispered Elizabeth, 'if only I could stay with you, and not go back to Leeds.'

'You can, you can!' he exclaimed hoarsely. 'We can be wed whenever you want.'

'No. I gave my word to Uncle Nathan that I'd stay two years as his housekeeper, until Christiana's old enough to take my place,' she said reluctantly. 'Besides, Uncle pays me a wage and, as my keep is provided, I'm able to bank it all for when we're married.'

'That day can't come too soon for me, love. Aah wish it could be tomorrow,' he said fervently, as he squeezed her hands again.

'Get yourself back to work, George Oaks,' she laughed, 'and stop trying to make a young lady blush.'

'Aah'll see thi at tea-time,' he called, as he returned to his work.

The rest of the afternoon seemed to fly past and the last haycock was made just as Tamar came to call them in for tea.

'Good!' grunted George, as he and Jonna walked companionably across the field towards the house. 'We shan't have this to finish tonight.' He looked with pride at the rows. 'Aah wish as how Faither could see it,' he said regretfully.

'Aye. It'd do his heart good,' agreed his brother.

When they entered the kitchen and began to wash at the sink, George was surprised to see no sign of Elizabeth.

'Where's Elizabeth?' he asked, glancing round.

'In t'parlour, talking to your Faither,' his mother answered. 'Take in his tea and tell her how it's ready in here.' Her tone was so acid that he looked at her curiously. She flushed and turned away.

'She doesn't like Elizabeth,' George thought with incredulity. How anyone could fail to care for his beloved was utterly beyond his understanding.

He could not know that, deep in his mother's heart, she blamed Mary Butler for taking away Joseph, her eldest son. Now Mary's sister had ensnared George, and his mother could only regard it as an older woman setting out to catch a younger man, when she was left on the shelf.

Taking the tin tray, laid out with his father's tea, George pushed open the parlour door. He was relieved to find his father and Elizabeth deep in conversation and that Jonadab was actually smiling. This was the first time since his accident that he had shown any lightness of spirit. It seemed to George, therefore, that his father must have a liking for Elizabeth, even if his mother had none.

'Go get thi tea, lass, and then come back and talk ti mi, while oor George helps wi' t'stock,' he instructed, as he picked up the knife and fork to tackle his tea.

Round the kitchen table, the atmosphere was strained. Most of the conversation was led by Elizabeth, who worked hard to include everybody in her remarks. Little Molly Waind chattered away but Tamar and Martha, sensing their mother's disapproval of the visitor, held back at first. Annie Oaks was civil but nothing more, so that Elizabeth was forced to rack her brains to find topics of conversation.

As for George, he was bewildered. Ever since he had realised that his love for Elizabeth was returned, he had daydreamed about the time that she would live in his home, as part of the family. Now here she was and instead of welcoming her, his mother was stony-faced and monosyllabic. The food stuck in his throat and he felt unable to take part in the talk.

'What's it like in Leeds?' asked Tamar suddenly. She envied Elizabeth's city life and felt that she would do anything to escape from the dale.

This gave Elizabeth her chance to talk to all of them. In her descriptions of a world beyond their ken, she was careful not to sound superior. Gradually, she got them laughing at the tales told against herself and at her ignorance when she had first gone to live in Leeds. Even her hostess went so far as to allow her face to break into a smile, once or twice. Eventually, when Elizabeth said, 'Oh, Mrs Oaks, you must give me your chutney recipe. It's the best I've ever tasted,' Annie visibly relaxed and responded to the flattery by offering to give Elizabeth a jar to take back to Leeds.

By the time that George and Jonna went out to help with the bedding-down and foddering-up, the womenfolk round the table were 'clacking like a gaggle o' geese', as Jonadab would have said.

When Tamar brought out her father's tray and took him another mug of tea, he said, 'Tell that lass to come back here and talk ti mi.'

'Don't you mean, "ask her", Faither?' Tamar pertly chided.

Jonadab's brows drew together over the piercing blue eyes. 'Tell! Ask! It makes no difference,' he protested. 'I want her to come and sit wi' mi, so that's that.'

Tamar smiled. Her father would never change. He demanded implicit obedience from all his household and employees but somehow, Tamar thought that in Elizabeth, he'd met his match.

As George and Jonna walked towards the stables, Jonna said, almost shyly: 'Aah'm sorry Aah said she were old, George. Aah'd never really looked at her. She's real bonnie, and clever an' all,' he apologised.

George was grateful to his brother, realising what it had cost the younger lad to say it. Like his father, whom he resembled so greatly, Jonna found it hard to admit being wrong.

When George got washed and changed his shirt, ready to walk Elizabeth home, his mother felt that she should protest. After all, it was not seemly for a couple to be alone before they were married. Indeed, look at their Joe and Mary Butler . . .

Before they set off, she went into the parlour to speak to her husband. 'He's walking her home!' she expostulated.

'Well?' demanded Jonadab.

'It isn't right. Shall I send young Jonadab with 'em?' she suggested.

'They'll have learned from Joseph's mistake,' comforted her husband. 'He's got his head screwed on right, has oor George. She has an' all,' he added. Seeing his wife's worried expression, he went on, 'Them as wants to sin'll sin. They'll find time and t'opportunity, never fear. Them two has got more sense.' So saying, he leaned back and closed his eyes, as if to dismiss his wife.

As the couple went towards the door, Annie glanced at the clock. Elizabeth followed her eyes and realising that she intended to time George's absence said, 'We shall tell my parents of our betrothal tonight, Mrs Oaks, so George may be a little late back.' With which statement she led the way to the door, where she paused to say 'Goodnight,' all round, before preceding George outside.

They set off in comfortable silence, no words being necessary to express their pleasure in being together. As they started up the hill, she slipped her arm into his. George took her hand and studied it.

'Such a little hand,' he whispered, 'and yet it holds my heart.' Elizabeth felt rather surprised at this statement from the practical George. 'Come and sit down a few minutes.' He led her by the hand into the trees at the side of the road.

As they sank into the fragrant bracken, George ran his finger along the line of her chin and moved it caressingly on her neck.

'You're so lovely,' he whispered. 'We can't wait another eighteen months to be married.'

'We must, George. I've explained it to you,' she insisted.

'Your Christie's nearly nineteen. Many a girl's in service at twelve. Why can't she go to Leeds?' He was almost sulky. While Elizabeth had been beyond his reach, he was content to wait patiently for her return. Now that she was here beside him, however, the urgency of his love was beyond endurance.

'George, darling, please try to understand.' She took both his hands in hers and gazed into his eyes. 'As I've told you, Uncle is a wealthy man with a large draper's shop in Briggate, one of the main

239

shopping streets. It's not a maid he wants – we
have two. He needs a housekeeper to see that the
household runs smoothly, and, also, a hostess for
when he entertains guests. A girl of Christie's inexperience just couldn't cope.'

'Well, how is she going to get experience?' he
demanded. 'How's she going to learn to cope?' He
suddenly looked deep into her eyes. 'You're not
having me on? You do really love me, don't you,
Elizabeth?'

Her eyes brimmed over with tears. 'How can you
doubt me, George?' she murmured, taking his face
between her hands. 'You know I love you,' she whispered fiercely, as she pressed her lips to his. The
strength of her passion was a revelation to George.
He eased her down into the ferns and rained kisses
on her eyes, the tip of her nose, her chin and, finally,
her lips.

'Oh, Elizabeth,' he breathed, 'you're more to me
than all the world. I love you! Only God knows how
much I love you.'

Elizabeth trembled as she drew him closer, and
returned his kisses with an ardour which left her
shaken.

It was not the first physical contact between them
but they were unprepared for the desire which swept
through them. George buried his face in her hair,
whispering in her ears and nibbling the lobes. She
was swept away in ecstasy and felt that their hunger
for each other must be assuaged. She made no protest as George started to unbutton her bodice and
began to kiss the creamy softness of her breasts as
they rose above the whiteness of her camisole.

Elizabeth showered kisses on his hair, and passed
her hands down his muscular back, before tightening
her arms around him, fiercely. Their bodies were

pressed together until she felt that she could hardly breathe and yet, she could not let him go.

George felt as though his entire body was about to explode with love. He had yearned and waited for Elizabeth ever since he had reached manhood, but he had never envisaged a feeling such as the one which now engulfed him. His wait was over. Elizabeth lay, willing, in his arms.

As he pulled at the ribbons which would totally lay bare her breasts, Elizabeth seemed to bring herself back with a colossal effort.

'George! George! No!' she cried, struggling in his arms. The strength of George's desire would brook no refusal and he ignored her protests, holding her close. 'No, please, George. This is madness,' she insisted, 'we must control ourselves.'

He released her so suddenly that she fell back. As Elizabeth looked up into his face, so dear and so considerate, her thoughts travelled back to her encounter with Sir William Forster. He would never have answered her pleas to be released . . . She would have been only too willing to succumb to George, until commonsense overcame her passion. George's desire sprang from true love and it had been surmounted by his wish to please her.

George, meanwhile, was overcome with embarrassment. Could she ever forgive him, he wondered miserably. 'I'm sorry, Elizabeth. Please, please forgive me,' he said huskily. 'I don't know what came over me.'

'The same passion that overcame me,' she said, as she hurriedly fastened her buttons. 'We placed ourselves in the way of temptation and it nearly overcame us. At any rate, George, you can never again doubt the strength of my love for you.' She smiled tremulously. 'We know, now, what awaits us when we do get married.'

To George, robbed of the ultimate culmination of his desire, this was but little consolation. He had to admit, however, that he felt relieved when Elizabeth brought their lovemaking to a halt before they'd gone too far. He couldn't bear the thought of folk sniggering if Elizabeth had become pregnant.

Their walk up the hill and on to Fadmoor was passed in near-silence. George walked with his arm round her shoulders and, just before they entered the village, they stopped to inspect each other, to remove any telltale fronds of bracken. Elizabeth tidied her hair as best she could and they continued on their way to the Butlers' farm.

Elizabeth had not confided to her family about her understanding with George, and they expressed their surprise. Her parents, indeed, showed a marked lack of enthusiasm for the forthcoming wedding. It had been obvious for some years that they were 'partial to each other' as her father put it, but the Butlers were still upset by George's apparently violent and unprovoked attack on Sir William.

Mrs Butler had always expected Elizabeth to remain unmarried and look after her parents in their old age but, even after Jane's wedding, which was to take place in the following spring, there would be Christiana and Sarah left at home. Perhaps one of them would remain an old maid, she consoled herself. Upon reflection, however, she realised that all her girls were attractive and that she would probably be in the care of Jack's wife when she became too old to run the house. 'If he ever gets round to choosing a wife,' she thought, glancing across at her son.

Jack, the Butlers' only boy, was a couple of years older than George, to whom he was now talking animatedly. He was telling George of a recent letter he'd had from Joseph, and how well the couple were doing in Canada.

George was surprised. His parents usually received a couple of letters a year from Joseph, which they exchanged with the Butlers, for those which they had received from Mary. This way, both families were kept up to date with the news. George had not known that Joseph wrote to Jack Butler, and felt a little piqued that his brother had never written to him, personally.

After having a cup of tea with Elizabeth's family, he got up to go. 'I'd better be off,' he said. 'I can't be too late ti bed. We've another field to rake into cocks, yet, before we've finished.'

As he held Elizabeth in his arms by the gate, he kissed her tenderly, not wanting to arouse passion in either of them. 'When will you come home again?' he asked.

'I can't say, George,' she answered. 'I had hoped that Uncle would come home with me for two days at Christmas, but I haven't managed to persuade him, yet. He doesn't like the country.'

'Not like the country? What is there to dislike?' He could not understand how anyone could dislike the country. Elizabeth laughed. Remembering George's wonderment at the size of Whitby, she wondered what he would think of Leeds.

With a heavy heart, George held her close. He had been quite resigned to the wait of two years, when they had first planned to marry. Now, after the bliss of their lovemaking in the wood, he was miserable at the thought of life without her.

Elizabeth gently disengaged herself from his arms. She stretched on tiptoe and took his face in her hands, looking earnestly at his features and into the steady, brown eyes.

'Sometimes when I'm away, I can't recall your face and it upsets me,' she said. 'I must impress it on my mind, George, so that I only need to close my eyes and it's there.'

George swallowed hard and gazed back at her beseechingly. 'I've loved you since the first time I set eyes on you,' he whispered. 'Please come back soon and wed me, Elizabeth.'

She kissed him lightly on the lips and then drew back before he could sweep her once more into his arms. 'You must go, George. I'll write to you as soon as I get back to Leeds. I'm due to set off on tomorrow's stage-coach. Never forget this evening and how much I love you. You'll find that the weeks and months will fly,' she promised.

George turned away, his heart full and his eyes moist. Suddenly, he turned. 'I'll come and see you off,' he offered eagerly.

'No,' she answered reluctantly. 'You can't leave the farm, especially with your father laid up. Prove that he can trust you, George, to run the farm as he would do himself.'

With that, she turned and walked briskly into the house. Before rejoining the family in the kitchen, she stood with her back pressed against the scullery door, to regain her composure. She knew that her face was flushed and could feel her heart beating so fiercely that she imagined it could be heard aloud. Elizabeth had had plenty of suitors in her time, but had never known that she was capable of such passion as George had aroused in her.

George strode out for home, his thoughts in a tumult. He realised that, if it had not been for her strong will, the power of their love would have driven them too far. How often had his father instilled into his children that the road to wrongdoing was a wide and pleasant one? Since Joseph's fall from grace, Jonadab had often urged his flock to choose the narrow and twisted path and here was

George, a hair's-breadth from what he realised to be sinful conduct.

Even though his marriage to Elizabeth was more than a year away, and his sadness at the parting had filled him with gloom, he was of a cheerful nature, and was soon determined to make the best of the long absence by concentrating on the time when they would be reunited.

'I'm a lucky chap,' he thought, as he recalled with longing the feel of Elizabeth in his arms. 'Time'll soon pass, if I fill it with hard work.'

When he reached home, his mother was still sitting beside the fire with her knitting, although the others had gone to bed.

After George and Elizabeth's departure, Annie Oaks had gone into the parlour and poured out to Jonadab all her reservations about her son's choice of a wife. 'She's getting on for thirty!' she had concluded.

Her husband frowned and the blue eyes bored into her. 'She's a good catch, woman. Make no mistake about that,' he answered forcefully. 'Oor George is lucky to get such a wife. She's all her buttons on and will see 'e's all right. She might come in for a bit o' brass from yon Uncle i' Leeds, but that's neither 'ere nor there. She'll make t'lad a good wife, so you'll make an effort to welcome 'er into oor family when t'time comes.' With which admonition he had closed his eyes and left her to return to the kitchen, feeling hurt at his lack of support.

However, as she thought over the events of the afternoon and realised how hard Elizabeth had worked to overcome what Annie could only acknowledge to be rudeness on her part, her attitude softened.

When George entered the kitchen, she raised her

head from her knitting and greeted him with a smile. 'Now, lad, how about a cup of tea?' she asked.

'I had one up at t'Butlers', thanks,' he replied. 'I'll just have a drink of milk before I go up.' He rose and, taking a pint pot from a hook on the dresser, he went into the dairy. Coming back, he sat in a wooden fireside chair, opposite his mother.

'I love her, you know, Mam. I always have.' As he spoke, he looked at her pleadingly.

Annie leaned forward and placed a hand on his knee. 'If she's your choice, George, she's mine,' she declared, adding, 'Don't worry, lad. Your wife'll be made as welcome here as I was, when I came.'

Relief flowed over George and, as he rose to go to bed, he leaned over and kissed his mother's forehead. 'Thanks, Mam,' he said.

It was the first kiss he'd given his mother since he became a man, and Annie realised that her change of attitude towards Elizabeth was appreciated and was thankful that she'd made the effort.

As George slipped between the sheets, he reflected on the day. It had started unpromisingly as a routine working day but had ended as one of the most momentous of his life. He drifted off with his thoughts filled with Elizabeth's presence and seemed to hear her whispering his name, as he fell asleep.

CHAPTER TWENTY

The day after Elizabeth's departure to Leeds, Jonadab called George into the parlour, before he went back into the hayfields after dinner.

'Can thoo spare Toby this afternoon?' demanded his father.

'Aye, Faither. We s'll finish cocking t'hay today and in any case, we get on as quick wi'out him as with him,' he chuckled.

Jonadab sighed and made an uncharacteristic admission. 'Aah doubts he was a bad choice. Anyroad,' he went on, 'send him down t'dale to James Waring's, and ask James to come and have a word with me, when he's got time.'

'Aye, that I will,' answered George, as he went out.

What could be his father's business with Waring, he reflected, remembering that his father's accident had occurred on the way to Cherry Tree Farm. 'Anyroad, it's nowt to do with me,' he thought, as he sent Tobias on his errand. The rest of the afternoon was spent in the task of raking the last field up into haycocks, and as George's mind was too full of daydreams about Elizabeth Butler to concern itself with his father's business, he thought no more about Tobias' errand to Waring's farm.

The following Sunday afternoon, however, James and Minnie Waring strolled up the valley on a very rare visit to their neighbours. While James was closeted in the parlour, his wife stayed in the kitchen with Annie Oaks and the rest of the family. George considered this, but could see no reason why his father should wish to speak privately to James Waring. The families were good neighbours, but not close friends.

When George and Jonna returned to the house in the evening, after attending to the stock, their mother glanced up from her knitting. 'Thi faither wants a word with you both,' she announced. As they dried their hands, they looked at each other. George shook his head in answer to the question in his brother's eyes. He could think of no way in which they could have incurred their father's displeasure. The haymaking had gone well and the men had worked hard under George's direction. Nevertheless, as they entered the parlour, each had a leaden feeling in the pit of his stomach.

As they approached the sofa, Jonadab eased himself into a more comfortable position. On the small table beside him was a sealed document together with the ink and a quill pen.

'Now then, what's on tomorrow, George?' he demanded.

'There's t'turnips to second and t'corn to luke,' answered George. 'There's plenty to do, Faither, never fear.' He thought his father had formed the opinion that without him to oversee them, they were slacking.

'Aye, well, thoo can dole t'jobs out and see to everything tomorrow, Jonadab,' he said to his youngest son. Young Jonna glowed with pleasure. He could not believe that he alone was to be entrusted to run the farm, even for a day.

George felt even more uneasy. Was he to be demoted in favour of his younger brother? He could not for the life of him imagine any way in which his work had been beneath the standards set by his father.

Jonadab held up his hand to silence young Jonna's

thanks and assurances that he would live up to his father's confidence in him. 'Hold thi noise!' he cut in. 'Get thissen back to t'kitchen and leave me to talk to George.' Jonna subsided into embarrassed silence and went out, leaving George and his father together.

Jonadab picked up the sealed letter. 'Tomorrow, Aah wants thi to take this letter to Sir Francis Sturdy.'

George was aghast. The Sturdys were gentry and he was nervous at the thought of going to the Towers, Sir Francis' home. Besides, he thought, what if he should meet James Sturdy or his friend, that Forster fellow? It would be far different from an encounter in the dale, if he should bump into them in Sir Francis' own grounds.

Jonadab watched as various expressions passed across George's face. His face always mirrored every emotion that he felt, deep inside and not for the first time did his father reflect that he could read George like a book. He was the only one of Jonadab's children whom their father believed to be entirely open. 'But is he?' wondered Jonadab, remembering how George had concealed the fact that he and Elizabeth Butler were to marry.

Suddenly, realising that his father was watching him, George looked uncomfortable. 'Will it be all right, me going to t'Towers and asking to see him?' he queried.

'Aye. Just ask t'manservant if you can see Sir Francis. If 'e's out, or not available, leave t'letter, but Aah'd rather have an answer as soon as we can. Try ti see 'im,' he urged.

George still felt uneasy at the thought of visiting the Towers, but realised that it was important to his father, so determined to face up to it. 'You can depend on me, Faither, to see him if at all possible,' he assured him and picked up the document and went out.

Jonna looked at him with curiosity when he re-entered the kitchen. 'What's up? You look as if you've lost a penny and found a farthing,' he asked, looking at George's face.

'I've a letter to take to t'Towers to Sir Francis,' he answered. 'After hitting Sir William, Master James' pal, I can't say as how I'm too keen to go.'

Their mother could not help but hear their exchange. 'You've done nowt to be ashamed of,' she declared stoutly. 'Sir Francis is a good man and won't hold ought against thi.'

Although consumed with curiosity, the family could not think of any reason why Jonadab should send a letter to his landlord.

'He's a close man,' mused Annie Oaks. 'He never discusses his business, even wi' me.'

As George rode up out of the dale the following morning, his heart was heavy. Not only did he feel nervous at visiting the 'big house' but he was not happy to leave the farm for the best part of a day. He chided himself that this was unfair to his brother who was, after all, now seventeen.

It was a balmy morning, not too hot and yet the air was clear and the sun bright. His spirits rose as his horse trotted along at a brisk pace, once the hill out of the dale had been surmounted.

With no farmwork to occupy his mind, George allowed his thoughts to dwell lovingly on Elizabeth. He imagined them living in his parents' farmhouse down in Sleightholmedale, as his sister Ann and John Waind had done. He was sure that his mother would welcome Elizabeth once they were married.

Slowing his pace as he passed through Kirkbymoorside, he exchanged greetings with many acquaintances. As his thoughts were deflected from Elizabeth, he considered the work of the farm. It would be time to sell the lambs in a week or two, and George decided that, on his way back, he would call in at the bank and draw out enough money to buy some of his father's lambs. His bank balance had built up nicely through his pig-breeding and dealing and he wanted to branch out and increase his savings before his marriage.

The further George rode, the less he urged the horse, until it was merely dawdling through the lanes. What if he should encounter William Forster come to visit his friend? It would be bad enough meeting James Sturdy, but the thought of coming face to face with the man for whom he felt an implacable hatred brought beads of perspiration to George's upper lip. His whole body suddenly burned with fury as Elizabeth's faltering account of the brute's conduct came into his mind.

Unaware that both young noblemen were down in London, various versions of how he would handle a meeting with either, or both of them, ran through his imagination. He felt that he could not avoid hurling himself at Sir William and avenging, not only his intended bride but his sisters Beth and Tamar. However, he determined that he must exercise control for the sake of his father's business with Sir Francis, whatever that might be. 'Aah'll just ride by and ignore 'em,' was his final decision.

With his thoughts thus fully occupied, George was at the gates of the Towers before he realised it. As he rode up the drive, George felt overwhelmed by his surroundings.

Each side of the drive was lined with rhododendron bushes, past their best now, but with sufficient flowers still blooming here and there, to indicate the range of tints and shades – far different from the ordinary wild specimens which grew in the woods at home.

As the house came into view, George was staggered by the sheer size and elegance of it. 'Queen's palace can't be any bigger,' he thought. The nervousness he had felt before was nothing compared to his feelings as he approached the house.

Seeing an archway in the wall which had replaced the shrubs on his right, he turned the horse into what was a large yard surrounded by stables. Dismounting, he tied Topper to a ring in the wall, and then stood, debating with himself what to do next. One half of him felt that he should knock at the back door of the house, which he could see from the stable-yard. However, his father had drilled it into all his offspring that to be an Oaks was something special. 'Tell 'em who you are,' he had always enjoined his flock. Consequently, George walked back from the stable-yard up the drive and mounted the wide steps which led up to the terrace and the elegant front door. If he felt overawed as he stood on the top step and rang the bell, it was nothing to his feeling of inadequacy when the door swung open and he was confronted by Sir Francis Sturdy's butler.

This supercilious-looking individual eyed him disdainfully, with raised eyebrows, before uttering the single word: 'Well?'

George cleared his throat, but his voice still came out on a higher note than usual. 'I wish to see Sir Francis Sturdy on business,' he announced.

'What name may I give Sir Francis?' asked the butler.

'Oaks. George Oaks. Mi faither's one of Sir Francis' tenants at Sleightholmedale.'

The butler stood aside and George stepped into

the hall. 'Wait here. I will see if Sir Francis is available,' he said, as he mounted the stairs.

George looked round him with unashamed curiosity. He had never imagined such luxury and his gaze took in the rich carpets scattered over the marble floor, the oak-panelled walls covered with pictures and the glass-fronted cabinets filled with oriental porcelain.

He suddenly realised that Sir Francis was accompanying the butler down the wide staircase.

'Good morning, Oaks,' he greeted George, as he approached with hand outstretched. George shook hands awkwardly, conscious of the roughness of his hand as it was grasped by the soft one of his host.

'Send a tray into my study, Carson,' Sturdy instructed the butler, as he opened a door and ushered George into a cosy, booklined room.

While Sir Francis read Jonadab's letter, George cautiously sipped his tea from the fragile china cup. 'There was nobbut a swallow in it,' he was to remark to his mother, later.

Sir Francis swiftly penned a reply and impressed the sealing-wax with a seal of his family coat-of-arms. 'There you are, and the best of luck to you, young man,' he said, as he handed it over.

George pondered over the remark as he was shown out by the butler, and most of the way home. Why should Sir Francis wish me luck? 'Happen 'e's heard I'm ti be wed,' he thought.

When he reached home, he found that his father was waiting impatiently for his return. Although it was midafternoon by now and George's dinner had been keeping warm since twelve, Jonadab called out peremptorily as soon as he heard the sound of his son's voice. 'Come in here, George!' he demanded.

As George entered, his father held out his hand. 'Did he send an answer? Didst thoo see him?'

He almost snatched the reply from George and slid his thumb under the seal to break it. As he held the letter towards the window, in order to see it more clearly, George turned to go back to the kitchen and his belated dinner.

'No! Wait!' his father ordered, not looking up. George sighed, but sat down. Even though he was famished, he was used to obeying his father's commands.

Jonadab finished reading the letter and then, with a smile of contentment, sank back on to his pillows. Only then did he turn to look at his son. 'How soon can yon wench finish at Leeds?' he asked.

Reference to Elizabeth was the last thing George expected at that particular moment. In what way could his errand to the Towers concern Elizabeth? Before he could answer, however, his father continued: 'Aah'm taking over Waring's farm and Aah wants you and 'er to live in t'house. We'll run t'land in wi' this, but Aah'd want thoo in t'house by Martinmas, when Aah gets possession.'

George could not believe his ears. He had resigned himself to another eighteen months' wait before his marriage and here was his father calmly talking about it taking place in early November of this year! Jonadab continued to amaze his family. Even though he was bedridden with his injuries, he had managed to arrange to take over James Waring's farm.

'I did ask if Elizabeth could leave earlier, but she says their Christie's not up to t'job yet.' George dared not hope that an earlier marriage could be arranged.

'Get thi dinner, lad, and then ride up and ask John Butler if he can come down and have a word wi' me, this evening.' Jonadab looked better than he had done since the accident. His eyes had regained their fire and he had lost the air of apathy which had overtaken him during his enforced idleness. As

George reached the door, his father twisted to look at him. 'George.'

'Aye, Faither?'

'Say nowt to t'Butlers as to what it's about,' cautioned Jonadab.

When George reached the kitchen, his mother clicked her tongue with exasperation as she placed his dinner on the table. 'Doesn't he realise what time it is?' She rarely criticised her husband and never in front of their family, but she knew how hungry George must be by now. 'Anyway, what's it all about?' she asked curiously, as she sat down opposite George.

He hesitated. If his father had not already discussed the plan with his mother, perhaps she too was included in the stricture for secrecy. It was, however, a plan which concerned the whole family so, as he ate his meal, he told his mother the arrangement.

Her face was a study. It was clear she had had no suspicion of Jonadab's scheme. 'It's a bad time for farmers. What if he's ruined? Whatever shall we do?'

She became more agitated as George revealed his father's dealings. 'Oh, dearie me! Oh, dear! Oh, dear!' she repeated, several times. 'What if we lose t'lot?'

'Nay, Mother,' George comforted her. 'Faither's got his head screwed on all right. We shall do well with the extra land.'

Just as George had placated her, he dropped the final blow. 'I've to go up to Butlers when I've had mi dinner. Faither wants me and Elizabeth wed before Martinmas, to live in t'Warings' house. Leastways, it'll be our house,' he added, with sudden wonder.

Annie Oaks stiffened and compressed her lips. She had still clung to the hope that George would meet a younger woman before the time of his marriage arrived. 'We've had one hasty wedding with a Butler. What's folk going to think?' she demanded.

The realisation that if everything went as his father planned, he would be married to Elizabeth in less than five months, had left George's mind in a whirl. 'Who cares what folks think?' he demanded. 'The sooner Elizabeth and me can be wed, the better I'll be pleased.'

His mother sighed. She realised that she had no alternative but to accept Elizabeth Butler into the family, as she had promised to George and Jonadab. She was, however, disappointed that George would not live in the Oaks' home after his marriage.

'Happen it's for t'best,' she consoled herself, recollecting Elizabeth's spirit.

As soon as George had finished eating, he went out to the stable and saddled up Topper again. As he rode from the valley for the second time that day, his thoughts dwelt in admiration upon his father. Even when laid up, with a broken thigh, Jonadab continued to manipulate events and organise the lives of his family.

'By 'eck,' George thought to himself, 'I wonder if Faither can get Elizabeth home to be wed sooner.' He had little doubt that if that was his father's intention, he would be successful. Failure was a word which Jonadab's family never associated with their father. He exuded such confidence that they believed implicitly that whatever he attempted would be successfully concluded.

John Butler agreed, reluctantly, to come down after tea and visit Jonadab. 'I'm in t'midst of haymaking and cannot really spare t'time,' he demurred ungraciously.

'Faither said to tell you it's urgent,' pressed George.

'What's it about then?' Butler passed a 'kerchief over his dripping brow as he leaned on his hayfork.

'Aah can't really say, Mr Butler, sir,' George hedged, as he looked reflectively at the older man whose jowls were so crimson as to be almost purple and whose face was running with sweat.

'Go on then. Tell him I'll come.' He looked across at his son. 'Our Jack can see to things here. They should finish this field tonight.'

'Thank you, Mr Butler,' said George, turning away and crossing to the gate where he'd tied Topper.

As he rode back towards Sleightholmedale, he compared John Butler to his own father. Jonadab's lean, sinewy frame carried not an ounce of fat and he could toil all day with the best of men, thought George proudly, not knowing of his father's troublesome shoulder. 'Faither could work him into 'ground,' mused George. 'Happen he'll be glad to get out of tonight's work.'

Entering the dark, precipitous tunnel of trees which led down into the valley, he allowed the horse to amble at its own pace. As he emerged into the dale, he was disturbed to find that the sky had darkened ominously and the sun was hidden by heavy, almost coppery clouds rolling over the moors.

A click of his tongue and a dig of his heels urged the horse into a trot as George heard the growl and roll of thunder, each rumble louder and closer than the last. Topper snickered nervously and flicked her ears.

Then the rain came!

When the first great spots began to fall, almost lazily, George quickened Topper's gait into a gallop, but before he reached the farm buildings the storm was upon them. A fearsome fork of lightning seemed to split the sky almost above their heads, accompanied by a deafening roll of thunder, which reverberated round the enclosing hills, echoing and re-echoing in a terrifying orchestration of sound.

Although normally the most placid of animals, despite the episode with Jonadab, Topper was now almost uncontrollable. She reared in terror, her front legs pawing the air, as George struggled to stay in the saddle. His ears caught the sound of her frantic whinnies over the tumult of the storm, as she brought her front legs down and kicked out with her back ones.

'Whoa! Whoa, lass!' George stroked the horse's neck and spoke to her soothingly. Under his firm touch, she became calmer, although she still trembled. 'Go on.' George urged her forward again, though they could hardly see through the veil of torrential rain.

The air all around him was sulphurous from the lightning, which actually sizzled along the road. George had never before in his life experienced such a storm. He heard a crash to his rear as a great oak tree was split in two by another great bolt of lightning. Thankfully, he reached the buildings and Topper turned into the yard of her own accord.

George leapt from the horse and they dashed into the stable, to find young Jonna and the farmworkers sheltering there.

'This has made a mess o' t'haymaking,' announced Jonna. 'Luckily, we saw it coming and managed to get back before it began.' He looked at George, who was soaked to the skin, his clothes and hair plastered wetly against him.

George motioned to Tobias. 'Unsaddle Topper and rub her down,' he instructed, 'I'm fair done.' He leaned against a cornbin and ran the back of his hand ineffectually across his soaking forehead.

Suddenly, he stopped and looked around at the

men. 'Sheep'll have to be moved!' he announced. He glanced across at Bert Weald. 'You moved 'em into t'Beck Side field, ready for selling, didn't you?'

'Aye, George,' Weald answered ruefully. 'If t'beck comes up they won't stand a chance. Yon field's too low-lying.'

'Come on, then! It'll take practically all of us,' George decided. 'Stay here, Tobias, and finish Topper. Give her a few oats.'

Jonna looked mutinous. It was all right for George, he thought, he was already soaked. George caught his eye. 'Come on, Jonna, you know how quick t'beck can come up,' he reminded him. 'If we lose just one o' them sheep, I wouldn't be in our shoes when Faither finds out.'

This admonition was enough for young Jonna, who feared their father's wrath.

Although the rain had abated slightly, it was still a heavy downpour and the men were wet through before they had run many yards. As they passed the orchard, George veered across and opened the gate.

'It's t'only place I can think of to put 'em,' he panted, as he ran back alongside Bert Weald.

'They won't be in long. It'll last 'em a day or two,' replied the hind.

When they reached the field, it was to find the flock in a distressed state. They were huddled together in the furthest corner from the gate, milling round in a tight-knit group, giving forth a melancholy bleating. As the men fanned out to approach them, the sheep moved away, still in the restless circle, until they found their way blocked by the field-hedge on one side and the rushing stream with which it formed an angle.

'Hold on a minute!' George had to bawl to make himself heard, as he motioned his men to halt. He could see that in their nervous state, the animals were poised to dash into the water if the men drew any closer.

'We mun turn 'em away from t'beck!' he shouted to his brother. 'Come down along t'bank wi' me and get between 'em and t'water.' He realised that Hodge Beck was now running so swiftly that, if any sheep entered, it would be swept off its feet. Once this happened and the fleece became waterlogged, there was no hope.

Jonna sprinted across to him and the two brothers began to work their way carefully along the water's edge to position themselves between the bank and the sheep.

Bert Weald signalled to the rest of the men to open up a gap between the sheep and the widely-gaping gate, while the sheep moved their heads and swivelled their eyes, trying in vain to keep both lots of men in view.

George had deliberately decided not to bring the dogs, in order to avoid any sudden movement which would excite the sheep even more. Now, as he and Jonna inched their way behind the sheep, cutting them off from the water, he knew, from the squelching beneath his feet, that the beck was already creeping above the bank.

Glancing across to where Jonna was peering back at him through the rain, George nodded and they both gave a great shout and waved their arms. After only a momentary hesitation, the flock surged forward, united in their terror. As they were ushered across the field, Weald placed himself in the lane to cut off their path down the valley.

Halfway across the field, George was satisfied that the sheep were moving well in the right direction. He paused and looked back, to see that the beck was, by now, spilling over: the corner where the sheep had sought refuge was already under water.

'We're only just in time,' he commented to his brother as they trudged together in the wake of the flock.

'Aye. We could easy have lost t'lot,' rejoined Jonna. 'It's a blessing thoo remembered 'em.'

It did not take long to move the little flock along the lane and turn them into the orchard, where the gate was secured behind them.

As soon as they entered the kitchen, their father's voice rang from the parlour. 'Where's thoo been? What's going on?' he demanded impatiently.

'Nay, Jonadab,' remonstrated Annie, 'they're both soaked through. Wait till they've got dry and put fresh clothes on.'

'It's all right, Mam. I'll go.' Young Jonna slipped off his wet boots and went through the parlour door in his equally wet socks. As George mounted the stairs, his brother's voice came to him clearly. 'If it hadn't been for oor George, we'd have lost all yon sheep that's ready for market.' All resentment was forgotten and he was full of admiration for his older brother's quick thinking and leadership.

When George came down to report on his trip to the Butlers, his father grasped his hand. 'Well done, lad.' The praise was appreciated because it was so rarely given. Jonadab expected the family to do their best, both for him and each other, so considered praise unnecessary.

Although the centre of the storm had passed, the rain was still falling steadily. 'I can't see Mr Butler coming down tonight, Faither,' warned George and his prediction proved correct.

Jonadab grew more tetchy and demanding as the evening wore on. He had little Lydia running in and out of the parlour with mugs of tea and snacks all evening and read the previous week's *Malton Messen-*

ger over and over again until, as Annie put it, "'e'll read t'print off it.'

There was, however, no way he could further his plans until he could discuss them with Elizabeth's father. He had, therefore, to try to contain himself in patience until John Butler's visit.

Not for the first time in his life was it brought home to Jonadab that Nature always had the last word . . .

CHAPTER TWENTY-ONE

The following day dawned bright and clear, as though the previous afternoon's tumult had never occurred. George had a word with the hind. 'Let the men get on wi' sorting and mending t'grain sacks, while I have a look round and see what damage has been done,' he instructed.

His first concern was for the sheep in the orchard. To his relief, they were grazing placidly and there was sufficient grass to last them for a few days, giving him time to review the problem. When he reached the narrow Beck Side field, he found it flooded almost to the gate, and it was brought home to him how easily the whole flock could have been lost. George had a sick feeling in the pit of his stomach when he remembered how tempted he had been to go straight home from the Butlers' farm and change into dry clothing.

As he gazed across the expanse of floodwater, he began to worry about the hay crop. Long Meadow, where the men had spent the previous day cocking the hay, also ran alongside Hodge Beck.

George turned from the gate and began to run back down the lane. He checked himself, however, before he reached the farmhouse, realising that his father would be looking out of the parlour window from his bed on the sofa.

'What's done's done,' he thought to himself. 'There's no rush. Nowt can be done to alter it now.' He realised that the sight of him running down the lane would only cause concern, so he put on a jaunty air and raised a hand to his father as he passed.

When he reached the hayfield, the scene of devas
tation was worse than he had feared. More than hal
the haycocks had been swept away and the edge o
the floodwater was lapping the bases of the next row

George leaned on the gate and contemplated the
scene. He dropped his head on to his hands and
heaved a sigh. The loss of much of the hay crop wa
a blow which would cut the farm's profits, just a
Jonadab was hoping to expand.

Gloomily, he turned away and trudged toward
the corner where the bolt of lightning had struck or
his homeward ride. When he rounded the bend, he
saw that the road was completely blocked. The hug
oak tree had been split in two when the lightnin;
struck: the road was filled with half the trunk and
colossal mound of boughs and branches, the debri
from which was scattered over a wide area. Georg
regarded the scene soberly, realising how close h
had been to death.

Before going into the house to relate the catalogu
of calamities to his father, he despatched the men
with Bonnie and Bluebell, to clear the road. 'Dra
it all down to t'stickheap and it can be sawn u
later,' he instructed. 'Thoo might need Rosie an
Violet an' all for t'trunk. Anyhow, you'll see whe
you've shifted t'rest.'

So saying, he went indoors with a heavy heart t
report to his father. Jonadab was upset at the loss c
so much hay, but consoled himself that at least th
sheep had been saved. When George described th
extent of the flooding, his father shook his head i
amazement. 'Hodge Beck's nivver come up as far a
that in all my lifetime. We're lucky it didn't reac
t'house.'

His wife came into the parlour in time to hear th
comment. 'Aye, and if it's happened once, it ca
happen again,' she said, thrusting a pint mug of te

towards her husband. 'Aah dissn't know why thoo wants ti tek over Cherry Tree Farm, Jonadab. We're all right as we are, surely.'

Jonadab's blue eyes flashed with the old fire. 'Nay, woman! Thoo run t'house and leave t'farm ti me,' he protested. His wife gave a sniff and went back to her kitchen. It could not be said that she banged the door, but she shut it firmly behind her.

Jonadab sighed. 'Women nivver wants change,' he complained. 'Aah want thoo ti have t'pigs and t'sheep down yonder and we shall work all t'arable land from 'ere and carry on wi' t'dairy cows. There'll be no hard and fast rules wi' labour. We s'll run both spots as one, where work's concerned.'

George didn't really care how the work was shared out. All he could think of was setting up in his own home with Elizabeth. He was brought back to earth by a sudden change of tone as Jonadab demanded, 'Are they spreading t'hay out ti dry?'

'No, Faither – ' began George, but was interrupted by an outburst.

'No? *No*? – and why not, I want ti know! What hay we've got left is vital, and must be saved. I s'll have ti buy in, as it is, and can't afford ti lose any more.'

'Nay, Faither, don't tek on so,' protested George. 'There's a nice breeze getting up and t'sky's clear. We s'll get t'hay spread, nivver fear. A tree was struck in t'storm, and t'road's blocked, so I thought it best to set t'men on clearing it. After all, we want John Butler to be able to get through, don't we?' he added slyly.

Jonadab thought for a moment. 'Aye, lad. Thoo's right,' he acknowledged, 'Aah lies 'ere, feeling helpless, and happen Aah feels that nobody but me can do owt. Anyroad, if they clear a way through this morning, t'haycocks can be pulled apart and spread out ti dry this afternoon.' He lay back on the pillows and smiled ruefully as George rose to go.

'Do as thoo thinks, George. Aah knows as how it'll be for t'best.'

When George reached the door, his father added with the old fire, 'Thoo's only t'boss while Aah'm laid up and even now, thoo's not t'boss in this room,' with which parting shot, he smiled ironically at his son.

George smiled back. 'Thoo knows me better than that, Faither. There can be only one boss on a farm, and on this one, that boss'll always be you.'

He left the house and went up the road to see how the men were getting on. The smaller sticks and branches had been dragged on to the roadside grass out of the way. These Tobias was gathering together and binding into sizeable bundles, ready to go down to the stick-heap – a huge pile of logs, branches and kindling that occupied a large portion of the grass near the pond.

Bert Weald and young Jonna were using a logging-saw to cut up boughs and branches which were too tangled to drag apart. When freed, these were chained together and dragged down the road by one of the horses. The waggoner was leading one while the other was led by a boy known as 'Tommy Owt'. There was one on every farm – a worker who was expected to turn his hand to anything. The other men usually called them Tommy and probably only their masters knew their proper names.

As George approached, he assessed the situation and decided that, with the help of an extra pair of hands, the road would be clear by dinnertime. He had intended to take over Jonna's end of the logging-saw, but changed his mind. His brother's growing maturity had overcome his juvenile jealousy and George had no wish to upset the delicate balance of the new, friendlier relationship which was blossoming between them. Instead, he began to drag and pile the freed timber so that, as each horse returned, there was a load of wood ready and waiting, thus speeding up the whole operation.

By the time Lydia ran up the road to tell them that dinner was ready, the last twigs and sticks were being gathered up to carry home, leaving the road clear.

As they ambled down towards the farm, George said, 'I s'll want you all in t'hayfield after dinner. We must get yon haycocks opened up and spread out before dark.' He glaced up at the clear blue of the sky and added, 'It looks settled, but then, so it did yesterday. I hopes I never sees a storm like yon, again.'

He had set his Uncle George to work clearing the gutters which drained the surplus water from the road to the ditches which ran alongside the hedges. Though younger than his brother Jonadab, Uncle George seemed to be frail and George tended to choose the less strenuous jobs for him.

When they entered the hayfield after dinner, George was surprised to see that the floodwater had hardly subsided from its level of the morning.

'That's funny.' He scratched his head in perplexity. 'There's been no rain since last night – I'd have thought it would have practically gone down by now.'

He had left Uncle George clearing out the gutters. As the workers in the field included his mother and two sisters, he explained what was needed.

'Use your forks to lift t'haycocks apart and spread it out to dry,' he instructed. 'Only put it where t'ground's got dried out and spread it well.' He turned to his brother. 'Come on, Jonna. Tek thi boots and stockings off and roll your britches up to t'knees. We'll go down to t'beck and see if we can find why t'water hasn't drained away.'

The two brothers stuffed their woollen stockings into their boots, which they then placed on the hedge-top, out of the way of the hay-tedders. They then picked their way across the field and, after a momentary hesitation, stepped into the floodwater. The sunshine of the morning had warmed the water so that it felt quite pleasant to paddle through, after the initial shock of entry.

As they drew nearer to the course of the stream, Jonna pointed to where Hodge Beck curved in what was almost an ox-bow.

'Look yonder,' he directed. 'It seems to be blocked with hay, as if all t'haycocks that were washed away has stuck there.'

'Aye.' George paused and studied the dam. 'They're caught on summat and that's why t'water can't get away. We s'll have to free it.' He looked back towards the road, trying to assess their progress through the water. 'Tek things steady,' he cautioned. 'We must be fairly near t'stream bed and don't want to fall down t'bank.'

Although the stream was normally quite shallow and the bank at this side only about a foot above the surface, to come across the drop unexpectedly would cause them to stumble and end up in the water. George grasped his brother's arm and they began to proceed more warily, supporting each other and feeling the ground cautiously with each foot, before setting it down. This slowed them up considerably but, as George put it, 'Better to be safe than sorry.'

Jonna suddenly stopped and felt around with his foot. 'We're 'ere,' he warned. Both halted. The water was already almost up to their knees, so they stopped and rolled their trousers as high up their thighs as possible, before stepping down on to the bed of the stream.

The going was now more difficult, impeded as they were by the stones on the beck bottom. However, by testing with each bare foot before stepping forward, they slowly made their way towards the blockage. Upon drawing closer, they could see that a large branch had been washed down by the storm and become wedged at the sharp bend in the stream. This had caught the haycocks as they had been swept along in the stream's torrent and the hay was now piled up against the branch, damming the progress of the stream.

'Come on, let's get it shifted,' urged Jonna.

'Wait a minute,' George held back. 'You go and fetch Bonnie and Bluebell and as many traces as you can lay your hands on. We shall never move that without 'osses and it'll take as many chains as we've got to snig it out. I'll be fishing some of yon hay out to try and let some of t'water through.'

While Jonna made his way back, George began to tackle the build-up of hay. Saturated as it was, it was terrifically heavy but, by dint of seizing it in his arms and taking each load to the opposite bank, he slowly began to move a considerable amount. At the start, he just dumped it in piles on the unflooded, higher bank.

Ignoring the fact that, for the second time in two days, he was soaked to the skin, George plodded on, realising that the more hay he could move from the dam, the easier it would be for the horses to move what he could now see was almost a whole tree.

Looking at the hay piled on the grass at the moor bottom, he thought of all the work which had been wasted, in addition to the expense of buying-in more hay. Suddenly, he was struck by an idea. 'We can save most of it!' he thought. Looking across, he saw his brother on his way towards him. Cupping his hands to his mouth, George shouted to him: 'Jonna! Jonna!'

Jonna looked up. 'What?'

'Fetch a couple of hay forks with you!'

With his brother's arrival, George said, 'Tie t'hosses up to yon tree on t'bank and help me to get t'rest o' this hay out.'

'Once we've moved yon tree, all t'hay'll be carried away in t'rush of water,' objected Jonna, who had no wish to end up as soaked as his brother was.

George however, was adamant. 'If we can lift most of that hay and spread it out on this bank, it should dry, given a bit of luck with t'weather. That way, it won't be a total loss.'

Although they knew that the hay would have lost some of its goodness and the seeds would be lost in the water, the brothers set to work with a will, dumping each dripping armful.

'We needn't have bothered to roll us britches up,' grunted Jonna, as he surveyed their clothes.

When most of the hay had been dumped on the bank in soggy bundles, the horses were yoked up to the chains, ready to dislodge the tree. Much of the water had already begun to swirl its way through the branches, now that the choking hay had been removed.

Now the two great shires were yoked to the tree; Jonna took one and George the other, urging them forward. As the chains tightened, the tree began to move and, with a rush, the undammed water surged through.

'We'd better just leave it ont 'far bank,' George panted, 'then we'll get this hay spread out.'

By the time they had finished their task, the floodwater from Long Meadow had almost completely drained away and Hodge Beck was, once more, gurgling merrily between its banks.

Squelching through the newly-drained field, they rejoined the others who were still working, higher up.

'Our Mam's gone in,' said Martha, ''cos Elizabeth's faither came.'

George felt an upsurge of excitement. John Butler was even now talking to his father about their future – his and Elizabeth's!

'We'd better stop for tea,' he said in what he hoped was a casual tone. 'Me and Jonna'll have to get changed. Will and Toby, see to t'horses and we'll finish this lot off before dark.'

As they trudged wearily towards the house, he fell in beside Tamar. 'When did John Butler arrive?' he wanted to know.

'Aah thinks it'd be about half an hour ago,' answered his sister. 'Mam thought Lydia might forget to give him some tea, or happen thought she'd give him a pint pot,' she added, with a grin.

As soon as they entered the kitchen, George and Jonna went up to get changed. Luckily, the shirts and trousers which had been soaked on the previous day had dried on the line in the warm sun and gentle breeze. Now they were on their beds, dry and inviting.

Annie had already spread bread, butter and jam out on the kitchen table. Now, as her sons mounted the stairs, she tipped the boiling water from the heavy iron kettle into the big brown teapot. 'There, that'll be mashing,' she said to the girls.

The meal was a subdued affair, passed in almost total silence as the adults round the table strained to distinguish what was being said in the parlour. So far, all they had heard was a mumble, first one voice, then the other. Occasionally, both men spoke simultaneously, and yet nothing they said was decipherable.

Tamar rose and, placing her finger to her lips, tiptoed to the parlour door and pressed her ear against it. After a moment or two, she returned to the table. The rest leaned forward to catch her whisper.

'Aah can't mek out what they're saying, but it sounds like an argument.'

'An argument?' George was dumbfounded. What could there be to argue about? It was a straightforward plan.

Just then, Jonadab's voice rose in a crescendo, so that he was clearly heard by the listeners in the kitchen. 'Good grief, man!' he thundered. 'Does thoo mean ti say that thoo lets thi own lass defy thi?'

'Now, now, Jonadab,' came John Butler's soothing tones, as both voices sank again to an unintelligible murmur.

George's heart was racing. He was not sure whether to be pleased that neither of the men was now shouting, or sorry that he could no longer hear what was being said.

Before he could decide, however, his father's voice rang out again. 'George! George! Get thissen in 'ere!'

All eyes were on George as he pushed back his chair and walked towards the door which led into the parlour. Looking round, he addressed his brother: 'If I'm not back when you're finished tending to t'stock, get on with tedding yon hay.' He turned to his mother. 'When you and t'lasses have done t'poultry and dairywork, Mam, give 'em a hand with the hay, will you?'

With that, he opened the door and entered the parlour, leaving the rest of the family consumed with curiosity.

'What's going on, Mam?' Tamar muttered.

Her mother merely looked round the table with a shake of her head. 'We'd best be on. There's a lot t'do,' was her only answer. 'Lydia, tek little Molly and feed t'hens and collect t'eggs, while we see t'milking and dairywork. We s'll be working till dark as it is.'

When George went into the best room, the atmosphere was strained. His father was white with anger, and his brows were drawn together over the vivid blue eyes, which were now flashing with icy coldness.

John Butler's display of displeasure was in direct contrast. His cheeks were mottled with crimson, verging on purple, and there was a blue tinge to his compressed lips.

Both men turned towards George for support, as he came through the door.

'George,' they chorused, in unison.

George held up his hand. 'Just a minute, if you don't mind, Faither, Mr Butler,' turning from one to the other. He pulled up a chair beside the sofa and sat down next to John Butler and facing his father. 'Now then, what's up?' he demanded.

'John, 'ere, won't give his consent ti t'marriage,' burst out Jonadab. George could not believe his ears.

'Nay, nay, Jonadab. That's not what I said,' replied Butler. He looked at George and spoke pleadingly. 'You and our Elizabeth agreed to wait until Christiana was old enough to take her place at Nathan's in Leeds.'

George thought for a moment. 'That's not quite right.' He felt that he was fighting for his future. 'I didn't exactly agree. It was Elizabeth who persuaded me. I told her your Christie's old enough to go out to work. Besides,' he added, 'we hadn't got t'chance of Cherry Tree Farm, then. Having a house of your own makes a difference.'

Jonadab broke in, testily. 'I've a great respect for

273

t'wench. She's a good head on 'er shoulders but think about it, man! She's knocking on for thirty and my lad's only twenty-three. 'E's not going ti wait for ever.'

Both George and John Butler flushed at this slur to Elizabeth. George opened his mouth to protest that his love was unswerving, but Jonadab caught his eye and, with a slight shake of his head, motioned him to silence.

John Butler began to splutter. 'Nay, I'll not have that! Our Elizabeth's a good catch for any chap.' He bridled. 'Let's face it – your George has spent a night in jail and folks don't forget that.'

Jonadab broke in, placatingly. 'Aah'm not criticising her. She's a handsome woman and Aah've a high opinion of her. However, you must admit, John, that it's high time she was wed. As for oor George's night in t'cell, you know 'ow that came about and Aah understands t'same chap tried to attack your Elizabeth.'

George butted in. 'Waring wants ti leave his farm at Martinmas, Mr Butler, so there's no time ti lose.'

It was obvious to both the Oaks that John Butler considered he was being treated in a high-handed fashion and was objecting on principle. As the argument was bandied back and forth, George felt desperate. He was, after all, the one most concerned and was determined to have his say.

'Wait a minute!' he suddenly broke in. 'Now, I've got an idea. I think a lot about Elizabeth, as you both know.' Not for the life of him could he use the word 'love' to these two older men, even though his love for her was so strong that he felt suffocation at the thought that he might lose her yet.

'How about,' he looked from one to the other, 'how about this. Christie could go to Leeds for a month, or even six weeks, and work alongside Elizabeth. That way, she'll learn what to do and not feel so lonely when she first gets there.' He warmed to his theme as he realised that both fathers were listening to him with attention. 'As well as teaching her how to go about t'job, Elizabeth would have the chance to introduce her to friends. That way, she'd settle down and Elizabeth could come back to get ready for t'wedding and help to get t'house fettled.'

He turned his gaze from his father to John Butler, to see that each was digesting the suggestion.

'Elizabeth wants to be wed just as much as I do, and I'm sure she'll think it's a good idea, Mr Butler.' George began to press his point harder, as he realised that his plea was being considered by John Butler.

'Aye, there's summat in what you say.' It was with seeming reluctance that he apparently agreed with George. It was not total capitulation however, as he continued, 'I s'll talk it over with t'missus and we'll let you know what we decide.'

George was nonplussed at this rebuff, just as he thought he had talked John Butler into his way of thinking. His confidence was, however, boosted as he recalled Elizabeth's spirit and determination. 'You do that, Mr Butler,' he said, as he rose to leave the parlour. 'Meanwhile, I'll write to Elizabeth and we'll let you know what *she* decides.' With which parting shot he went to rejoin the others in the hayfield.

As he worked, he was in a turmoil of indecision. Had he gone too far, he wondered. Perhaps the Butlers would think he was too impertinent for Elizabeth.

However, his father laughed later that evening when he recounted Butler's reaction. 'He was as red as a cockscomb. In fact, Aah thought 'e would bust!' he chuckled. 'Nivver fear! He knows it's too good a chance for that lass of his ti miss. There's not many as gets their own home when they wed.'

That night, George wrote to Elizabeth – an impassioned plea for her to come back, so that they could marry in the autumn. He then had to await her reply in an agony of hope.

CHAPTER TWENTY-TWO

After the day of the disastrous storm, the remainder of the summer unfolded in golden months of shimmering heat.

Although George Oaks could not have put the thought into words, the summer months seemed to echo the present tenor of his life – warm, peaceful and forward-looking.

A reluctant Christie Butler was despatched to Leeds to be groomed for Elizabeth's position as Uncle Nathan's companion/housekeeper. When the news was brought to Jonadab by Tamar, one market day, he sighed with relief. 'Thank goodness John Butler had the sense to put his foot down,' he remarked.

'By 'eck, she was carrying on and no mistake,' Tamar told them gleefully. 'She says she hates you an' all,' she added, looking at George.

'Her opinion matters little to me,' he retorted, 'as long as her sister doesn't.'

Early in August, just before the beginning of harvest, James Waring walked up the valley one evening to visit Jonadab.

'Now Jim,' said his host, as Annie settled them with pint pots of tea. 'Dost thoo think we could share a valuer ti go round t'farm? That way, it'd save us both a bit of brass.'

'Nay, Jonadab.' James Waring looked uncomfortable. 'That's one o' t'things Aah've come about. It'll be all right by me, if your lad comes round wi' me and we come to an agreement between us.'

Jonadab realised that Waring must be even more

pressed for money than he had realised and could not really afford to pay for the farm to be valued.

'Aye. That'll suit me,' he agreed. 'There'll be no falling out between us.'

James Waring had not, however, finished with the reasons for his visit. 'There's summat else,' he persisted. 'Mi rent's paid up ti Martinmas but me and t'missus has the chance ti live with t'daughter at Castleton, so we wondered if you could tek over at Michaelmas and pay me that part o' t'rent?'

Things must be bad, Jonadab thought, if the Warings were so desperate for money. From Michaelmas on 29 September to Martinmas on 11 November was nobbut a few weeks. He felt deep sympathy for the other man, not many years his senior, and knew that there were many more farmers like him, who were going under in these difficult times.

It was agreed that George should ride down the valley to look over Cherry Tree Farm, one evening early in the following week. He and James Waring would appraise the things which were part of the farm's valuation. The two men then settled down to chat about farming matters and their neighbours, before Waring left to stroll back down the dale, through the waning light.

When Annie came in for a last chat and to make her husband comfortable for the night, she found him in a pensive mood.

'Waring seems to be in deep trouble, money-wise,' he remarked. 'From what I can gather, 'e'll be lucky to come out of it with much.'

'Oh, Jonadab,' she again voiced her fears, 'do you think you're doing a wise thing, ti tek it on?'

Jonadab gingerly hoisted himself into a more comfortable position, as he smiled at her. 'Dost thoo not trust me, woman? Aah've nivver let thi down, has I? No! It's a right decision. Them as is going ti t'wall hasn't moved wi' t'times. T'days of oxen is over. Heavy 'osses is what t'future's about and Aah've built up good stock. There's new machinery coming in, an' all, and that must be looked into.'

Annie sighed. She was satisfied with life in her own safe little niche. What Jonadab called 'progress' worried her, but she had respect for his farming ability and his acumen so, if he thought that they should expand and change their methods, she supposed that he was right. She realised that his enforced idleness from farmwork had given free rein to his active mind. He now filled his days with ideas of how, not only to keep his farm viable when others were losing theirs, but to increase and enrich his business.

Before harvest-time was due to start, George went down to Cherry Tree Farm. He had rarely passed the house and had never been inside, so was eager to view it. First, however, there was the ritual of walking round the fields to look over the land. It was soon obvious to him that James Waring must have been struggling for some time. He had not employed hired help for almost two years and had laid most of the land down to grass.

'It hasn't had much muck on these last few years,' explained Waring apologetically. 'I've just this small flock of sheep left, a few pigs and t'house-cow.'

George thought he could, perhaps, buy the cow but kept his own counsel until he'd discussed things with his father. He was pleased to see that there was a range of good buildings, surrounding a sheltered fold-yard.

The farmhouse was solid but attractive. Built of local stone, it was square and nestled snugly under a thatched roof. The front of the house faced due south and the door opened into a fair-sized living kitchen with a flagged floor. The parlour opened off and there was a long dairy running along the north side of the house.

George took in as much as he could, looking round surreptitiously as James Waring discussed the farm. He would have liked to see the four bedrooms, but felt too embarrassed to ask.

'The garden's looking well,' he observed.

'Aye. 'E's a keen gardener, is James,' the wife replied, while her husband looked suitably modest. George had, indeed, been impressed by the neatness and quality of the garden patch which held an abundance of all kinds of fruits and vegetables.

As he made his way back home, George was divided over the acquisition of Cherry Tree Farm. The house and buildings were, in his opinion, a desirable asset and he could just picture himself living there with Elizabeth. What of the land, however? It was obvious that it had not managed to pay its rent for Waring. Could his own father fare any better, or would it drag down their own prosperous farm?

When he reached home, he was still deep in thought and gave a start at his father's tap on the parlour window. As he looked up, Jonadab beckoned him in. 'Well? What's it like? Have you agreed t'valuation?'

The questions were rattled out, one after the other, before he could answer. 'No, Faither. There's not a lot to value: not even a muck-heap.' George sat for a moment, twisting his cap in his hands while he pondered how best to present his fears to his father. He raised his eyes to find his father's vivid blue ones boring into him.

'Come on, lad! Spit it out! What's up?' Jonadab was becoming impatient.

'Well,' George hesitated and then the words came

tumbling out. 'Oh, Faither, I think happen it's been a mistake! It's not in good fettle and – '

His father's upheld hand halted the spate. 'Don't get thissen flummoxed. Just tek it steady and spell it out. What's t'house and buildings like? They used ti be good. Is it that they're run down?'

'Nay. They're good,' admitted George.

'Well, then, what ails t'spot?'

'It's t'land, Faither. He's laid it all down ti grass and it's poor: covered in thistles, too.'

'Land that'll grow thistles'll grow crops.' Jonadab began to look more satisfied. 'Waring hadn't enough behind him ti tide him over a bad year and once he let his men go and his cattle, he was neither working his land nor muckin' it and land needs both. Never fear, lad. We'll pull it round. It's just a nice acreage to build this farm up.'

As his father talked, George found his fears allayed. Jonadab had known Cherry Tree Farm when it was a good holding and he had both the money and expertise to restore the land.

'Jim Waring's certainly got some good crops in his garden,' he remarked.

'There thoo is, then!' Jonadab exclaimed. 'We'll be all right, nivver fear.'

George explained that James Waring would call and give his valuation and see whether they agreed. As there were no growing crops and the land had not been manured, there was not a great deal to value.

'Whativver 'e says, Aah s'll agree,' Jonadab decided. ''E's been a good neighbour and Aah'm sorry ti see any farmer go under. There's many more'll sink afore we're through, but Aah'm determined t'Oaks' s'll swim.'

He noted the relief in George's face. 'Mek no mistake, lad. Thi faither's more brass put by than most folks would dream. Enough ti weather many a storm, anyroad, and what we lost on t'roundabout, we s'll gain on t'swings.'

When next the doctor visited, Jonadab's splints were removed and he began to make his tentative way about the farm, with the aid of two walking sticks. He was worried and rather embarrassed at first, to find himself so weakened by his enforced idleness that he had to rest after a few uncertain steps. However, driven on by his steely determination, he made rapid progress and could soon walk as far as the fields where harvesting was in full swing.

The only work which was carried out on Sundays was the essential tending of the livestock. No matter how vital the struggle between work and weather in the fields, the Lord's day was set apart. Consequently, on the first Sunday that he was up and about again, Jonadab Oaks sat in his accustomed place at the head of the dinner-table. After saying Grace, he looked round his family. His eyes softened and he spoke more gently than usual. 'Aah'm proud of you all,' he said, as his eyes moved from one to the other. His listeners glanced at each other. Was this sarcasm on their father's part? However, upon looking towards him they realised, by his expression, that his tribute came from the heart.

'This farm's in as good fettle as if Aah'd been in charge missen these last few weeks. You've done well – true Oaks.' This final accolade proved the depth of his feelings. To be an Oaks was to be among the elite of mankind, in Jonadab's estimation. His family felt gratified at his appreciation of their efforts.

When the meal was over, Jonadab motioned to George. 'Bring t'pony and trap round to t'door and thoo and me'll slip down ti Waring's. Aah wants ti

look over Cherry Tree Farm and we'll agree t'valuation with him.'

George allowed the pony to amble through the
dale at her own pace. The valley pulsated with heat
and the bees moved heavily among the hedgerow
flowers, as father and son sat in silence, each
wrapped in his own thoughts.

The silence was broken first by Jonadab. 'Dids't
thoo mek a bid for Waring's sheep?'

'No,' answered George. 'I've bought twenty from
you and I've got mi pigs. I want ti keep a bit of
brass behind me for when I gets wed.'

Jonadab eyed his son. 'Nay, George! Stock's as
good as brass. Money's only good for what it can
buy. If t'Warings is going ti live with their lass,
maybe thoo can buy a lot of what it takes ti furnish
a home from them, at a tidy price. That way, thoo'll
mebbe manage ti buy t'sheep an' all.'

George reflected for a moment. 'I'll see how much
he wants. They're not as good as ours, but they're
not bad. It's a good little house-cow an' all. I s'll see
what he'll tek for 'er.'

They had, by now, reached the farmhouse and
George reined the pony to a halt. Jumping down, he
gave his father a hand out of the trap.

Jonadab stood leaning on his sticks and considered
the house. 'Aye – it's none so bad,' was his summing
up. 'Thoo and Elizabeth'll be real cosy 'ere.' He had
only just finished this comment when Mrs Waring
came out of the door, removing her apron.

'It's grand ti see thoo up and about again, Mr
Oaks,' she greeted. 'Aah'm afeard James has gone
for a walk round t'fields. 'E's tekkin' it bad, having
ti leave t'farm,' she added sadly.

'Aye, and so would any man.' Jonadab's reply was
heartfelt. The love he felt for his own land was an

intense and personal feeling, even though it was not actually owned by his family.

He and George set off to go round the fields in the pony-trap, picking up James Waring on the way. While the two older men discussed the farm, George allowed his thoughts to drift to Elizabeth. He found it hard to grasp the fact that his years of adoration were to bear fruit – that his waiting would soon be over and that, in a few weeks, he and Elizabeth Butler would be married.

When they drew up once again in front of the house, Waring helped Jonadab to alight, while George tied up the pony.

Mrs Waring bustled to the door. 'Come in, Mr Oaks, George. Aah've just mashed a pot o' tea.' She ushered them inside as she spoke.

To George's secret gratification, his father expressed a wish to be shown round the house. As they moved from room to room, he could visualise, in his mind's eye, Elizabeth making a home for them within the cosiness of its walls. Upstairs, while his father and Mrs Waring discussed the merits of south-facing bedrooms, George's thoughts lingered on passion-filled nights. He glanced guiltily at his father, as though the older man could read his mind.

When they left, George had arranged to buy any furniture which the Warings would not be taking, in addition to the cow and a few hens. Jonadab had agreed a valuation with James Waring and was also to purchase the small flock of sheep.

As the pony sauntered home through the limpid heat of the peaceful valley, Jonadab's two hands were clasped round the handle of his walking stick, his chin resting on them and his eyes closed in thought.

George studied his father and realised the toll that the last few years had taken on him. The once-raven hair was now flecked with grey and there was a wing of silver at each temple. The time spent indoors while his leg was mending had caused his customary tan to fade and the lines were etched deeper in his face. When he suddenly opened his eyes however, they were as vivid blue as ever and seemed to see into George's very soul.

'What's thoo thinking on, George?' he demanded.

'I'm thinking how lucky I am, Faither. I'm grateful for you getting Cherry Tree Farm for me and Elizabeth and making it possible for us to be wed sooner than I'd expected.'

'Luck? Luck?' Jonadab was full of scorn. 'Thoo makes thi own luck, lad. Luck is superstition and t'Devil's work. Thoo must make thi own luck in this world.'

Life was a constant challenge to Jonadab Oaks and he was determined that, with his God's help, he would not only survive, but triumph.

'Aye, Faither.' George was suitably chastened.

'Thoo must work hard and justify my faith,' continued Jonadab. 'We'll show 'em what sort of stuff t'Oaks is made of.'

George felt a swell of pride that his father had acknowledged his faith in him. 'Nivver fear, Faither. We'll do our best.' As he felt at the present moment, nothing was beyond him. With Elizabeth beside him, there was no task they could not accomplish.

As the harvest progressed, Jonadab became more involved with the work. He did not, this year, become sufficiently nimble to work on the corn stacks, but George was proficient and his father expressed himself satisfied with the shape and dimensions of the round, thatched pikes, which were built in the field along the roadside for passersby to admire.

'Things seem ti be going better for us,' Jonadab

told Annie one evening and, indeed, life did seem to be running more smoothly.

Only a day or two later, however, as they were sitting down to breakfast, Tamar hurriedly left her seat at the table and rushed outside.

'Whatever's up?' Annie followed her daughter through the door to find her leaning against the house wall, pale and trembling after a bout of vomiting.

'Now, lass, what's wrong?' asked her mother solicitously.

Tamar would not meet her eyes. 'It's nowt, Mam. It must be summat I've eaten,' she answered shakily.

Annie Oaks looked at her daughter's face and noticed, for the first time, how drawn Tamar had become. She was suddenly filled with a dreadful suspicion. 'Tamar! Look at me!' she said sharply.

Tamar raised her eyes reluctantly, and her mother saw the guilt and fear in her daughter's face. 'Oh, no,' Annie whispered. 'You can't be.'

'I don't know what you're on about, Mam.' The girl spoke defensively, but Annie knew that her suspicions were confirmed.

When they re-entered the kitchen, Jonadab looked up with a frown. 'What ails thi, lass?' he queried.

'Nowt, Faither. I must have eaten summat that disagreed with me.' So saying, she began to busy herself in clearing the table.

Annie laid her hand on Jonadab's arm as the men prepared to go about their daily work. 'Come into t'parlour, Jonadab. Aah've summat ti say.' Although outwardly calm, she felt that her world was once again, in total devastation.

'What is it?' he asked, but turned back and crossed the kitchen.

When they reached the door into the parlour, Annie spoke again. 'Come here, Tamar.' With an effort she kept her voice steady.

When they were all in the parlour out of earshot of Martha and Lydia, she turned to her husband. 'Tamar has summat ti say,' she announced.

They both turned to their daughter, but Tamar had decided to brazen it out. 'I don't know what you mean!' she protested. 'I've nowt ti say.'

Jonadab looked from one to the other in puzzlement. 'Aah've no time ti play guessing games. Aah've plenty ti do today,' he said. 'If there's owt Aah should know, spit it out.'

Annie took a deep breath. 'Oor Tamar's in t'family way,' she blurted. Jonadab could not believe his ears. Despite all his efforts to raise his children in a decent and God-fearing fashion, could there be another who had let him down?

Tamar flushed and stiffened. 'I'm no such thing, our Mam,' she denied flatly, but though she tried to sound innocent and offended, her face gave the lie to her protestations.

'It's no use trying ti pull t'wool over us eyes,' said her mother sadly. 'Truth will out.'

Tamar drew herself up to her full height and a spot of colour appeared in each cheek. 'All right! So I am!' she retorted defiantly. 'He'll marry me, when 'e knows and make me a lady.'

Jonadab was seized with a terrible rage. He sprang across to his daughter and, seizing her by the shoulders, began to shake her with a violence that robbed her of her breath.

'Strumpet!' he roared. 'Thoo's well-named! Tamar in t'Bible was a harlot, an' all.' His voice rang through the house, to the consternation of those in the kitchen.

'Whatever's up?' whispered Martha.

'Heaven knows,' answered Lydia, 'but t'Maister sounds ti be in a rage.'

When her father paused to regain his breath,

Tamar twisted from his grasp. Looking from one to the other of her parents, challengingly, she burst out: 'If t'truth's to be told, I'm glad it's out in t'open. I'm sick of living down 'ere. It's dull and dreary and I want more out of life.'

Jonadab lifted his hand and brought it across her face, sending her spinning. She quickly recovered herself and faced him. Though her hand caressed the cheek which he had struck, her eyes flashed her defiance. 'It's no good going on like this, Faither. What's done cannot be undone and I s'll be away from here before long and out of your sight.'

Annie had stood, a mute witness to the scene, but now began to sob. 'Whatever are we ti do?' Her question fell on unheeding ears as Tamar and her father faced each other, hostility in every line of their bodies.

'Who is the man? Tell me!' He reached forward, intent upon shaking her again. Tamar, however, dodged from his grasp and faced him, hands on hips.

She leaned forward from the waist and eyes flashing, hissed, 'Sir William Forster.' She tossed her head as she spoke. 'He'll marry me, never fear, and I'll be Lady Forster.'

Jonadab sank into a chair with a groan, shaking his head. 'Thoo's not only a sinner, thoo's a fool an' all.' He looked across at her. 'The one he's going ti mek a lady is Sir Francis' daughter, Miss Rowena.'

Tamar blanched. 'No! That can't be true! He's promised me so often!' she cried.

'T'likes of him don't marry t'likes of thoo,' Jonadab said heavily. ''E's been young Master James' friend since schooldays. That's why he spends so much time at t'Towers. When Miss Rowena came back from school, they became betrothed and are ti be wed afore long.'

He spoke with such authority that Tamar knew

what she was hearing was not just hearsay. 'It was in t'*Messenger* only last week,' her father confirmed, tossing the paper to her.

All the fire left her and she slumped down on to the sofa, weeping hysterically. 'I'll kill myself! I can't go on!' she cried.

As her mother held her, she poured out the whole sorry tale. In answer to Annie's questioning she confessed that she had been meeting Sir William in the quarry during his stays at the Towers, ever since George had knocked the young nobleman down.

With a flash of insight, Annie realised that these clandestine meetings accounted for Tamar's supposed new interest in the gathering of herbs. From time to time, she had taken to going out with a basket to collect whatever was in season: comfrey, yarrow, elderflowers for use in herbal remedies, in addition to seasonal fruits for jam and preserve-making. Her mother had often remarked how helpful and dependable she had become. 'She's been deceiving us all this time,' she thought sadly.

'He does love me,' Tamar protested wildly. 'He's told me so, many a time.'

Jonadab rose to his feet and went over to the door. 'Aah'll not be long,' he told his wife. Nodding towards Tamar, he added, 'Put 'er ti bed.' After leaving the room, he turned back and looked at his wife. 'Lock 'er in,' he instructed. 'We don't want er doing owt daft.'

While Annie accompanied the distraught girl upstairs, Jonadab saddled his horse for the journey up to the Towers. He knew his visit could do no good, but was determined to see Forster, whom he new from the newspaper article, to be staying there or the betrothal party, which was to take place that weekend.

As he rode, his head was bowed and he asked

himself where he had gone wrong in the upbringing of his family, that two should bring disgrace upon him. That Tamar should have an affair with the blackguard who had attacked her sister was beyond his understanding.

As he entered the drive leading to the Towers, he was still undecided as to how he should proceed. Should he see Sir Francis and tell him the whole tale, or should he ask to speak to Sir William, leaving the Sturdys to wonder what his business could be.

Before he could come to a decision, however, the matter was resolved. Rounding a bend in the drive, he saw, walking towards him, William Forster and James Sturdy, each carrying a gun and accompanied by two or three retrievers.

Jonadab dismounted and stood holding the reins while they approached.

'Good morning, Oaks. Whom do you wish to see?' asked James Sturdy.

Jonadab inclined his head towards William. 'Sir William Forster, sir,' he answered. James Sturdy raised his eyebrows and looked from one to the other. He could not imagine what Jonadab could have to say to his friend. The incident with the Oaks was now water under the bridge, as far as he was aware.

'Go ahead, James,' instructed his future brother-in-law. 'I'll catch you up.'

Neither spoke until James was out of earshot. Then William raised one eyebrow in a supercilious manner. 'Well?' he drawled. 'What can you possibly want with me?'

'Thoo knows!' affirmed Jonadab. 'Thoo's got my lass into trouble.'

Forster gave a smile. 'And you've interrupted my morning's shooting for that? The silly girl is n

290

better than she should be. Who is to say the bastard is mine?'

The veins in Jonadab's forehead stood out as he struggled to maintain his composure. He realised how George had felt when he had knocked this arrogant man to the ground. He clenched his hands and answered, in a controlled tone: 'I've come to see what thoo's going ti do about it.'

'Do? *Do*? What on earth do you think I'm going to do? What's done cannot be undone. Now, I'd like to rejoin my companion. I may say,' he added, 'that the wench was willing enough.'

This was untrue. The seduction of Tamar had taken far longer than he had ever envisaged. Despite the fact that she was passionate and tempestuous, Tamar had a lifetime of her father's strict upbringing behind her, which caused her to draw back at the last moment.

At their first clandestine meeting in the quarry, Forster had never had any intention of taking Tamar against her will. His eventual success had strengthened his feeling of victorious revenge over her family. She had surrendered her virginity to him of her own free will – that this had been achieved by false promises of marriage was merely a source of amusement to him. The first erotic excitement of their early meetings had palled and Sir William's attentions were now all to his future. The girl's fate was of no interest to him.

As he made to walk away, Jonadab moved in front of him. It was not often that William Forster encountered a man of his own height, but Jonadab Oaks was equally tall. The implacable, vivid blue eyes bored into his pale ones, making him feel a twinge of unease. He knew, to his cost, the strength of these dales farmers: he had not forgotten his encounter with this man's son.

He brought his shotgun down from his shoulder, cradling it loosely in the crook of his elbow, to draw Jonadab's attention to the fact that he was armed. Jonadab's eyes narrowed and his mouth curled mockingly.

'Aah'm not a man of violence,' he said in a quiet voice, 'so you don't need that gun. All Aah've come for was ti see what thoo's going ti do about my lass.'

'I do not intend to do anything at all,' stated Forster. Suddenly, a look of understanding dawned upon his face. 'Oh, of course,' he said speculatively. 'This is what you mean, is it not?' Upon which he drew a small leather money bag from his pocket and offered it to Jonadab. 'Pay your daughter for her favours and let's end the matter, man,' he said impatiently.

Jonadab made no attempt to take the money. In silence, he mounted his horse and then, from his greater height, looked down at the younger man.

'We don't want your brass,' he stated with dignity. 'We didn't want your bastard, but we've got it and when it comes we shall rear it without owt from you.'

'Why bother me with your petty problems?' demanded Forster, anxious to be away from the accusing blue eyes and beginning to be troubled lest Rowena should learn of the scene.

Jonadab's lip curled disdainfully. 'Aah came ti see if you'd do right by the lass and wed 'er, as thoo pledged. I can see, though, that it's too much to expect of a – a person like thoo.' His voice rose, as the pent-up anger surged forth. 'Aah was going ti say "a man", but thoo's no man, much less a gentleman, as thoo's supposed ti be.' He pointed his riding crop at the younger man, whose face purpled with rage.

'How dare you speak to me like that?' he hissed.

'Oh, Aah dare, all right, because, though thoo may be a "Sir", thoo's *scum*!' Jonadab almost spat the word. 'And as for marriage – Aah wouldn't let 'er marry thoo, if thoo was t'last man on earth.'

Before Forster could think of a reply, Jonadab continued, 'And thoo needn't worry. Aah s'll see the child never knows who sired it. Keep away from us and oors and, once thoo's wed, don't let us see thoo up 'ere again, or Aah can't promise your safety.'

As he turned the horse, he spoke over his shoulder. 'Aah only hopes as how t'bairn's a better person than its faither – it can hardly be worse.' Riding down the drive, he added under his breath, 'And God help poor Miss Rowena.'

CHAPTER TWENTY-THREE

Before harvest was quite finished, Elizabeth came
home to prepare for the wedding. As she and George
strolled down the lane towards their future home,
George went into details about its good features.

'There's a good garden at t'front, facing south,
where I can grow all our fruit and vegetables,' he
enthused, 'and, at t'north side, there's a belt of pine
trees that protect it from the wind.'

Elizabeth smiled and squeezed his hand. 'I have
seen Cherry Tree Farm, you know, George,' she
smiled. 'I've passed the back of it on my way to the
healing-well.'

'I know, but – ' George sought in his mind how
to express what he felt. Words, however, did not
come easily to him. 'It's different when I know it's
where we're going to live.' He smiled at her tenderly
and a little shyly. 'You and me, Elizabeth. It'll be
our home.'

She sighed as they turned down the track which
led to the farmyard. 'I often thought the time would
never come, George. Thank you for waiting for me,'
and she smiled tremulously up at him.

George was overwhelmed that she should express
her thanks to him. He regarded himself as the luckiest man in the world that Elizabeth should consent
to marry him. He lifted her effortlessly in his arms
and spun her round, planting a kiss full on her lips
as he set her down.

'You know I'd have waited for ever,' he pledged
'Since the first time I set eyes on you, it's been you

nobody.' With which declaration, he took her arm
and they approached the house.

Elizabeth was sensitive to the Warings' feelings,
merely staying long enough to see what George was
buying from them and what else she would need.
Before leaving, she shook hands with the couple and
wished them well in their new life.

'Don't worry, Mr and Mrs Waring. We shall look
after the place,' she assured them.

As the couple strolled along the mile of meandering lane which separated the two farms, both were
deep in thought. George eventually broke the silence. 'Is it all right for you, Elizabeth? I don't want
you to be lonely.'

She turned a radiant face to him. 'It's lovely,
George. It's like the Garden of Eden, but without
the serpent. I shall be busy all day, waiting for you
to come back in the evening.' With mounting colour
in her cheeks, she added: 'And perhaps it won't be
long before there's a baby for me to look after.'

George felt that he would burst with happiness.
He did not care what his father had said – he *was*
the luckiest man alive. There was only one blot on
his landscape. He felt reluctant to broach the subject
of Tamar's downfall, especially as he was all too
conscious that, in John and Ann Butler's estimation,
the Oaks' family's standards of behaviour were well
below what was expected. He felt that her parents
considered that Elizabeth was marrying beneath her,
and he was only too thankful that they would be
safely married before Tamar's condition became
apparent.

When they reached the gate which crossed the
road between the two farms, he drew to a halt. 'Wait
a minute, Elizabeth, love,' he said, 'Aah've summat
to tell you.'

She turned towards him, a loving smile spreading

over her face. 'Yes, George?' she murmured miscl
ievously, as she raised her lips to his. He bent an
kissed her, but then drew back apologetically.

'No, I didn't want to say I love you. Though
do, of course,' he added hastily. 'It's summat not –
he paused. 'I don't know how to say it, but it's n
as pleasant as what our life is.'

She gently placed her hand across his lips. 'Nov
begin from the beginning, George,' she prompte
seeing that something was troubling him deeply.

'It's our Tamar.' He flushed miserably as he sea
ched for words. 'She's in t'family way.'

'Oh!' Elizabeth breathed the word in disbelie
She knew how strict Jonadab Oaks was with his gir
– how fiercely protective. 'Who is the man, Georg
Does your father know?'

'Aye, he does, an' all. It's *him*!'

'Who?' She wrinkled her brows in puzzlement.

'Sir William Forster – the one who tried to for
himself on you – and our Beth.'

Elizabeth was devastated at this news. She realis
immediately that there was no possibility of Sir W
liam ever marrying Tamar and could imagine Jona
ab's humiliation. Tamar had always been wayway
and headstrong, but Elizabeth had not thought h
capable of such defiance of the code of conduct s
by her father.

'Whatever will she do?' she asked.

George was silent for a moment, then a long si
escaped him. 'At first, she threatened to do aw
with herself,' he admitted, 'but she's gone quiet ar
broods a lot. Faither won't speak to her.'

Elizabeth could not believe her ears. 'How can
ignore his own daughter, living in the same house
she asked incredulously. 'Our father wouldn't ha
done that to Mary.'

'Well, our Dad can do what he wants.' Geor

made the statement flatly, in a tone that would brook no denial. 'She told me that there's no way she'll stay down here, once she's had the bairn, but I can't see how she'll get away. It's not as if she's got any money.'

He was desperately worried about his sister. All the fire had gone out of her and she dragged herself through her days in a state of hopeless misery. At the beginning of her pregnancy, she had been buoyed up by the expectancy of marriage to Sir William Forster, and rising beyond her humble background. Once this hope was dashed from her, she had sunk into hopeless lethargy, rarely speaking and totally ignored by Jonadab, who acted as though she did not exist.

George kissed Elizabeth again. 'We can worry about our Tamar after we're wed,' he said. 'There's nowt we can do at the moment and we've our lives ahead of us.'

The wedding was set for Michaelmas, and September disappeared with unbelievable speed. The Warings' son-in-law came with a flat cart which was loaded with the few possessions that could be accommodated in his wife's home. They called with the key, on their way out of the valley, and Jonadab eyed them with compassion as the cart moved off.

'It's not much for a man to have left, after a lifetime of hard graft,' he observed softly.

'Nay, Jonadab. I only hopes as how we can end oor lives in this place,' answered Annie, looking round her cosy kitchen.

Her husband laid an arm across her shoulders in an unexpectedly tender gesture. 'Have no fear, lass. We shall always be comfortably off.' He spoke reassuringly, confident in his ability to look after his own.

The hard, dawn to dusk work of harvesting culminated once more in the Mell Supper and George had more spare time. On the first Wednesday after the end of harvest, he approached his father. 'Is it all right if I go into Kirkby today, Faither? I want to see if I can get a decent tup.'

'Nay, lad. Save thi money. Thoo can use one of my tups.'

George, however, was determined. He wanted to buy as good quality ram as he could afford, to upgrade his flock. He had another reason, also, to go into the town before his marriage.

The Windsor chair standing beside the fire had always, in his eyes, been a symbol of authority. Even when Jonadab was confined to the parlour sofa with a broken thigh, no one else had dared to sit in 'Faither's chair'. Now that George was to have a home of his own, he had set his heart on a Windsor, and matching rocking-chair, to place beside the fireplace as a surprise for Elizabeth.

'If you don't mind, Faither, I'd rather buy a tup of my own,' he insisted. 'That way, I've my own flock, complete.'

Jonadab admired George's independence and gave him permission to have a day off work.

'Aah'll tell thee what Aah told thi brother when 'e got wed,' he cautioned. 'Look after thi brass. Don't be tempted ti fritter it away.'

'Nivver fear, Faither. I haven't much, but I s'll mek every penny count.' With which assurance, George strode out to bring round the pony and trap, to take his mother into Kirkby to stand the market.

As they turned into Dale End, at the entrance to the little town, he drew the pony to a halt. 'I'll not be a minute, Mam. I just want a word with Tom Smithies,' he said, as he dismounted and went to knock on a cottage door. Thomas Smithies, one of the town's carriers, answered it. 'Now, George. What can Aah do for thi?' he queried.

'I want a good Windsor chair and a rocker to match, Mr Smithies,' George replied.

'Aah can recommend Sunley's, at Nawton,' the other man said. 'Aah'm in Nawton tomorrow, on t'way ti 'Elmsley. Dust want mi ti give him an order?'

'Yes, please, and if you can collect them and bring them down to Cherry Tree Farm, I'd be pleased. I expect Elizabeth will be getting in touch before we're wed. I know she'll have some stuff to move.'

'Right thoo is, then.' Smithies could be relied upon to do his best, George knew.

When he rejoined his mother, she did not ask what his business with the carrier had been, for which he was thankful. He had no wish to remind her of his move from the family home, which she was taking badly, though she said little. He also felt self-conscious about the purchase of a Windsor chair but, in his estimation, it would set the seal on his position as master in his own house.

In the days leading up to the wedding, Elizabeth spent most of her time at Cherry Tree Farm. She scrubbed and polished until everything in the house shone, and burnished the windows until they sparkled in the late summer sun.

On each trip, the pony-trap was laden with things she had collected over the years for her bottom drawer. Whenever George could spare some time to visit the house, there was more evidence of her home-making efforts to delight his eyes.

About a week before the wedding, came the time for which George had been waiting. Thomas Smithies, the carrier, called one evening at the Oaks' house. 'Is thoo coming down ti give me an 'and, or s t'house oppen?' he wanted to know.

'No! I'll come!' George snatched the key from the dresser where Elizabeth had left it on her way home.

He joined Smithies on the cart and they trundled their way down the dale.

As George unlocked the door, the chairs were unloaded. He proudly tried the elm seat and ran his fingers over the smooth ash of the arms. With a smile of satisfaction, he carried them in and placed them upon the new, brightly-coloured clip rug in front of the kitchen fireplace.

'There!' he breathed, as he stepped back to admire them, feeling that they completed the picture of domesticity.

'Thoo'll want this lot in t'parlour, Aah reckons,' came the carrier's voice from the doorway.

'No! This is where I want them,' answered George, indicating the chairs with a sweep of his arm.

'This lot, Aah means.' Smithies pointed with his clay pipe towards the cart. George joined him at the door and regarded the remainder of the load. 'That's not for here,' he protested.

'Oh, aye, it is!' The answer was emphatic. 'It were dropped off at my place by a carrier from Malton ti be brought 'ere.'

George scratched his head in puzzlement. 'Is there anything to pay?'

'Nowt! All's paid for.'

'Well, we'd best put it in t'parlour, then.'

The seven-piece suite, which they unloaded and placed in the parlour was, to George's unsophisticated mind, the grandest, nay, the most magnificent furniture he had ever laid eyes upon. The sofa, two armchairs and four dining chairs were framed in luminous dark wood which was polished to a deep glow. The upholstery was of deep, rich crimson velvet.

'By 'eck!' George reverted to dialect, so great was his amazement. 'What's ti do, then? Where's i from?' He expected no answer from Thomas Smithies and, indeed, got none.

The way back was passed in almost total silence, except when George asked, 'Was there enough for the chairs from Sunley's and the carriage, Mr Smithies?'

'Oh, aye! Thoo's a few coppers ti come back,' was his response.

'Keep it for yourself, and thank you very much,' said George, thinking how scandalised his father would be to hear such prodigality.

He did not mention the new furniture to his family. He was, if the truth were told, rather embarrassed to be the owner of such fine possessions. The suite was Elizabeth's wedding present from her Uncle Nathan but, although George later came to accept it as a normal part of his household, in the beginning he felt that it was far too grand for a country lad, as he knew himself to be.

During her time down at Cherry Tree Farm, Elizabeth had the eggs to collect and the hens to feed; the cow to milk and butter and cheese to make. By now, George had moved his pigs into the farm buildings, and Elizabeth fed these too, while George came to clean them out and to turn over the garden whenever he had some spare hours.

The morning of Michaelmas Day was overcast, much to George's disappointment. There was, however, far too much work to be rushed through for him to dwell upon the weather.

During the morning, his mind frequently went back to the occasion of Joseph's marriage to Mary Butler. Not only had this marked his first realisation of Elizabeth's existence, but he could not avoid the comparison between this autumn wedding and their spring one.

They had decided upon a quiet ceremony, with

only immediate family invited to the reception afterwards.

As George sat in the church at Gillamoor with his brother Jonadab beside him, he thought again of Joe's wedding when he had supported his brother as best man. Was Jonna as nervous as he had been? A glance at his brother revealed nothing. He sat, one hand on each knee, a younger replica of their father, his face inscrutable.

The vicar motioned them to rise, whereon George glanced towards the door. His heartbeat quickened as Elizabeth seemed to glide up the aisle on her father's arm.

She wore a jacket and skirt of deep chestnut velvet and a matching bonnet, perched on her head. The colour was an ideal foil for her olive skin and lustrous dark eyes. She carried no flowers and, in George's eyes, needed none. Her appearance was perfection, he considered. As she took her place at his side, their eyes met and she gave him a smile which radiated love and confidence.

George swallowed a lump in his throat but, even so, was so overcome with emotion that, at first, he had difficulty in making his responses. His confidence grew, however, when he felt Elizabeth's firm little hand placed in his, and his voice became strong and clear.

The wedding breakfast which followed the ceremony passed like a dream to George. He later recalled that several relatives from both sides had pressed money into his hand and that someone – he was never sure who – had told him there was a crate in the yard containing a trio of geese.

When people began to take their leave, he was relieved that he and Elizabeth were going to their own home, rather than remaining with the Butler as had been his brother Joseph's lot.

It seemed strange to drive straight past Aumery Park Farm and to realise that it was no longer his home. As they drove down the dale, the sun broke through the clouds and lit the whole scene with a golden glow.

'There!' said George. 'That's what our life's going to be – sunshine all the way!'

Elizabeth threw back her head and laughed with delight. 'They say "Happy is the bride the sun shines on" and no one could be happier than I am,' she announced, as they drove into the yard.

While George put the trap into an open shed and stabled and attended to the pony, having first found a suitable home for the geese, Elizabeth went into the house and lit the kitchen fire, which she had laid the previous day.

Upon following her into the house, George was greeted by the scent of beeswax polish, while the flames seemed to dance on gleaming wood and shining utensils.

'The Queen in her castles couldn't be happier than I am, George.' Elizabeth placed her arms round his neck and raised her lips for his kiss.

He clasped her tightly to him and rained kisses upon her face and neck. Elizabeth, however, gently disengaged herself and gave him a little push.

'We'd better change, George. There's the stock to see to,' she protested as she turned towards the stairs. As she disappeared, George turned the key in the front door and, with a smile, followed her.

When he reached the bedroom, Elizabeth had already removed the brown velvet outfit and stood looking out of the window in a froth of white undergarments.

'You'll not gainsay me this time, Mrs Oaks,' said George, taking her hand and leading her to the bed. 'I am determined to be master in my own house.'

'Yes, George,' she responded in mock meekness, as she held out her arms for him.

Later that evening, as they walked hand in hand along the beckside, George gazed round at what he regarded as his land, lit by the pearly rays of the setting sun. He agreed with Elizabeth. Life was good – and there could be no one happier in the whole world.